If you're looking for love this Valentine's Day, take a peek...

Behind the Red Doors

Heaven Scent

An exclusive perfumery featuring only the most seductive, enticing fragrances. A consumer is encouraged to experiment, discovering for herself which scent will drive her lover wild. And it doesn't take Jamie Ruskin long to find out....

Diamond Mine

A collection of the finest pieces of jewelry, all designed to inspire that special man to pop the question. But what happens when that man is planning to pop...to the wrong woman?

Sheer Delights

The ultimate indulgence. A lingerie boutique that decorates beautiful models with creations of silk, satin and lace. Too bad one of those models doesn't know just how much she's revealing....

Bestselling author **Vicki Lewis Thompson** believes writing romance is the most fun you can have while vertical. With more than sixty books in print, she's having a whale of a good time, and her frequent appearances on the Waldenbooks bestseller list indicate that her readers are partying right along with her. An eight-time finalist for Romance Writers of America's RITA® Award, she's also been honored by *Romantic Times* magazine, including receiving their Career Achievement Award.

Stephanie Bond has an affinity for Valentine's Day because that's when the love of her life proposed on one knee! An incurable romantic who has never been able to make it past the Godiva store without a flyby, Stephanie considers writing sexy comedies the ultimate indulgence. In the summer of 2003, look for *Lovestruck,* a collection of three of her funniest Harlequin books ever! Stephanie lives with her valentine in Atlanta, Georgia. Readers can contact her at www.stephaniebond.com.

Leslie Kelly is a stay-at-home mother of three who says she started writing as a creative outlet after one too many games of Chutes & Ladders. Since the publication of her first book in 1999, she's gained a reputation for writing hot and funny books in the Temptation line. Her first two books were honored with numerous awards, including two Barclay Gold Top 10 Favorite Romances of the Year, the Aspen Gold and the National Reader's Choice Award. Leslie has recently branched out into the Blaze line and is working on special projects with Harlequin for 2003.

Vicki Lewis Thompson
Stephanie Bond
Leslie Kelly

Behind the Red Doors

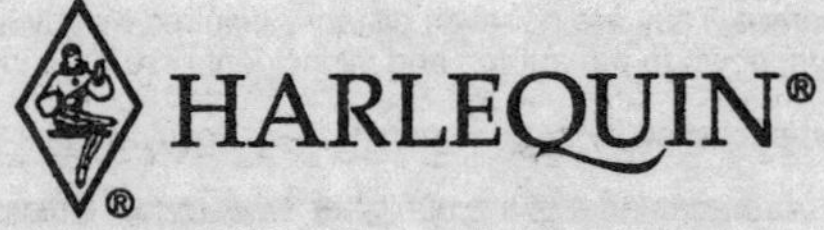

TORONTO • NEW YORK • LONDON
AMSTERDAM • PARIS • SYDNEY • HAMBURG
STOCKHOLM • ATHENS • TOKYO • MILAN • MADRID
PRAGUE • WARSAW • BUDAPEST • AUCKLAND

ISBN 0-373-83569-8

BEHIND THE RED DOORS

This edition published by arrangement with Harlequin Books S.A.

Visit us at www.eHarlequin.com

Printed in U.S.A.

CONTENTS

HEAVEN SCENT

Vicki Lewis Thompson

For John Kudjer, a Chicago boy
and a terrific brother-in-law.
Hey, John, life is gooood.

PROLOGUE

Valentine's Day, 2001

IF MONEY COULDN'T BUY happiness, it sure could buy a kick-ass bottle of champagne. And sipping pricey bubbles in Chicago's famous Pump Room was making Jamie feel extremely happy. To think that she, a janitor's daughter, could now afford a meal here. Even more astounding, Dev Sherman, the man of her dreams, sat across the linen-draped table from her.

If Jamie raised her champagne glass to block out her view of Dev's sister, Faith, sitting on her right, her fantasy of a Valentine's evening with Dev was complete. But since Faith was Jamie's best friend, it didn't seem right to do such a thing. Besides, taking Dev to the Pump Room had been Faith's idea, a way of thanking him for turning both Faith and Jamie onto some wildly profitable dot.com stocks.

They'd bought low and sold high on Dev's advice. Now they were ready to kiss his feet. They called him Broker Man, able to pierce the veil of the future with a single glance of his laser-blue eyes. Jamie was ready to kiss more than his feet, actually. Dev owned the franchise on tall, dark and delicious.

For years she'd been careful not to let either Dev or, more important, Faith, know about her gargantuan crush. Dev was a Sherman, of the Evansville Shermans. His dates played tennis at old-money clubs and sailed yachts on Lake Michigan. Jamie was a Ruskin, of the Irving Park Ruskins. Her dates played basketball in the park and fished off the pier.

Jamie Marie Ruskin had nothing in common with Deverell Heathcliff Sherman the Fourth except, potentially, sex. When people were naked they lost their class distinctions, or so she liked to think, and a hot session between the sheets required more moaning than sophisticated conversation.

But she'd never get there with Dev, because her lack of glamour and polish rendered her nearly invisible to him, she was sure. She was so out of his league that she didn't try to pretend otherwise. Joking about her lack of sophistication had become her special brand of self-protection.

Dev put down his champagne glass and leaned his forearms on the table. "So, have you two decided what business you're going into?"

"I'm still deciding what fork to use for the dessert I just ordered," Jamie said. "Who knew dining out could get so complicated?"

"She's trying to change the subject," Faith said. "I've come up with a dynamite concept, but Jamie has yet to see how great it is."

"I'm not *that* negative about it," Jamie said, glancing at her friend. Faith had inherited the Sherman genes for height and dark hair. The hair was okay with Faith, but she complained about her height, especially to Jamie, who was five-three.

"You're not particularly positive, either," Faith said. "Okay, picture this, Dev. Three boutiques under one roof, each with glamorous gift items for women. We rent the bottom two floors of the Sherman Building, right in the Loop so businessmen will use it to shop for their wives and girlfriends."

"There's an art gallery in there," Dev said.

"I already checked with them, and they're not renewing. Think Dad would give us a break? Assuming I can arm-wrestle Jamie into going along with the idea, that is."

"Dad's always a question mark, but maybe." Dev didn't look enthusiastic. "What kind of gift items?"

"Lingerie, jewelry and fragrances. One-stop shopping for that special woman." Faith blew out a breath. "Dev, your eyes are glazing over."

"Sorry. Just not my area, I guess."

"Now you see why Faith has to put a hammerlock on me," Jamie said. "For a gemologist and glamour-puss like her, it makes sense. For a computer nerd and female jock like me, who thinks carats are what you put in stew and facets are what you turn on to get water—"

"You're into aromatherapy!" Faith said. "The fragrance boutique would be a natural for you."

"Wrong," Jamie said. "I like fooling with essential oils because it reminds me of chemistry class. I would be useless trying to sell the stuff. I'd probably bore people to death trying to explain the inherent properties of each oil when all the customer wants is to smell good.''

''You don't have to sell,'' Faith said. ''You can consult. You can—''

''You know what's wrong with girlie stores like that?'' Dev laid his knife across his plate. ''Sorting through racks of women's underwear is not a manly thing to do. And how the hell do I know what jewelry would look good? And perfume is another land mine. After I've smelled three different kinds, my nose turns off. I know women are experts at all of this, but—''

''I'm not.'' Then Jamie noticed how discouraged Faith looked and felt sorry that she'd been such a wet blanket. ''But I'm trainable.''

Faith brightened. ''Yes, you definitely are that.''

''And I'm sure a store like this would be perfect on Michigan Avenue.''

''Plus your current job sucks,'' Faith offered helpfully.

''Yes, my current job sucks, so peddling undies and good-smelling stuff to urban professional guys would be a step up.''

''I just don't know how you're going to get the guys in there,'' Dev said. ''Now if you could computerize it so all they had to do was push a button, then you'd have something.''

''How romantic.'' Faith sounded testy. ''You remind me of Dad. I—''

''Wait a minute.'' Jamie's ears started to buzz, the way they did when a most excellent idea was incoming. Or maybe it was the champagne. At any rate, her brain was heating up. At times like this, her brothers swore that even her hair got redder. "Wait a minute!" She looked at Dev and Faith, her heart pounding with either excitement or too much booze, hard to tell which. What the hell, might as well share. "I have an idea."

Faith shook her head. "I don't want to get into mail order."

"We wouldn't do mail order." Her idea might look stupid in the morning, but after three glasses of champagne, it ranked right up there with the theory of relativity. "We have the shops, like you said, but in a different part we have computer kiosks. Guys feed info in, get gift suggestions out, order them, have them delivered to an order desk. No racks of underwear to face."

Dev and Faith stared at her, their mouths open.

"Wow," Faith said. "That's...that's a groundbreaking idea, Jamie."

"It's more than that," Dev said. "It's your ticket. You lay that idea in front of Dad, and I guarantee he'll cut you a deal on the rent. He'll want to see that place open just so he can use it to buy gifts for Mom."

Jamie peered at them. "Are you just saying that because you're a little tipsy, too?"

"Faith will have to speak for herself," Dev said. "Guys don't get tipsy. They get wasted—which I'm not."

"Me, either." Faith glanced at Jamie. "Are you?"

"Maybe. Yeah, I think so."

Faith grinned at her and shook her head. ''Still trying to keep up with the big dogs. Tiny people can't drink as much as big people.''

''If drinking champagne gives you ideas like this,'' Dev said. ''We should have it piped into your apartment.''

''That's for sure.'' Faith gazed at Jamie. ''You may have just secured our future.''

Jamie giggled and raised her glass. ''I'll drink to that.''

As she lifted her glass and touched it to Faith's and Dev's, she noticed the gleam in Dev's eyes as he looked at her. She knew it was interest in her idea, not interest in her, but that gleam made her feel wonderful, anyway. He had more of an effect on her than champagne. She doubted the day would come when he'd look at her like that for personal reasons, but if he ever should, she'd probably ruin the moment by fainting dead away.

CHAPTER ONE

January 27, 2003

JAMIE HURRIED DOWN Michigan Avenue on Monday, her collar turned up against a serious morning wind coming off the lake. No place did wind like Chicago. Her eyes watered and her lashes froze. Inside her fur-lined boots, her toes were numb. So were her gloved fingers and the tip of her nose. Even her nipples were rigid.

But when she came in sight of the cherry-red double doors set into the imposing granite facade of the Sherman Building, she forgot the cold blast in a rush of pride. The Red Doors was spelled out in brass on a marble plaque to the right of the entrance, as if this were an exclusive club instead of a trio of boutiques.

Faith had suggested that plaque. Naturally most of the elegant touches were compliments of Faith, but Jamie held on to her nerd territory and took credit for the computer shopping concept. Coming up with that idea, booze-induced or not, had made her feel like an equal partner in the commercial venture. The concept of being a bona fide entrepreneur never failed to blow her away.

Some snow had fallen during the night, and the drifts beside the doors reminded her of lace decorating a valentine, not that she was the type to inspire frilly valentines. One boyfriend had gone so far as to eat the chocolates from a heart-shaped box before filling it with the new pairs of gym socks that he just knew she'd rather have.

Valentine's Day. A queasy feeling dimmed the excitement she usually felt walking through these red doors. Valentine's Day revenues were critical in the first year of operation. The Red Doors sold merchandise that moved best during a holiday, and a romantic one like this should spike sales. Although it was still January, the normal after-Christmas slump should be long over and the Valentine's Day upsurge well in progress. It wasn't.

The Red Doors had opened in time for the Christmas season, and sales had been decent in November and December. The Valentine season was supposed to be even better. They'd had a minor jump, but not enough for Jamie to feel comfortable. If traffic didn't pick up soon, she would no longer be a bona fide entrepreneur. She would be a bona fide bag lady.

She used her key to open the door. Yes, she could go in the back way and straight up to her office, but she loved the front entrance so much she couldn't bear not to enjoy it every morning. Stepping into the entry and stomping the snow and slush off her boots, she pushed through the brass-trimmed revolving door.

A tantalizing aroma drifted from the coffee bar she and Faith had dubbed The Red Bean. This was her favorite moment of the day, before the lights came up to full power, before the customers arrived.

Standing just inside the revolving door and gazing up the red-carpeted winding staircase to the mezzanine, she thought what a fantastic job Faith had done in designing this store so it appealed to both men and women. With dark wood and soft leather, Faith had given the coffee bar and computer kiosks on the main floor a masculine look.

But the mezzanine, accessed by the staircase or a glass-and-brass elevator, was totally feminine. Each boutique had its own unique character. On the right, Sheer Delights oozed sensuality, the display windows piled with silk pillows and lingerie draped over antique privacy screens. This month the theme obviously was red.

The middle store, The Diamond Mine, was Faith's baby, and it glittered and gleamed like an heiress at a fancy-dress ball. The windows were empty now, but in an hour they'd be filled with jewelry that made Jamie gasp in wonder. Each piece was showcased on black velvet under high-intensity lights. Breathtaking.

Faith's latest brainstorm involved bringing in a novelty gem to display. She hoped the impressive Valentino diamond would attract more people into the store and put them in the mood to buy fabulous rocks. She'd also come up with a "wish list" concept, where women's gift preferences would be recorded in a databank that husbands and boyfriends could call up on the computer.

The "wish list" concept would be implemented

in all three boutiques, but Jamie wondered if that would be enough to boost revenues in Heaven Scent. Custom fragrances made with essential oils had been a major gift item during Christmas, but so far the same rush hadn't taken place for Valentine's Day. Heaven Scent looked like a garden, with potted flowers blooming throughout the space. Even the boutique name was spelled out in stylized leaves and flowers created in hammered brass.

Jamie couldn't understand how people could come into The Red Doors and not buy something fragrant to take home. Dev said that people didn't buy perfume in the winter because their noses were too stuffed up to be able to smell anything.

And speaking of the man who made her heart go pitter-pat, he sat at his usual table in The Red Bean, his dark hair tousled from the wind. He was drinking coffee with Faith and Dixie Merriweather, the fifty-something woman Jamie and Faith had hired to oversee sales in all three boutiques, although she paid particular attention to Sheer Delights. From her bleached-blond hair to her colorful clothes, she brought a spark to the operation that everyone depended on.

Dixie had been one of Faith's contacts, a bartender at a restaurant Faith liked. Faith's instincts about hiring her had been right on. Jamie had fallen in love with Dixie from the minute the woman had opened her mouth and all those long Southern vowels had spilled out. Even better, she had a wicked sense of humor.

Dixie had been a widow for many years, and said

she wasn't in the mood to train another man, but Jamie wondered about that line. Jamie told people all the time that she wasn't interested in a boyfriend right now. She had the perfect excuse—working to make this business a success—but if a certain Dev Sherman crooked his finger, she'd find the time for canoodling. In a heartbeat.

Dixie, Faith, Jamie and Dev often gathered for an early morning cup of coffee before The Red Doors opened. Then Dev would go upstairs to his office at Sherman Investments. Jamie counted herself lucky to see Dev first thing nearly every workday morning, but she didn't think it meant much to him. He simply loved the coffee.

Today, however, even the excellent coffee didn't seem to be lifting anyone's mood. Their expressions were grim as they studied something they'd found in the *Tribune.*

Faith glanced up and saw Jamie. "Good. You're here. You'd better come and take a look at this."

"Okay." Jamie unwrapped her scarf and flipped back her hood as she wound her way through the groupings of leather chairs and chunky wooden tables. She combed her short red hair with her fingers, but doubted anything she did to it would matter to Dev. She assumed he liked long hair, as did most men. Faith had gorgeous long hair, but Jamie's had so much natural curl that if she let it grow she'd look like Little Orphan Annie.

Dev reached out and snagged a chair from the next table and pulled it over beside him. "Maybe we shouldn't let Jamie see this until she's had her caffeine."

"A double espresso won't prepare her for this piece of Shinola," Dixie said.

Jamie stuck her purse under her chair and slipped out of her coat as she sat. Dev, raised as a gentleman, helped her with the coat. The casual way he managed it reminded her that, from his standpoint, there were no sparks. A guy with lust on his mind would allow his hand to linger, maybe only for a nanosecond, but Jamie would feel that pause. With Dev, there was no pause.

As for Jamie, sitting next to Dev always changed the rate of her breathing. She had to adjust to his thigh brushing hers—ooh—and his aftershave tempting her—aah—before she could turn her attention to the full-page ad Dixie had shoved in front of her.

And she still could barely focus, with such a hunk-a-munk right there beside her. Dev always smelled so sexy. After aromatherapy had become her hobby and she'd studied pheromones, she'd understood why. From her standpoint, he was mate material. It didn't seem to work in reverse, though. She'd never caught him breathing deeply and sighing around her.

She finally forced herself to concentrate on the *Tribune* ad that had upset everyone. Large type across the top of the page read Guys! Take The Guesswork Out Of Gifts For Her! A few cheesy graphics of women in lingerie followed, then came the words "Stumped for the perfect Valentine's Day gift? Hate to shop in lingerie stores? Let our software help you choose her soft wear!''

As rage slowly replaced her dreamy state, Jamie scanned the rest of the ad for a name and address. The place was called The Gift Program and it was about six blocks away. Almost close enough for lobbing a hand grenade. Someone had stolen her brilliant idea. ''Talk about solid-brass *cojones.*''

''My thoughts exactly,'' Dixie said. ''Think you could hack your way into their database and give them a nasty virus?''

''I'm thinking legal action.'' Faith tapped at the paper with one manicured fingernail. ''They can't get away with this, can they, Dev?''

''I'm pretty sure they can,'' Dev said. ''It's hard to claim ownership of a general concept like this. Go ahead and ask Dad's lawyers if you want, but I'll bet they'll tell you to ignore it.''

''How are we supposed to ignore it?'' Dixie asked. ''We've been screwed without being kissed!''

Alfred Willis, the distinguished-looking widower they'd hired to run The Red Bean, set an espresso down next to Jamie. He'd made a point of knowing what each of them liked and always brought it over whenever they appeared in his territory. The tinge of red on his ears meant he'd heard Dixie's last remark.

Dixie might have said it partly to get a rise out of him. Because he was so formal in his bearing, everyone except Dixie called him Mr. Willis. She insisted on using his first name and seemed to enjoy knocking him off-kilter.

Jamie took pity on him and gave him a smile. "Thanks, Mr. Willis. I can really use this today. Did you notice that we have competition?"

He gave the ad a disdainful glance. "I wouldn't trouble myself with that lot."

"You wouldn't?" Listening to his Britspeak always made her feel more civilized. "Why not?"

He waved a hand at the ad. "It's obviously an inferior establishment. The Red Doors's clientele wouldn't dream of popping in there. Now, may I offer anyone a bit more coffee?"

"Thanks, but I have to get up to my office," Dev said.

"I think we all do," Faith said, but she made no move to leave.

"Then perhaps I'll check on a bagel delivery that seems to have gone missing." Mr. Willis headed back toward the counter area.

"He has a point about the new store," Dev said after he left. "They may be copycats, but from the looks of this ad, they're underfunded copycats, so you may just have to outlast them. And if the store looks as cheap as this ad, customers won't enjoy going there."

Jamie sighed. "I wouldn't be so sure. Maybe your friends wouldn't be caught dead in there, but I can picture my dad and two brothers giving it a shot."

Dixie frowned. "I think you're wrong, sugar. They seemed to be enjoying themselves when they were here at Christmas."

''They did, but my dad commented on the overhead we must be paying. My family doesn't mind a warehouse atmosphere if they think they're getting a deal. And we can't survive by attracting only upscale customers. We need the working-class shopper, too.''

Faith nodded. ''You're right. So what can we do to make The Red Doors a better alternative to—'' she glanced at the ad and grimaced ''—The Gift Program?''

''You go them one better,'' Dixie said. ''What if a woman could go into the kiosk, answer questions about her particular guy—like his hobbies, his job, his general attitude about life—and the computer would tell her what to buy for themselves to turn him on?''

''So the women start using the kiosks, too,'' Jamie said, liking the idea already. ''But we'd have to gather some data on types of men and what gets them hot.''

''Dev can help with that,'' Faith said immediately.

''Hey, wait a minute.'' Dev pushed back his chair. ''I agree that the idea has promise, but I do work for a living, you know. In fact, the stock market opens in ten minutes and I—''

''It won't take long.'' Faith grabbed the sleeve of his suit jacket. ''This doesn't have to be totally scientific. It's a fun thing. Lighthearted.''

''It has to be sort of scientific,'' Jamie said. ''I mean, we don't want to mislead—''

"It's simple," Dixie said. "Men are much easier to figure out than women."

"Now I'm really leaving," Dev said.

"And I'm *really* leaving," Dixie said. "I have several things to do before we open this morning. You kids fight this out, but I really think it would work." She pushed back her chair, grabbed her fake chinchilla coat and headed for the winding staircase. "Just like Tara," she said with a grin as she started up it.

"Please, Dev," Faith said to her brother after Dixie left. "This is a really good idea, and we don't have much time. Think about your friends and what type of women they're attracted to. I guarantee the men will fall into general categories."

"I think you're right." Jamie started getting excited about the concept. "If I take my brothers and their friends as examples, I can see patterns. The program should be easy to get up and running, and we can fine-tune it as we go."

"And when am I supposed to do all of this?" Dev asked. "With the market the way it's been, I'm up to my ears dealing with my clients."

Faith waved away his protest. "The market closes every afternoon. You could get together with Jamie in the evenings. Jamie, you could meet with Dev at night to work on this, right?"

Jamie opened her mouth and prayed that an answer would come out. Something light and breezy. Something about checking her calendar. Something—*anything*—that would keep Dev from suspecting that the idea of spending an evening alone with him had just fried her circuits.

She gulped. ‘‘Uh, Faith, you’ll come over, too, right?’’

CHAPTER TWO

SHE DIDN'T WANT *to be alone with him.* The truth hit Dev like a hockey puck to the gut. For weeks he'd been working up his courage to make a tiny move in her direction, such as suggesting they walk down to the deli together for a sandwich. He'd never been this nervous about asking a woman out, but Jamie was so damned smart that he figured he'd make a fool of himself if he ever had to carry on a solo conversation with her.

He'd been almost ready to chance it, anyway, because there was this sexual thing that happened every time he looked at her. That sleek little body of hers turned him on, and he'd become obsessed with the idea of making love to her. He'd never been attracted to a tomboy before, but lately the image of being in bed with Jamie had become a major component of his fantasy life.

If he could avoid acting too stupid when they were alone, then maybe eventually she'd let him kiss her. Once they got into that and moved beyond into getting naked, her superior brain power might not matter.

But if she didn't want to be alone with him, he'd never get out of the starting gate. "I, um, have stuff to do this week,'' he said to salvage his pride. ''Tonight I was supposed to—''

''Never mind, then,'' Jamie said too quickly. ''I'll just work with my brothers and their friends.''

''Don't let him back out now,'' Faith said. ''Turns out I'm busy tonight, but I think you should make the effort, Dev. Couldn't you switch some things around so you can go over to Jamie's?''

Dev could cheerfully wring Faith's neck. ''I wouldn't have time to talk to the guys by tonight.''

''Really, Faith, I can get Justin and Brad to—''

''Sure you can, but we have Dev in our sights. Why not start with him?''

''Because I want a willing subject?''

Jamie's innocent comment started his engines all over again.

''Dev will be willing, won't you, Dev?''

You have no idea, baby sister.

''You wouldn't jeopardize this chance to get a jump on the competition, would you?''

Dev's eyes narrowed as he gazed at Faith. Now his suspicions were aroused along with the rest of him. She was too damned eager about his participation. ''Are you sure there's not something else going on here?''

She blinked, all innocence. ''What else could be going on?''

He'd seen that look too many times, and it always meant Faith was up to something. ''You could be getting Jamie to be your stool pigeon.''

''What?'' Jamie and Faith said together.

"It's possible. The whole family wants to marry me off. They're not even subtle about it anymore."

His sister relaxed back in her chair with a big grin. "I know what this is about. Helena."

"Who's Helena?" Jamie asked.

"I still say Mom and Aunt Judi sabotaged the motor on that boat," Dev said, trying to stare Faith down, but she'd had a lot of practice in these staring contests of theirs and she held her ground.

"That's possible," Faith said, still smiling.

"What boat?" Jamie asked.

Faith turned to her. "Last summer my mom and aunt Judi set Dev up with Helena Throckmorton."

"*Set up* being the operative term." Dev scowled at her. "So, under protest, I took her out sailing, but the wind died."

"Which you can't blame Mom for."

"No, but she sure as hell could've been listening to the weather reports and known that was due to happen. And she could have had something to do with the motor acting up."

Faith started laughing. "Poor boy." She glanced over at Jamie. "He got stranded with a wild woman who tried to take advantage of him."

"Isn't that every guy's fantasy?" Jamie looked at Dev with an impish smile.

If his sister hadn't been there, he'd have leaned over and kissed that saucy expression right off her face.

"Not my brother's fantasy, apparently."

"I didn't even know the woman! Just you try being stranded on a thirty-footer with a woman who's flinging off her clothes.''

Jamie's eyes widened. ''She really took off her clothes?''

''So he claims,'' Faith said. ''I think she was planning to seduce him and then demand that he make an honest woman of her.''

''Oh, do you think?'' Dev folded his arms over his chest. ''After that, you can't call me paranoid for being wary of this latest project. If I give a list of my favorite turn-ons to Jamie and she passes them over to you, I can imagine that being used against me.''

''Dev, Dev, Dev.'' Faith shook her head. ''As if I would ever go to that much trouble to find out your weak spots with women.''

He decided not to look at Jamie, who still wore that cute little smile that made him want to kiss the living daylights out of her. ''So none of you will make use of this information to set a trap for me?''

Faith made an *X* over her heart. ''Cross my heart and hope to die, stick a needle in my eye. This info will not be used to create the perfect marriage candidate for my brother. Why should I want you to get married? Once you do, Mom and Dad will turn their attention to me and want to know why I don't have a husband on the horizon. C'mon, Dev. This is important.''

He couldn't see any way to wiggle out of it. Jamie would have to tolerate his presence. He just hoped she wouldn't smile like that tonight, or he might have trouble controlling himself. ''Then I'll do it.''

He pushed back his chair. "I gotta go. Jamie, I'll see you at seven-thirty tonight."

"You remember where I live, right?"

He stood and retrieved his topcoat and briefcase. "Are you still in that apartment just off of Addison?"

"Yep. Third floor, 6C."

"See you then." He walked toward an exit on the far side of the coffee bar that opened onto the ground-floor lobby of the Sherman Building. From there he would take an elevator to his offices on the sixty-fifth floor. Technically he'd be far away from Jamie, but he knew he'd be thinking about her all day long.

JAMIE WATCHED until he was out of sight. Then she turned to Faith. "Okay, *is* there something fishy going on?"

"No." But mischief danced in Faith's blue eyes. "At least not yet."

"Faith Sherman, if you're trying to get Dev married off on my watch, so help me—"

"I wouldn't do that."

Jamie sighed with relief. "Good."

"What I would do is use this perfectly legitimate excuse to get you two alone together."

Jamie stared at her, and all the blood left her brain. "What...what do you mean?"

Faith leaned closer. "We've been friends for almost twelve years. I would have to be beyond dense not to know you have a thing for my brother."

Jamie could see there was no sense in denying it.

She buried her face in her hands and groaned. "Does he know?"

"Of course not. Guys don't pick up on that stuff."

Jamie lifted her head. "You're sure?"

"Absolutely. Furthermore, he's intrigued by you, too."

"He is not."

"He's my brother, and I say he is. I've seen the looks he gives you, and I don't think he comes for coffee every morning for Dixie's and my company."

"Well, duh! He comes for the *coffee.* You've heard him rave about the cherry-bark blend."

"Okay, he likes the cherry-bark blend, but he also likes you. You scare him a little bit because you're so bright, but that's good for him. He thinks he wants somebody who won't challenge him intellectually, but I think that's why he's bounced from woman to woman. He gets bored."

"*Faith!* You sound like you're trying to set us up!"

"Why not?" Faith smiled at her. "Why wouldn't I want my best friend to date my brother?"

"Oh, I dunno. Because I'm not remotely, by any stretch of the imagination, your brother's type?"

"I don't think he knows his type. But his answers to the questions might give you some ideas."

"I'm supposed to be creating a program for The Red Doors!"

"So, multitask!"

Still unable to believe they were having this conversation, Jamie gazed at her friend in astonishment. "Okay, let's try this discussion from a different angle. I don't seem to be getting through. Here's the deal. I don't fit into Dev's world."

Faith stared at her. "What is that supposed to mean?"

"You know perfectly well." Jamie sighed impatiently. "I'm not glamorous. I'm not..."

"Rich?"

"There is that. The dot.com windfall was the first serious money I've ever seen in my life, and it's all sunk into the business."

"You and I are friends." There was an edge to Faith's voice. "Has that been a problem for you?"

"No, but—"

"I don't know what you've been telling yourself about Dev, but he's no snob. If he dates women from a certain level of society, that's probably because those are the ones he comes in contact with. But he values people, not social position. You've created something in that fertile brain of yours that isn't even a problem."

Jamie couldn't very well continue the argument without risk of insulting both Faith and her brother. "All that aside, I'll guarantee he likes a woman who wears silk instead of cotton and who knows her way around the cosmetics counter."

"And that is exactly what you're going to find out tonight." Faith glanced at her watch. "Come on, partner. It's time to get to work."

DURING A VERY LONG DAY at the office, Jamie's lack of enthusiasm about seeing him tonight kept flashing into Dev's mind like a brake light, warning him not to get too excited about the appointment. He wasn't used to women shying away, and that's what Jamie had done from the beginning.

He'd kidded himself that she wasn't skilled at the man-woman thing, but now he had to face the possibility that she didn't like him much. So tonight would be complicated. He'd been attracted to Jamie ever since that Valentine's dinner at the Pump Room.

He still remembered how she'd looked that night. Her white knit dress had shown off subtle curves he hadn't noticed before. He'd loved watching her enjoy herself and become adorably snockered. But when her green eyes had started glowing with excitement over her new idea, she'd gone from cute to beautiful. He was attracted, all right.

If only she weren't so damned smart. Although he had an instinct for the stock market that had made him a decent living, he'd slid through Northwestern's business college without distinction. Jamie's grades had earned her an academic scholarship four years in a row. Her computer skills had saved Faith from flunking a class, which was when they'd become friends. Jamie had graduated magna cum something-or-other.

Dev figured she saw him as a frat guy and a party animal, which he'd been, no doubt about it. In those days he hadn't expected that he'd ever want to impress a smart cookie like Jamie. And he couldn't hide a single flaw from her, because she was best friends with his sister, who had probably cataloged every one of Dev's failings for Jamie over the years.

By the time Dev left his Lakeshore Drive apartment in a taxi bound for Jamie's place, he'd convinced himself that he'd be a fool to let her know he was attracted to her. She'd shoot him down, and then where would he be? The morning coffee sessions he'd come to relish would be ruined. He'd have to avoid her, which would be next to impossible considering her personal and business connection to Faith.

To add to the complications, he wasn't completely convinced that tonight wasn't a scheme to get vital info out of him. Faith could be in league with his mother, no matter what she claimed to the contrary. Jamie might be in on it or she might only be the messenger.

Therefore he'd not only play it cool with Jamie, he'd fake his answers to her questions. Then if some woman came onto him while wearing some overwhelming perfume, he'd know she'd been primed by his answers to the questionnaire.

The cab heater blasted him from the moment he'd climbed inside, so he unzipped his black leather jacket. He'd spent way too much time deciding what to wear tonight and had finally chosen his favorite ivory sweater and black cords. From listening to Jamie over the last several months, he'd figured out that looks didn't count for nearly as much with her as character and smarts.

That was another thing he liked about her. He'd grown tired of the parade of designer dresses on the women he dated. Even sex couldn't be spontaneous when a woman was zipped into something worth thousands that could not, under any circumstances, end up on the floor. He'd broken up with his last girlfriend over that very issue. He'd accidentally spilled something on her Vera Wang, and she'd screeched and hollered as if he'd murdered a close relative.

After paying the cab fare, Dev climbed out onto the icy sidewalk and headed toward the four-story brick apartment complex where Jamie lived. His loafers crunched against the hard-packed snow accumulated during the Chicago winter and he quickly got chilled again. He wondered if Jamie would have some hot coffee made. Maybe he should have brought something, such as cookies from the deli.

Oh, to hell with it. This wasn't a date. It wasn't even something Jamie particularly wanted to do. He'd answer the questions just to get Faith off his back and to test the conspiracy theory. Then he was outta here.

He'd been to Jamie's apartment once, when Faith had asked him to come over to help them haul a gigantic bookcase up the stairs. The place had looked functional, like Jamie, without a lot of extraneous stuff lying around. Also, it had smelled great, like pies baking, although she'd said nothing was in the oven.

He hoped she had coffee. It would give him something to do with his hands. And his mouth.

Inside the vestibule with its row of mailboxes and doorbells, he buzzed her apartment.

"Yes?" Her voice on the intercom sounded as though she'd been running.

"It's me."

"Right."

Another buzz and he was admitted inside the building, but her curt little "Right" hadn't made him feel exactly welcome. It wouldn't have killed her to say a friendly hi or glad-you-made-it. With a sigh, he started up the carpeted stairs. If only Faith hadn't made this sound like the critical ingredient to saving The Red Doors.

He had to agree that the business needed a kick in the pants if it was going to survive this first year, and Dixie's idea to get the women into the computer kiosks had merit. But he felt like a damned guinea pig. That was probably exactly how Jamie saw him, too.

Shoving a thumb against her doorbell, he stood back, hands in the pockets of his jacket, and waited for her to open the door. Maybe she hated giving up her evening. For all he knew, she was missing a favorite TV show. He pictured her glued to a documentary on the life of Einstein.

The door opened and she stood there in jeans and a well-worn N.U. sweatshirt. Although she'd put on lipstick, which surprised him, she didn't have on any other makeup that he could tell. Between her freckles and the college sweatshirt, she looked more like twenty-two than thirty-two.

He had a sudden attack of lust. Her outfit emphasized the slender, wholesome look that made him salivate. Maybe, too, her outfit reminded him of his college days when sex had happened in the back seat of cars and on blankets in the grass. Now it took place in civilized spots such as bedrooms or hot tubs. He'd thought the thrill had disappeared because he was older and more jaded, but maybe it had more to do with who he'd been with.

"Come in." She didn't smile, which was probably a good thing.

"I'm sure this is a real pain in the patoot for you," he said.

"No, it's fine. The idea's a good one. Here, let me take your jacket."

"Thanks." Shrugging out of it, he handed it to her. At the same moment, he registered the aroma of coffee and that scent of baking pie from the last time.

She turned and hung his jacket on the antlers of a fake moose head mounted on the wall.

"I like your moose." He couldn't think of a single woman he'd dated who would hang a grinning moose head on the wall as a coat tree. Jamie really fascinated him. He sure wished that he fascinated her, too.

"That's Gerald." A hint of a smile flitted over her mouth.

He looked away from that potential smile, which could have a lethal effect on his restraint. "What's that I smell?"

"Coffee?"

"No, the other thing."

"Must be the blend of cinnamon and cloves in the diffuser. Does it bother you?"

Even without the smile, it makes me want to strip you naked and make love until we're cross-eyed, even if there is a moose watching. "No, I like it. I just remembered the last time I was here your apartment smelled the same way, and I thought you were baking something."

"Oh, yeah—the bookcase-moving caper." She swept a hand toward her small living room. "See? All filled up."

He glanced at the bookcase that took up most of one wall and, sure enough, it was jammed with books—hardbacks and paperbacks, thick volumes and thin, some scuffed and ragged, others shiny and new.

He turned to her. "What now? You stop buying books?"

"Oh, no." She remained serious. "I have a smaller bookcase in my bedroom, but it's almost full, too. Unless I can figure out where to put another bookcase, I might have to move into a two bedroom."

"You'd move just to have more space for *books?*"

She gave him a puzzled glance. "What else can I do?"

"Get rid of some." From her look of horror he quickly figured out that wasn't an option. "Okay, so I don't get it. Obviously I'm not big on reading like you are." *Obviously I'm also forty points below you on the IQ scale.*

"It's not only the reading." She seemed eager to have him understand. "It's the way they look on the shelves, marching along side by side, all that delicious knowledge captured inside those colorful covers. And I love the way books smell. I don't know if it's the glue, the paper or the ink, or the combination, but I've been thinking that the aromatherapy folks should look into creating a booklover's blend.''

She had that glow going on in her eyes again, and her cheeks were flushed with enthusiasm. Her topic didn't matter to him, and she could have been speaking in Portuguese for all he cared. When she got enthusiastic about something, he began to heat up. Maybe her smile wasn't required for him to combust, after all.

''Coffee!'' She snapped her fingers. ''Here I am blabbing away and I haven't even offered you a cup. Some hostess I am. Have a seat anywhere and I'll be right back.''

Before he could say anything, she'd darted out of the room and through an archway on the left into the kitchen.

ONCE INSIDE THE KITCHEN, Jamie slapped her forehead in frustration. Had she just stood there and given him a minilecture on the appeal of *books?* Yes, she had. Her Royal Nerdiness had done exactly that. Wow, talk about putting the moves on a guy. Stand there and rave about the scent of book bindings, and he'll be all over you.

As if Dev would ever have such an impulse under the best of conditions. No, that would be her projecting her lust on him. The minute he'd stepped into her apartment, her body had started to hum. That pheromone situation had gone straight through her, activating all her special places.

Apparently intense arousal made her go insane and babble about the spines of books. Who knew? At least Dev wouldn't recognize her reaction for a passionate response. No normal woman would go into lecture mode when she really craved a permanent liplock.

And she'd had something positive going with the moose head, too. The moose head had surprised him and might have even made him think she had a wild-and-crazy side. But then she'd had to turn into Professor Bookworm. Gee, he must have been thrilled down to his toes.

Well, she'd probably killed the evening dead, but at least she had the cherry-bark coffee he loved so much, so she'd serve him that, just as soon as she found a tray. Dev came from the land of household help and serving trays. She couldn't just march in there with two bare cups. She had a tray around somewhere. Yes, it was metal and had the Chicago skyline on it, but it was better than nothing.

She was determined to find it, even if it meant emptying out every damned cupboard. Of course, the longer she left him in there alone, the more time he had to dwell on her eggheaded behavior. She'd known tonight would be a disaster and, sure enough, the disaster was proceeding right on schedule.

CHAPTER THREE

DEV WANTED TO FOLLOW HER into the kitchen. He wanted to follow her everywhere, most especially into her bedroom. This was bad. She had no interest in him and he was fast becoming loony over her.

Wandering over to the bookcase, he listened to her bang and clatter around in the kitchen while he looked at the wall of knowledge. To think it was so much a part of Jamie that she'd pay more rent instead of giving up any of it. He tried to think of whether he had any books in his apartment.

He had magazines and newspapers, a whole collection of movies on DVD, but books…oh, yeah. Faith had given him that Tom Wolfe book, *Bonfire of the Vanities.* Dev had watched the video instead. No wonder Jamie wasn't interested in him, an intellectual bottom-feeder.

The racket in the kitchen continued, and he wondered if she was stalling. It sounded as if she was building a set of steel shelves instead of making coffee.

He turned, looking for a place to sit. Against the wall opposite the bookcase was a love seat flanked by two overstuffed chairs, all of them covered in some beige slipcover thing that looked very eco-friendly. He picked out a chair and discovered it was very body-friendly, too. The chair seemed to give him a hug.

Shoving himself out of the chair, he started to pace. A chair that cozy made him think of how else it could be used. If a woman happened to be small, like Jamie, and athletic, like Jamie, then the possibilities were endless.

Damn, Jamie sounded as though she was doing metal sculpture in the next room. He'd never heard a person make so much noise brewing coffee. And if he didn't stop staring at that comfy chair of hers, he'd be erecting his own personal sculpture.

He scanned the room, desperate for a distraction from thoughts of sex. There, that picture over the love seat might work if he could forget about the love seat and concentrate on the picture. Two little kids, a boy and a girl, skated on a pond. Jamie liked to skate. Faith had told him Jamie kept a pair of skates in the bottom drawer of her file cabinet at work. Sometimes on her lunch hour she'd go over to the McCormick Tribune rink right down the street.

He'd love to watch her skate, love to watch her lithe body glide across the ice. Maybe she wore a short little skating skirt. He licked dry lips and forced himself to concentrate on the kids in the picture instead of his mental image of Jamie flitting around the rink in a short skirt.

The little girl had red hair. The little boy had brown, like his used to be as a toddler. He caught himself wondering whether Jamie planned to have kids someday and turned away from the picture. As if it made any difference to him what her marriage and family plans were. He might have sexual fantasies about her, but he sure as hell wasn't dreaming of white picket fences. Not this boy. He wasn't ready for that.

Continuing his inventory of the room, he saw a little cranny beside the bookcase where she'd squeezed in a small computer table. The monitor was on, and a screen-saver graphic of time-lapse blooming flowers entertained him while he waited for Jamie to come in with the coffee. The flowers were about as neutral as he was going to get, so he focused on them.

"Here's the coffee." She finally came in holding two oversize pottery cups, one yellow and one blue. "I couldn't find my tray. I know I had one, but I don't use it much, make that never, so maybe in a weak moment I gave it to one of my brothers." She handed him the blue cup. "This is how the other half lives. No trays."

"Who needs trays?" But as he took the cup in both hands, he realized a tray would have provided a buffer and he wouldn't have touched her when he accepted the drink.

Could it be that he'd never touched her before? That seemed impossible, given how long he'd known her, but this contact felt new. The warmth of her skin zipped right through his fingers, up his arms, down his chest and across the Mason-Dixon line to rebel territory. He was not going to get an erection from touching a woman's fingers. He was not.

Okay, he was, but he would control it. "Thanks for the coffee." He cradled the large cup in both hands. He associated her with coffee, maybe because they'd spent so many mornings surrounded by the scent of it.

"It's cherry bark."

His glance flew to hers. She'd brought home his special preference on purpose. Nah, probably not. But if she had...

"I happened to have some on hand."

She hadn't done it on purpose. His tiny spark of hope died. She hadn't asked him about cream and sugar, either. He figured she'd noticed he took it black, not because she cared about him, but because she was so smart and observant.

"Okay." She stood in front of him, her cup clutched like a shield in front of her. "If you'd like to sit in that chair, I'll bring up the questionnaire on the computer. I created it today and it's probably not perfect because I had to rush a little, but it's a start."

Back to the hugging chair. He could do this. He settled into it without spilling his coffee and vowed to keep his chair-sex fantasies under control while he gave fake answers to her questions.

She looked so earnest that he felt guilty about misleading her, but he had to, for self-preservation. "Did Faith help you with the questions?"

"Yes, but that doesn't mean what you think it means."

"I hope not."

"Look, Dev, if you want to forget the whole thing, then—"

"No, I don't. Let's do it." Now there was a loaded suggestion.

"Right." Obviously her thoughts were miles away from his, because she became all business, turning away and slipping quickly into her secretary chair in front of the computer. "I'm sure you'd like to get this over with."

That was up for debate. Although he had to fight his attraction to her, she was unknowingly demonstrating the qualities he found so sexy. He'd been dating the wrong kind of women for years without realizing what the right kind was. He wanted someone unaffected, someone who entertained guests in jeans and an old sweatshirt, someone who picked out furniture for the way it felt when you sat on it instead of how it looked, someone who didn't take an hour to put on makeup and fix her hair.

Good thing she'd directed him to this chair. He could see her profile from this position, but he wouldn't seem to be watching her. From the love seat or the opposite chair, her back would have been to him. Of course, with this woman, a view of her straight spine and the tender nape of her neck would send him into overdrive.

"Are you ready for the first question?" she asked.

"Shoot."

"Who would you rather take to bed, Cleopatra or Joan of Arc?"

He barely kept from choking on his coffee. *Neither. You.* "Aren't they both dead?"

She swiveled the chair to look at him. "Yes, but I picked them out as archetypes. One is all about glamour and seduction, whereas the other one didn't care about that, but she had charisma and sacrificed herself for a noble cause."

He wondered what she wore under the sweatshirt. With her perky breasts, she really wouldn't need a bra. Then he realized she was waiting for his response. "I'm pretty sure they both sacrificed themselves. Didn't Cleo get way too chummy with a snake?"

Jamie frowned. "Yes, but forget about that. Just think of the image of Cleopatra floating down the Nile on her barge. Does that excite you?"

"No." Or she might be wearing one of those stretchy sports bras, the kind that displayed a woman's nipples when she was excited.

"Then you'd pick Joan of Arc?"

"No." He tried to tell from the drape of her worn sweatshirt if she had on a bra or not. He couldn't.

"Is it a bad question?" Uncertainty flashed in her eyes. "Maybe I don't have the right historical figures. Let's try Lady Godiva and Amelia Earhart."

He forced himself to concentrate on something besides her breasts. "Let's try Jennifer Lopez and Jodi Foster," he said gently. "Guys don't fantasize about famous dead women."

"Faith said that question might not fly, but I liked it. I was hoping—"

"Then maybe you should leave it in." He wasn't

quite sure when, but somewhere along the line he'd become protective of her feelings. She was proud of her question and he'd shot it down. Now he wished he hadn't. "I'm not very intellectual, so I'm not a good person to judge."

She turned back to stare at the screen. "Faith says you're smarter than you let on. She said if you didn't think that question would work, I should probably take it out. So I'm taking it out."

"Wait a minute. I—"

"Too late. It's gone. Okay, next question. Which part of a woman's anatomy do you notice first?"

He gasped, then covered his reaction with a coughing fit.

"Are you okay?"

He nodded and cleared his throat. She was so damned clinical that none of this must bother her, which meant she had zero interest in him as a man. He was only a specimen under a microscope. "Coffee went down wrong," he said in a thick voice.

"Would you like some water?"

"I'd like a different question."

She sat, her fingers poised over the computer keys, her gaze on the screen. "But this is important for a woman to know about her guy, don't you think? Just tell me. It's breasts, isn't it?"

"I am so not answering that."

"Come on, Dev." She scrolled up and down the document. "We're going to poll a bunch of guys and see if any of them choose something besides breasts. I'm doubting it, personally. I think a woman should always buy things to emphasize her breasts if she wants a guy to get turned on.''

If that was true, he wondered why he was sitting there in a state of arousal while Jamie wore a baggy sweatshirt that disguised her breasts. Still, he had been fixating on them. Maybe disguised breasts were underrated as a sexual turn-on.

But he was here to give her false info. ''All right,'' he said. ''Then put that down for me, too.''

She nodded and began typing. ''Breast man. And thank you for being honest.''

He winced. Honesty would have meant saying that the first thing he'd noticed about Jamie were her incredible green eyes, which were so expressive. Next he'd noticed her sweet little mouth, especially when she gave that saucy little smile of hers. He'd never really taken note of her breasts until she'd worn that slinky knit dress to the Pump Room. Now, of course, he was intensely interested in them.

''Would you find it sexy if a woman wore a necklace to bed and nothing else?''

He wasn't a fan of jewelry during sex. As far as he was concerned, the only hard object in the bed should be his penis. But here was a perfect opportunity to discover if his answers would find their way to the Sherman family matchmakers. If he said he loved seeing a naked woman wearing a necklace, and a naked woman in a necklace appeared, he'd have his proof.

''I think that's very sexy,'' he said.

''A choker style, or something long that dangled between her breasts?''

Well, he hadn't thought he liked jewelry in bed, but now he was imagining Jamie with emeralds that matched her eyes.... A choker would have kinky overtones, which would be sort of exciting, but a long necklace, with a teardrop emerald nestled right between her freckled breasts... He didn't know for sure they were freckled, but he could guess they might be.

"Dev? Which necklace?"

He jerked out of his daydream so quickly that he almost spilled his coffee. "Long and dangling." He still sounded hoarse, so he cleared his throat and said it again. "Dangling."

"Got it. Long and dangling between her breasts," she murmured, typing in the answer.

He was losing focus. He was supposed to be feeding her wrong answers, but when it came to thinking of having sex with Jamie, there were no wrong answers. "Rubies," he said, just to throw in something different from his emerald fantasy. "Rubies are sexy. The color of passion and all that."

Jamie typed some more. "Rubies it is. Next question. In women's negligees, do you prefer silk, lace, or a combination of the two?"

Apparently he'd groaned without knowing it, because she turned to him, alarm in her expression. "You aren't getting sick, are you?"

He sat up straighter. "Nope. No." He thought frantically of a way to cover his goof. "I, um, remembered I forgot to record the Bulls game." Another lie. His VCR was humming away at this very moment.

"Is it over?"

"No, just starting."

"Then it's not a problem." She jumped up. "What channel?"

"WGN. But that's okay." He glanced around for a TV and didn't see one. "You don't have to—"

"I'll record it for you."

"How? I don't see a set, let alone a VCR."

"I keep them in the bedroom."

He really didn't need to know that. Now he was picturing the two of them cuddled naked in bed watching an erotic flick.

"While I'm gone, be thinking about the silk versus lace question, okay? And the one after that has to do with your favorite color of negligee, so you can think of that, too. We'll be done before you know it." She took off down the hall.

Oh, sure, he was going to spend the time she was gone thinking about silk and lace, and she'd be the one wearing it in his sexually charged imagination. He'd bet a chunk of his portfolio that she wore cotton sleep shirts to bed, and even that image got his juices flowing. A cotton sleep shirt was uncomplicated. No elastic, no ties, no panties. Just up and over the head, and you were in business.

He had to set his coffee on the low table in front of him because his hands were shaking. All of him was shaking. He'd had no idea how erotic these questions would be. Many more of them and he'd have to do something drastic, such as kiss her. Kiss her or leave. Those seemed to be his only viable options.

JAMIE KNEW she was boring Dev to tears while she was getting all hot and bothered. She didn't know what to do about either problem. Her questions had sounded okay this afternoon in the office, fun and suggestive, the perfect icebreaker. But while she was squirming in her chair at the discussion they were having, he wasn't paying any attention at all.

She'd had to remind him to answer the necklace one, and he'd been thinking of a basketball game while she'd been trying to find out about lingerie. Maybe if he sat at the computer and worked through the questionnaire on his own, he'd find it a little more interesting.

Jamie grabbed her remote from the bedside table and popped a tape into the VCR. Then she started the recording process for the Bulls game. She didn't follow basketball, but her brothers did, and she knew how important it could be to a guy. At least she could make sure Dev didn't miss his game because of a questionnaire he had no interest in.

As she'd feared from the beginning, his answers weren't matching up with her reality at all. He'd admitted to being a breast man and she'd never been a real contender in that department. Hers were on the small side, nothing to make guys stare and drool.

And the thought of wearing cold metal jewelry to bed was ridiculous, especially the dangling kind. Supposing the woman got on top and leaned over? She could bloody his nose or knock out a tooth with a swinging ruby pendant. Oh, well, no surprise. She and Dev weren't meant for each other, no matter what Faith seemed to think about it.

Once she had the Bulls game under control, she hurried back to the living room, only to find Dev on his feet. Maybe he'd had enough boredom for one evening. "Did you decide to go home and watch the game, after all?" she asked.

"No, of course not. I just thought I'd get more coffee," he said. "If that's okay."

"I'll be glad to get you some." As she walked over to take his cup, she wondered if she wanted him to stay or not. Apparently he had to pump himself full of more caffeine so he wouldn't fall asleep out of sheer boredom.

"I can get the coffee, Jamie."

She thought he looked stressed. "You know, I probably have enough answers for now, if you'd like to get home. That way you'd only miss a part of the game, and I could give you the tape in the morning." She took hold of the cup, expecting him to let go, grab his jacket and take off.

Instead he held on to the cup. "We've made it this far. Might as well do the job right. And I really will get my own coffee. You can type in the answer to the silk or lace question. It's lace. I like lace the best because..." His voice trailed off and he stood there looking at her.

"Because?" She shouldn't stand this close to him, especially not when they were talking about negligees. It might not bother him, but she kept thinking of sex. Specifically, sex with Dev.

"Because it's not, um, solid...so you can see..." His blue eyes darkened, becoming almost black.

"Uh, yeah." Her heart thundered. If she hadn't

known better, she'd swear he was getting turned on. Was it possible? Maybe he wasn't as bored as she'd thought. "I—I know what you mean."

"Do you...wear lace?" His question had a funny squeak at the end, as if his vocal cords had refused to cooperate.

"No." She couldn't seem to break eye contact. Shivers started coursing through her.

"Why not?"

"Too, um, scratchy."

He cleared his throat. "Silk, then?"

"Too...slippery." She couldn't believe the reaction she was seeing in his eyes. Maybe, instead of disinterested, he'd been so interested that he hadn't been able to concentrate on the questions.

"Then...what do you like?" Unbelievably, his head began to lower. He was going to kiss her.

And she was going to let him. "C-cotton. Or... nothing." She closed her eyes, her whole body straining upward.

"Nothing?" His voice had become husky.

She sighed. "Nothing."

He groaned as his mouth came down on hers.

CHAPTER FOUR

JAMIE HAD FANTASIZED about Dev's kiss for twelve years, and it was every bit as wonderful as she'd imagined. Wonderful squared, in fact. His lips were soft, but the pressure was firm. She and Dev might have stumbled into this moment, but he was kissing her as though he meant business.

Probably he was imagining she was somebody else. Because they were pressed as tightly together as books on her shelf, he'd have trouble pretending she was Jennifer Lopez, but Jodi Foster was a possibility. If so, Jodi must really work for him, because he was packing iron under those cords.

She didn't care what was going through his head, though. She'd just reached one of her life goals and that was worth celebrating. Snuggling closer in what she hoped was a Jodi Foster-type move, she invited him to expand on what he was offering. At the moment when his tongue slipped inside her eager mouth, the cup landed on her wooden floor with a loud crack.

They both jumped back and stared at the blue cup, which had broken neatly in two, except for the handle, which lay a few inches away.

"Damn, I'm sorry," Dev muttered. "I thought you had it."

She'd been oblivious to everything but their full body contact. "It's only a cup." Heart racing, she crouched to pick it up at the same moment he did, and they knocked heads. She saw stars and lost her balance, sitting hard on the floor.

"Oh, God!" Kneeling, he reached for her, holding her by the shoulders. "Talk about clumsy—now I've hurt you!"

"It's okay." She rubbed her forehead and glanced up at him. "What about you?"

"I have a really hard head."

"So I just found out."

He winced. "Jamie, I feel terrible about this. Do you think I should take you to the E.R.?"

Although she felt wobbly and disoriented, she managed a smile. "It's only a little bump on the head, Dev. Even a head as hard as yours wouldn't give me a concussion." But the moment was gone, and she had sense enough to know it. "Maybe something's telling us we aren't supposed to be doing this."

He cradled her face in both hands and looked into her eyes. "Do you think?"

She gazed into those laser-blue eyes. His mouth was still moist from their enthusiastic exchange. She could reach up, cup his head and bring his lips back down to hers for more of the same. But she might find out that the first time had been an impulse created by the questionnaire and thoughts of women who ranked way higher on the sex-o-meter than she did. Now that the mood had shifted, he might not be into it.

He cleared his throat. "The questions were... I guess I got a little carried away."

Well, there it was, just as she'd feared. Luckily she hadn't tried to kiss him again. "Me, too."

"Yeah." His thumbs brushed her jawline and his gaze was tender. "I'm sure I'm not your type."

She had to admit that was gallant of him, when she was the one who wasn't his type. Dev was every woman's type. But if he wanted to back away from their encounter, she'd help him. "I suppose we can call this the Questionnaire Effect."

"Yeah." He looked into her eyes for a moment longer. "You're sure your head's okay?"

"I'm sure."

"Well, I owe you a new cup."

"You most certainly do not."

"I most certainly do." He got to his feet and held out his hand to help her up.

She decided to avoid his gaze as she put her hand in his and allowed him to pull her to her feet. She was still feeling the Questionnaire Effect, and now that she'd blown her chance to continue what they'd started, she was already having regrets. She didn't want him to look into her eyes and figure that out.

Instead, she had to find a graceful way out of this situation. "Tell you what." Releasing his hand, she walked over to the computer. "Why don't I e-mail you the rest of the questions, and you can fill them out and e-mail them back to me?"

"If that's what you want." He crouched and picked up the broken cup.

No, what I want is to kiss you again...and again, and see if we can segue right into the bedroom. But that train has left the station. "It makes sense to do that. In fact, if you'd be willing to e-mail the questions to your friends, that's the most efficient way to gather the information."

He stood, the broken pieces of the cup in one hand. "Their answers will be anonymous, right? They might not care one way or the other, but—"

"Oh, definitely anonymous. But I'd like a general profile of each guy, so I can create some composites for the program. I'll send you the form for the profile so they can fill that out, too." She sat at the computer.

"Wait a minute. You didn't ask for profile information from me."

"No, because Faith gave me that." Taking a steadying breath, she hit the enter key and the questionnaire popped back onto the screen.

His eyebrows lifted. "Oh, she did, did she? I want to see what she said."

"Now?"

"Absolutely." He crossed to the computer, set down the broken cup pieces and braced his arm on her desk, leaning over her shoulder to look at the screen. "Go ahead and bring it up."

He was within kissing range once again, and the scent of his aftershave made her giddy enough to consider risking it. The urge to ease back into the curve of his arm was almost irresistible. Almost. But she needed him to move away, because the name she'd given his file was...personal. "Let me look it up and print it out for you."

"No problem. You have the same operating system I have." He reached around her and manipulated the mouse until he had her directory on the screen.

Caught in the circle of his arm, she longed to stay right there. He radiated such heat, and she wanted that heat. What she didn't want was that incriminating directory on the screen where he could see it.

"Which one is it?"

"I'll find it." She pulled the mouse out of his hand and double clicked on the file as fast as she could, hoping he hadn't seen the designation.

He had. "'Hot Commodity'?"

"Just a little inside joke." Her face burned. "Protecting your anonymity."

"Yeah, right. I can just imagine you and Faith cracking up over it, too. Lord save me."

So he had taken it as a joke, she thought with relief. He'd never have to know she considered it a perfect description of him.

He cleared his throat and peered at the screen. "Okay, let's see what we have here. 'Astrology sign—Sagittarius.' That's right, for whatever difference it makes."

His cheek was inches from hers. His presence had a mesmerizing effect, even though she didn't want him to read what was coming up on the screen. She ought to do something, create a diversion, pull the plug. But instead she stayed very still, held in the tractor beam of his forceful sexuality.

"'Athletic, sports-minded.'" He nodded. "I'll go along with that. 'Good physique, highly...sexual.'"

Galvanized at last, she bolted from the chair just as he recoiled from the keyboard as if he'd had an electric shock.

He spun to face her. "Faith told you I was *highly sexual?* My baby sister told you that?"

Dammit, she should have taken that file off her C-drive and stored it on a disk, but she'd never envisioned this happening, and she'd been so rushed, getting everything ready....

"Did she?" he demanded again.

"In...in a way. She said you started dating early and girls seemed to flock to you from the beginning, like you gave off some sort of sexual energy...or something." She could certainly testify to that. The closer he came, the more she melted into a puddle, like the tea lights under her pottery diffusers.

"Sheesh." He rubbed the back of his neck and stared at her. "Honest to God, if the two of you are cooking up some matchmaking scheme for me..."

"We're not. I swear." Faith was, but Jamie hadn't ever said she'd go along with it. And Dev didn't have the slightest idea that she was the intended match. He'd never think of that.

"You'd better not be." He continued to gaze at her. "You know what? Maybe you should e-mail me that questionnaire. Here's my home e-mail address." He moved back to the desk and picked up a pen she had lying there.

"Fine." She'd become so sensitized that his quick scribbling on the notepad beside the computer became erotically charged. Watching him write, she imagined his hands on her and his fingers caressing her skin. She swallowed.

"I should probably take off."

He was leaving, and she had nothing to keep him here. Maybe he'd seen right through her. He could have thought back to the Hot Commodity thing, added that to the highly sexual description and come up with the conclusion that she had a mega crush on him. Maybe he was beating a quick retreat now before she could throw herself at him.

Desperate to erase that impression, she faked an elaborate yawn. "That's a wonderful idea. I'm totally exhausted, and I was hoping this wouldn't take too long. I'm ready for bed."

He looked even more agitated. "Right. I'm wiped out, myself. Long day." He headed for the moose head coat tree.

Oh, no. Maybe he'd thought she meant ready for *bed* as in ready to have sex. "Listen, Dev, I would hate for you to get the wrong idea from all this and think I'm attracted to you."

"No, I didn't get that. And, for the record, I'm not particularly attracted to you, either." He grabbed his coat and quickly unlocked her door. "That kiss was just…"

"A fluke."

"Exactly. A fluke."

"You know, it's a really good thing we're not

attracted to each other,'' she said. ''That would be awkward.''

''You said it.'' He opened the door. ''See you later.'' Then he was gone.

Dazed, Jamie stood motionless for several seconds. ''That certainly went well,'' she muttered at last. Then she walked over and sat at the computer.

She might as well e-mail him the questionnaire before she forgot. As if she would forget. Ha. She'd never forget a single thing about tonight, not even the embarrassing parts—especially not the embarrassing parts.

Logging onto the Internet, she glanced at Dev's e-mail address. Risk Taker. Well, there it was, spelled out. He was one and she wasn't. There had been a moment, when he'd cupped her head in both hands, when she could have gone for it. He might not be particularly attracted to her, but there had been a window of opportunity when he might have started to become attracted.

But she'd lost her nerve. Now the window of opportunity was closed, latched, and the shade pulled down.

SOME RISK TAKER HE WAS. Dev cursed himself for a coward as he flagged down a cab and headed back to his apartment. He was damned lucky he'd even found a cab, but he'd been so eager to make his exit that he hadn't wanted to call one from her place.

He'd been afraid that if he stayed any longer, he'd try to kiss her again, and she might reject him. He hadn't been willing to test it.

But he should have tested it. Jamie might have said she wasn't attracted to him, but she'd kissed him as if she might be, given some encouragement. And she'd typed in that "hot commodity" and "highly sexual" stuff, even if she and Faith had been giggling at the time. There was a chance he could have built on that.

But no, he'd been too worried about failure to give it a decent try. If he conducted himself that way in the market, he'd be toast. If he conducted himself that way with other women, he'd still be a virgin.

Jamie was just a woman. He sighed and leaned back against the cracked upholstery in the cab. Yeah, sure, and Sammy Sosa was just a baseball player.

This was all Faith's fault. For years she'd been raving about Jamie, who was so smart, so talented, so amazing. No wonder he couldn't follow his normal playbook with Jamie. She was several moves ahead of him.

Well, he was back in control of the situation now, or as much in control as possible, considering the schemes that could be going on behind his back. Jamie might not think she was part of Operation Marry Off Dev, but she was loyal to Faith, and Faith could be very convincing. He should know, because he'd backed more than one of Faith's schemes.

This collection of boutiques was an example, because he'd helped convince his dad to give Faith and Jamie the space for a ridiculously low rent. But he thought this particular concept had promise, so he wasn't sorry. Besides, his dad thought a lot of

Jamie and liked the idea of giving her a boost. The whole family liked Jamie.

Then, as the cab turned onto Lakeshore Drive, he had an inspiration.

If he became involved with Jamie, he could stymie the matchmakers on two fronts. Jamie wouldn't be part of a matchmaking scheme if he was dating her, and his mother and aunt would back off for a while, because they liked Jamie. The plan had merit. There was the small problem that Jamie didn't want anything to do with him, but maybe he could work around that.

He thought about it some more as he greeted the doorman, walked through the lobby and used his key to activate the elevator. The idea of getting involved with Jamie made his groin tingle in anticipation. He brushed his hand over his mouth, remembering the feel of her lips, and his pulse rate jumped several points.

The elevator arrived and whisked him up to his twenty-fifth-floor apartment. A short walk down a carpeted hallway brought him to his door. Unlocking it and going inside, he left the lights off. As big a fuss as he'd made about the Bulls game, he wasn't interested in turning it on. Instead, he moved over to the far side of the apartment, where a wall of windows looked out onto the inky expanse of Lake Michigan.

To his left, the Chicago skyline glittered, and the sight never failed to stir him. Wealth had always been a part of his life, and most of the time he didn't consider it the biggest part. But it could buy him this view, and for that he was grateful.

As always when he stood here, his gaze followed the shoreline north. Somewhere embedded in that brilliant necklace were the lights of his parents' lakefront home in Evansville. They'd told him once that during happy hour they always lifted a glass in his direction, and that had made him smile. He'd been lucky, being born to those two.

But as had most of his friends' parents, they were starting to moan about not having grandkids. It was normal, but Dev thought there was more to it than wanting to cuddle babies and root for Little Leaguers again. His mom and dad needed to know that there would be heirs to the Sherman empire for at least the next two generations. He didn't blame them but he didn't like being rushed, either.

Dating someone like Jamie would stall the marriage mobile for a little while, anyway. But if he had a prayer of succeeding, he'd have to stop being such a chicken shit and put a move on the woman that she wouldn't be able to resist. He'd have to forget about her brains and appeal to a more primitive part of her make-up. It was all about focus.

If he'd never kissed her, he'd doubt his ability to manage a seduction. But until they'd dropped the cup, she'd been into it. Without the cup incident, he might have been able to bypass that IQ of hers while he honed in on her libido.

All he needed to do was create a second chance. And the very cup that had spoiled the moment the first time around would be his entrée back into her apartment. He'd promised to replace it, and he always kept his promises.

DESPITE SPRITZING some lavender on her pillow, Jamie didn't sleep well. She was up early and checking her e-mail to see if Dev had sent anything back. Come to find out he'd sent his own questionnaire and two of his friends had sent theirs, as well.

Dev must have been a busy boy after leaving her, which only confirmed what she'd suspected—he hadn't been tired, only desperate to get away from her. At least she had a start on information she could use to modify The Red Doors program.

She'd hand the info over to Jason, a developer they'd kept on staff to maintain the program. With some late nights, which Jason seemed to love putting in, the revised program could be up and running in a couple of days. She'd talk to Faith today about getting some new ads in place.

Because she was weak, she took the time to glance over the rest of Dev's answers to her questions. She discovered that she and Dev were about as opposite as two people could get. She liked subtlety and he apparently went for the obvious.

She wasn't into lingerie, but if she were, she'd choose filmy white outfits that were semisheer. Dev admitted to liking leather, specifically a G-string and a push-up bra. And spike-heeled boots. Maybe even a whip, for all she knew.

As for fragrances, no delicate florals for him. Although he'd said he liked the cinnamon she'd had in the diffuser, he was turned on by heavy, exotic perfumes, the kind that would likely choke her to death. Oh, well. She'd asked, and if she was disappointed in his answers, they only emphasized how wrong she was for him.

After downloading all the information onto a disk, she got ready for work. She thought about Dev as she stood in front of her closet. Because she was fresh out of leather G-strings and push-up bras, she pulled out her favorite green suit. It was probably too conservative to get his attention, but it made her feel pretty, and she could use that right now.

She wondered how he would play things this morning. If he ducked out of their regular coffee gathering, she'd know that he was uncomfortable being with her after what had taken place in her apartment. Under the circumstances, she'd rather walk in a couple of minutes later than usual to give him a chance to commit himself one way or the other. If he bailed, she'd have an assistant deliver the tape of the Bulls game to his office.

When she stepped off the bus, she checked her watch and decided to window-shop on Michigan Avenue for a little while. Although it was still very cold, the wind had let up, so she should be able to dawdle without freezing to death.

Unfortunately, the constant reminder of Valentine's Day in every display window depressed her. Not only was she worried about how The Red Doors would do this holiday season, she was also reminded that she had no love life. Nobody was likely to send her gym socks in a heart-shaped box, let alone candy and flowers.

That was her own fault, she admitted as she gave up on window-shopping and headed down Michigan Avenue at a faster pace. She could have arranged her schedule around an occasional date.

But she hadn't.

Instead she'd compared every other guy with Dev and found them not worth the effort. Maybe it was time to be ruthlessly honest with herself. She'd been doing more than dreaming of Dev as the central player in her sexual fantasies. She'd been imagining him as the central player in her life, for the rest of her life—white lace, champagne toasts, happily ever after.

Talk about idiotic. But Faith had brought those unconscious dreams to the surface yesterday. Jamie and Dev as a couple. Not likely. She would love to share Dev's answers to the questionnaire with Faith, just to prove that a matchup was hopeless, but she'd promised Dev confidentiality, and she always kept her promises.

CHAPTER FIVE

DEV ARRIVED at the café early because he didn't want to miss Jamie. He wondered if she'd wimp out, come in the back and go straight up to her office. That would be a dead giveaway that she was avoiding him, because he knew how much she loved that front entrance. In a way, her ducking out might be a good sign, because he'd know that kiss had knocked her off balance, too.

As luck would have it, Faith showed up before Jamie. Whipping off her coat and gloves, she sat across from Dev, a gleam of anticipation in her eyes. "Did you and Jamie take care of the questionnaire last night?"

He kept his expression neutral. Faith wouldn't hear about the kiss from him. "We did." He glanced up as Mr. Willis approached with a steaming mug of coffee for each of them. Dev had never asked, but he would bet the guy had worked in at least one five-star restaurant in his career. His talent for anticipating a customer's wishes was uncanny. "Thanks, Mr. Willis."

"You're most welcome."

"You're wonderful, Mr. Willis." Faith gave the coffee bar manager a smile before zeroing in on Dev again. "That's good that you completed the questionnaire," she said. "We need that info."

"For the program."

"Of course for the program. Dev, I am not giving your answers to Mom. Considering the kinds of questions Jamie and I dreamed up, Mom would have a heart attack if she saw your answers."

"I don't want *anybody* to know what my answers were—except Jamie, of course."

"And that's the way it'll be. I promise."

Dev sipped his coffee and gazed at his sister. She'd also been raised to keep her promises, so he had to believe she meant what she said. But that didn't explain her cat-that-ate-the-canary expression. "You're up to something. I know that look."

"I'm excited about the additions to the program, that's all. Oh, here's Jamie."

Dev's pulse rate picked up. So she wasn't so rattled by their kiss that she'd skipped having the usual morning coffee. Okay, she was a cool customer, which made him even more determined to put his plan into action.

"Hi." Jamie flipped back her hood and unwound her scarf, which she'd done every workday morning since it had turned cold in November. Except this morning Dev saw it differently, as the first stage in undressing. As she took off her gloves and slipped out of her camel-colored coat, he pictured her reaching for the row of buttons on the jacket of her two-piece suit.

She'd undo them in a matter-of-fact way. A striptease wasn't Jamie's style. Underneath she'd be wearing cotton underwear, and that was fine with him. A woman who wore cotton underwear had suddenly become an irresistible challenge. He saw her as earthy and basic, someone who was into comfort. And he would make her so comfortable…after he turned her inside out.

"Dev says you finished the questionnaire," Faith said.

Dev forced his attention away from Jamie and hoped he hadn't been caught ogling.

"Yep, we finished it." Jamie saw Mr. Willis coming with her coffee and gave him a big grin. "Mr. Willis, you're a peach."

Dev felt an unreasonable spurt of jealousy, and toward a sixty-year-old man, for crying out loud. He was amazed at how quickly he'd settled into the idea of Jamie as his current girlfriend. But she had no idea of his intentions, and he didn't plan to be obvious about it. He'd leave himself room to back out if she vigorously hated the idea.

After Jamie sat, she rummaged in her large purse and pulled out a videotape. "Here's your Bulls game." She handed it to him.

"Thanks." He felt his sister's curiosity go up a notch. "I forgot to set my VCR before I left for Jamie's, so she offered to tape the game for me."

"So the interview took that long?" Faith asked.

"Oh, I'm sure Dev saw the last of the game when he got home, but this way he didn't have to miss any of it," Jamie said quickly. "By the way, where's Dixie this morning?"

Faith studied them both for a moment before answering. ''She's upstairs bugging our supplier for those red teddies we wanted to put on special, the ones that were supposed to arrive last week.'' Faith leaned forward. ''But if you ask me, she's hiding out. It seems she has a secret admirer, and she doesn't know quite what to make of it.''

''A secret admirer?'' Jamie's saucy grin appeared. ''That's cool. And she has no clue who it is?''

Jamie had a secret admirer, too, Dev thought, but not for long. Soon he'd swing into action. That grin of hers reminded him of how good her lips tasted, and he could hardly wait for more.

''She has no idea who it is,'' Faith said. ''But she's started getting little notes on elegant paper.''

''Are we supposed to know about this?'' Dev asked.

Faith nodded. ''She said I could tell you both, in case this admirer turns out to be a dirty old man and she needs backup.''

''I hope not.'' Jamie's green eyes sparkled. ''I hope he's someone wonderful.''

Dev wondered what he had to do to produce that sparkle in Jamie's eyes. He wasn't into notes on elegant stationery.

''I have a business decision to run past you, Faith,'' Jamie said. ''I'm thinking of using a patchouli blend in the diffusers at Heaven Scent for the Valentine push. It'll ratchet up the intensity, and I think we need that extra punch.''

''Good thinking, Jamie,'' Faith said. ''Patchouli's a great idea.''

Dev didn't have much to add to the conversation,

but he wanted to see if he could get Jamie to look at him. So far she hadn't met his gaze. "Sounds like patchouli would make you sneeze."

"If it does," Faith said with a smile, "that's a sure sign your love life sucks."

"Why am I so positive you made that up?"

"She did," Jamie said, laughing. Yet her cheeks turned pink and her gaze skittered over to his and away again. "Faith, no fair harassing our best source of interviews."

"That's right," Dev said. "I'll have you know I talked two of my buddies into e-mailing Jamie their completed questionnaires last night."

"Absolutely true." Jamie's glance settled on him for a moment before veering over to Faith. "So far Dev and his friends have been a lot more helpful than my brothers, who whined about how they hate to fill out forms."

"Besides," Dev said, "if anybody should be sneezing when they smell patchouli it would be you, little sis."

Faith wrinkled her nose at him. "With what's going on around here, who has time for a love life?"

"Ain't that the truth," Jamie said. "In fact, I need to get upstairs and consult with Jason on retooling our program." She stood. Efficiency in motion, she hooked her purse strap over her shoulder, her coat over her arm, and picked up her coffee.

"I'll go with you," Faith said. "Elevator or stairs?"

"Stairs, of course."

"Of course," Faith said. "I don't know why I

even asked a woman who ice skates on her lunch hour. Okay, stairs it is. I can use the exercise. Bye, Dev.''

''Bye, Dev,'' Jamie echoed.

Dev stood, too. He'd hoped to subtly find out if Jamie would be home tonight without letting her know he'd be stopping by with the replacement for her cup. He didn't want to tell her what he planned because he was afraid she'd suggest that he bring the cup to the office instead. No, a surprise visit was best.

But here she was leaving already, and he had no idea what her plans were for tonight. He didn't want to go all the way over there and find her gone, or worse, discover Faith was there.

Finally, when she was partway up the stairs, he had no choice but to ask her straight out. ''Jamie, are you going to be home tonight?''

She froze. Then she glanced at him over her shoulder. ''Um, I think so. Why?''

Faith looked at him strangely. Well, he didn't have time to worry about that. He had a big hairy lie to tell. ''One guy I contacted about the questionnaire said his computer's in the shop, so he couldn't do the e-mail thing. But if I give him your number, you can ask him the questions over the phone.''

''That would be fine. I should be around.''

''Good. I'll tell him.'' If he didn't know better, he'd swear that she looked disappointed. Maybe she'd wanted his question to lead to something else, something involving him. But that was crazy. She'd had several chances the night before to encourage him, and other than the kiss she'd dismissed as a fluke, she'd kept her distance.

"Then it's off to work we go," Faith said brightly.

Mr. Willis hurried after Faith with a lidded coffee cup in his hand. "I wonder if you would be so kind as to deliver this to Mrs. Merriweather? I know how much everyone depends on a bracing cup of coffee in the morning."

Faith took the coffee. "I'm sure she'll appreciate that, Mr. Willis." Then she followed Jamie up the winding staircase.

Dev turned away, not wanting to be caught staring after Jamie as she climbed the stairs. But he wanted to watch. Each step she took made the material of her skirt cup her trim little bottom. Instead he polished off his coffee, stood and handed the mug to Mr. Willis.

"They all work too hard," the older man said.

"Sometimes you have to, if you want to get a business off the ground." Dev knew that was something else that attracted him to Jamie. She threw herself heart and soul into whatever she tackled.

"Yes, I suppose that's true. But I hate to see them missing out on the small pleasures of life."

Dev was touched by the older man's concern. Obviously he was in a service job because he was the soul of service. "Your coffee sure qualifies as one of the pleasures of life. I don't know how I lived without it before." He couldn't imagine going without his daily doses of Jamie, either, as they shared this morning ritual.

"Thank you, Mr. Sherman. That's kind of you to say so."

"It's Dev."

Mr. Willis gave him a rare smile. "Old habits are hard to break. Now if you'll excuse me, I need to go see to the espresso machine. It was acting up yesterday."

"I need to take off, myself." He glanced at the stairway. Jamie and Faith were gone. "Thanks again for the coffee."

"My pleasure, Mr. Sherman."

As Dev headed for the side entrance, making the same trip he had every morning since November when The Red Doors opened, he offered up a little prayer that the business would survive. Besides temporarily lowering the rent on the space, his father would do nothing else to shore up the venture.

Outsiders might think that with Faith as a partner in The Red Doors, the business was automatically backed with Sherman money. Not so. Even the break on the rent had been a hard-won concession. D. H. Sherman believed in educating his children and letting them make their own way.

Ten years ago Dev had resented the hell out of his father's attitude. After partying his way through college, he'd expected to slide right into a slot with the brokerage firm. He'd been convinced his father was bluffing.

Instead he'd been required to dig for every client, and he'd nearly bombed out. But he'd made it, made it very nicely. Grudgingly, he'd admitted to himself that his father had been right in forcing him to grow up.

He hadn't said so to the old man yet, but he would, eventually. Just not right now, when Faith was struggling. His father might get all full of himself and his excellent parenting skills and decide to hike the rent.

That would be horrendous for Faith, but even worse for Jamie, who had sunk everything she had into the business. Although it didn't make a lot of sense, he felt responsible for whether she made it or not. He'd helped her earn that original stake, and he'd been there when she'd had the brainstorm that could make her even more money. He didn't want to see her fail. That was another good reason to stay close to her, so he could keep an eye on things.

JAMIE WALKED with Faith down a hallway between Heaven Scent and The Diamond Mine. In allotting space, they'd reasoned out that Sheer Delights required the most floor space, so the other two boutiques had been scaled down to allow for a hallway that led back to a storeroom and office area.

"Okay, I think we're out of earshot now," Faith said. "Tell me about last night."

Jamie glanced at her. "Faith, it's hopeless. I think it's sweet, what you tried to do, but Dev and I are not meant for each other. I've known that all along."

"How can you be so sure? What happened? Did you fight?"

"No. But we're not on the same wavelength,

okay?'' She opened the door and immediately heard Dixie, her tone sweeter than a mint julep as she talked on the phone to the supplier. She was giving him hell, but he was probably so mesmerized by her accent that he didn't even realize it.

Dixie's cubby was off to the left, partitioned as was the rest of the area with portable walls that could be rearranged according to staffing needs.

If the elegant public areas of The Red Doors were Faith's natural environment, the back room was Jamie's. Practicality was the watchword. She'd made sure the desks, computers and telephones were reasonably priced and easy to use.

Because the business wouldn't open for another half hour, Jamie, Dixie and Faith were the only ones there. Jason, the person Jamie needed to consult about retooling the program, would arrive at any minute.

''Come sit with me until Jason gets here so you can tell me what happened,'' Faith said. She led the way past Dixie's cubby and deposited the coffee on Dixie's cluttered desk. Dixie waved her thanks.

Jamie obliged Faith's request because she wanted this to be over. Faith was going to embarrass her if she continued with the matchmaking plans. ''Just keep your voice down,'' she said softly. ''I really don't want Dixie to know about any of this, and I'm sure she could listen to us and ream the supplier at the same time.''

''Yes, ma'am.'' Faith continued past Jamie's cubicle to her own, and to her credit, she lowered her voice. ''When you didn't call me last night I was hoping you and Dev had become so involved that you forgot everything else.''

''You have to give it up.'' Jamie tossed her coat over the back of a chair in front of Faith's desk and sat. ''Trust me, I'm not the right woman for Dev.''

Faith sat across from her, took a sip of her coffee and made a face. ''Cold. We'll have to nuke these—but not now. Jason could show up anytime, and I'm dying to hear why you'd be so terrible for my big brother.''

''I'm not going to get specific.''

''His answers to the questionnaire, huh? Too far out?''

''Not me, not ever. Not by any stretch of the imagination.''

Faith rolled her eyes. ''You know guys. They think they want all this fantasy stuff, but what they really want is a good woman who will love them even when they leave socks on the floor and the toilet seat up. So what if you're not into his preferences? Use them to grab his interest. I can't believe you'll have to dress up like Xena the Warrior Princess very often after that.''

Jamie's jaw dropped. She didn't think Faith was a hacker, but the description was so on the nose, it was as if Faith had broken into Jamie's computer and read Dev's questionnaire.

''I guessed?'' Faith laughed. ''What a hoot.''

Jamie felt the heat rising to her cheeks. ''I'm not saying a word—not a single word.''

''You don't have to. One look at your face was all I needed. Oh, Jamie, he's not really into all that.

He's just being a guy." She eyed Jamie, her blue eyes merry. "We could organize an ensemble, you know. There's that little leather outfit we special-ordered for the woman who changed her mind. She was about your size, and I'm positive we haven't sent it back."

"This is getting way too weird for me. And if you say one word to Dev, I'm in such big trouble. I promised him that everything would be anonymous, *especially* in his case, because he's so paranoid about people trying to marry him off."

Faith shook her head. "I've never been part of that, which I keep trying to tell him. And why would I snitch on you? It would screw up any chance you have with him, and right now the only person I'd like to see dating my brother is you. I haven't liked anybody he's gone out with in the past five years. No, make that ten years. Actually, make that forever."

Jamie heard Jason's voice as he came in with Veronica, a clerk working the morning shift in Heaven Scent. "I have to go. All this aside, we have to get the revised program up and running."

"I know." Faith's expression sobered. "I went by the other store yesterday afternoon on my way home. It's cheesy, but I saw guys walking in there, guys we should have had coming to The Red Doors."

"I think Dixie's idea will work. Career women are busy, too, so why wouldn't they like a program that helps them pick out something sexy to wear for that certain man?"

"Indeed." The twinkle returned to Faith's eyes. "You would think that once a woman had that kind of information about a man who interests her, she'd put it to good use." She winked at Jamie. "At least, if she's as smart as I think she is."

Jamie groaned. "Do you have any idea how much courage it would take for me to do something like that?"

"Do you realize how many regrets you'll have if you fail to use the information that fate has dropped in your lap?"

Stuck for the answer, Jamie gazed at her friend. "I have to go talk with Jason."

"I know. I have to dream up a new ad. But you'll have a few spare moments to consider what I just said, so I hope you do think about it."

Jamie was sure she'd think of nothing else.

DEV SPENT his entire lunch hour looking for a blue cup. Twice he walked past the skating rink and saw Jamie there, her red hair catching the noon sunlight streaming down between the buildings. He stayed within the protective coloring of the passing crowd, not wanting her to notice him and later ask what he'd been doing.

He'd hoped to accomplish this cup-buying himself, without the help of his secretary Edna, but after looking through several department stores with no luck, he returned to the office in defeat. Mostly he tried to act like a grown-up around Edna, because she was old enough to be his mother and tended to treat him as if he were a little boy.

She'd been with Sherman Investments longer than he had. Recognizing gold when he saw it, Dev had talked her into working for him when one of the senior members retired. She was more efficient than he was, looked like Tootsie, and he paid her really, really well. He hoped she wouldn't quit until she was at least eighty.

"Edna, I'm looking for a blue cup." He took off his trench coat and came over to stand by her desk.

Edna adjusted her glasses and swung away from her computer screen to gaze at him. "Did you lose one?"

"No, I broke one. It looked like a giant teacup, but it was heavy, like a mug and...someone served me coffee in it. I dropped it and I want to replace it, but I don't know where to find one." He felt about six.

"What color blue?"

"Sky-blue. Or maybe lake-blue. Something along those lines. Not pale blue and not dark blue. In between."

"Would you like me to go buy you one?"

He gazed at her. "You're not gonna tell me where I can get it myself, are you?"

Her smile was prim. "If I told you all my secrets, then you wouldn't need me anymore."

"I will need you forever. But if you would take an hour off and go buy that cup from whatever secret source you have, I will give you stock options."

"I already have enough stock options."

"Then take time to get yourself a double mocha

espresso at The Red Bean while you're out, and charge it to me."

"Bingo." Edna turned off her computer and rummaged in her bottom desk drawer for her purse.

"How much money do you need?"

She glanced up at him with that same prim smile on her face. "I'll let you know."

"Thank you, Edna. I will be forever in your debt."

"That's my plan." Then she walked to the coatrack, took down her red wool coat, and left the office.

Forty-five minutes later she tapped on his office door. When she came in, she placed a gift-wrapped package on his desk. The gift wrapping was a nice touch that he never would have thought of.

"I assume the cup's in there?" he asked.

"It is."

Although he was glad it looked so festive, it was probably Edna's way of making sure he couldn't see inside so he had to take her word that she'd found the right cup. Silently she handed him the bill, and he reached for his wallet.

"Thank you," he said, giving her the money. "I love you to pieces, Edna, but you're a real control freak."

Behind her glasses, her eyes twinkled, as if he'd given her a compliment. "And that's why your office runs with the precision of a Rolex watch. Now, if you'll excuse me, I have a lot to do. Fortunately I now have enough caffeine in my system to get most of it done, despite the delay. Thank you for the espresso."

"You're welcome. And Edna, this cup thing... was important."

"I could tell."

As she walked out the door, Dev picked up the square package and took a closer look at the wrapping paper. It had wedding bells on it. "Edna! What's with the wrapping paper?"

She turned. "They had a special going. Anything that was a wedding gift they wrapped for free."

"But—"

"Don't you think it looks pretty?"

"Yes, I do, but this isn't—"

"Do you want me to take it back and get different wrapping paper?" She frowned at him exactly the way his mother used to when he'd been an ungrateful little kid. "Surely you wouldn't want to waste that beautiful job, not to mention my time?"

"No. This is fine." Dev decided it didn't matter all that much. At first glance he hadn't even noticed the wedding bells. Jamie might not, either, and he'd wad the paper up as soon as she unwrapped the box.

"Okay, then." Edna left the office.

So he had the cup. Now all he had to do was deliver it. Then he had another brainstorm. After work he'd use one of The Red Doors kiosks to order up something else for Jamie. He'd start with Heaven Scent, her favorite boutique.

If things went well tonight, he might consider a purchase from Sheer Delights next. Then maybe he'd go for something from The Diamond Mine.

Whoa. The Diamond Mine? He sat looking at the paper with the wedding bells on it. He thought about the picture over the love seat in Jamie's apartment. His stomach felt funny. Either he had a major case of indigestion from the chili dog he'd wolfed down at lunch, or he was getting in much deeper than he'd planned.

Probably the chili dog.

CHAPTER SIX

DURING THE DAY Jamie accessed her home computer's e-mail and discovered three more of Dev's friends had sent in answers to her questionnaire. She interviewed her brothers at home, and Faith forwarded answers from two men she used to work with. Jason offered to fill out a questionnaire, too, and he had some great ideas for tweaking the program. Thanks to everyone's cooperation, there was enough data to move forward.

By five, when she peeked into Jason's cubby on the way home, he was deep in his work and showed no signs of leaving.

''You don't have to burn the midnight oil on this, Jason.'' She said it to clear her conscience, but she knew he would anyway. Jason was so intense, but maybe that was partly because he was twenty-four, involved with his first live-in girlfriend, and determined to make good at his first real job.

He glanced up at her, his round face serious. ''You know I'm a midnight-oil kind of guy,'' he said. ''I do my best work between twelve and three.''

''What about Wendy? That can't be very popular

with her, you being at the office in the wee small hours.''

''She's cool with it,'' Jason said with a touch of pride. ''She understands my work is important to me. And I—'' he flushed slightly ''—I make it up to her on the weekends.''

Jamie smiled at him. ''That's good to know.'' She had a tough time imagining Jason as a great lover, but she'd seen his questionnaire answers and the guy had more imagination in that department than she'd given him credit for. ''Wendy's a lucky lady,'' she added. ''Well, guess I'll be taking off, then.''

''Have a good night.''

''Thanks.'' As she walked down the hallway she wondered how long it had been since she'd had what could be called a good night. Almost two years, come to think of it. Her last good night had been the Valentine's dinner with Faith and Dev.

She wouldn't call last night good. Overstimulation was more like it. By contrast, tonight would be understimulation, with nothing to look forward to except a phone call from one of Dev's friends with his questionnaire answers.

Jamie stepped out of the hallway into the well-lit mezzanine. The boutiques and coffee bar would remain open for another hour to catch the after-work shoppers. She glanced inside The Diamond Mine where Faith was helping a customer. Because Faith wasn't available to talk, Jamie went into Heaven Scent to pick up a small vial of patchouli oil to create the blend she had in mind.

Although she'd suggested using the new scent in

the shop diffusers during the Valentine season, she wanted to spend a few hours with it at home before making the final decision. Just as she was leaving the boutique, the phone rang, indicating an order was being placed from one of the kiosks. Every time that happened, she felt a personal glow of triumph. It was a damned good idea.

The vial in a small red shopping bag with The Red Doors logo printed on it in gold, she strolled past The Diamond Mine again. Faith was huddled over the display case with the same customer, and Jamie hoped she was making a big sale. In Sheer Delights, Dixie was packaging up something for two thirty-something women.

Jamie counted the number of customers, including the two who had been in Heaven Scent and the group of four guys in the café downstairs. She wouldn't have minded seeing Dev at one of the tables, but he wasn't there. Once in a while he stopped by The Red Bean after work, but not often. He was probably already heading home.

From the top of the stairs she couldn't tell if any of the computer kiosks were still in use, although she could be certain of at least one sale from them a moment ago. Still, she had to admit the place wasn't exactly bustling. Thank goodness they had a plan to increase business or she'd feel really depressed.

She felt better knowing that Jason was hard at work making that plan happen. And her current contribution was to go home and experiment with the patchouli. Maybe it would put her in the mood to try on the tiny red leather outfit she'd tucked into her oversize purse. Faith had dropped it on her desk earlier in the day, and she'd shoved it in her purse, more to get it out of sight than anything.

Well, okay, she was curious. She'd never worn intimate leather apparel. She didn't think of herself as an intimate-leather-apparel sort of woman. No doubt she'd put on the outfit, laugh herself silly, and take it off again. Or maybe she'd forget the whole thing. Descending the stairs, she walked into the frigid evening air and headed for the bus stop.

DEV STOOD in the small entryway of Jamie's apartment building, the gift-wrapped cup in one hand and a gift bag from The Red Doors containing a scented candle in the other. After ordering the candle from one of the kiosks late that afternoon, he'd stepped out in time to see Jamie leaving through the front entrance. He was glad they hadn't run into each other. Surprise was his secret weapon.

But secret weapon or not, he was still nervous. The whole idea of the wedding bell wrapping paper had been working on him. His stomach continued to feel funny, and he couldn't blame it on the chili dog anymore. Slowly but surely he was starting to connect Jamie with the M-word.

That was ridiculous, of course. He'd only kissed her once, and he couldn't possibly be so far gone after a single touch of the lips. But all the months of thinking about her without taking action must have done something to his brain, because the ever-popular word *affair* tasted bitter in his mouth this time, while the long-avoided M-word rested on his tongue like a piece of Godiva chocolate, rich and full of promise.

He'd never felt that way about a woman he wanted. About a good-looking stock, definitely, and he'd learned to trust his instincts when it came to the market. He wasn't nearly as sure of his instincts when it came to women. Still, he couldn't shake the feeling that tonight was huge in his life. His heart beat embarrassingly fast as he used the hand that held the gift bag to nudge her intercom button. What if she wouldn't see him?

After several seconds her voice floated from the intercom. "Who is it?" She sounded puzzled.

"Dev."

"Dev? Is something wrong? Is Faith—"

"Nothing's wrong. Faith's just fine. I happened to run across a replacement for your cup today, so I thought I'd bring it over."

"Oh! Um, okay, um, come on up." The door lock buzzed and he was let in.

Taking a deep breath, he crossed the small lobby and started up the stairs. Tonight he'd dressed down a little, putting on jeans that had been softened by a couple of hundred washings, and a sweater he'd had since college. He wanted Jamie to know that, like her, he wasn't overly clothes-conscious.

She opened her door wearing a furry white bathrobe that covered her from neck to ankles, but her feet were bare. Even more interesting, she had on more makeup than usual—dark red lipstick, mascara, even some blush.

She looked as if she was getting ready for a date, and yet she'd told him she'd be available for the phone call from his friend, the one he'd made up. Maybe this was a spur-of-the-moment date. Spur-of-the-moment or not, he didn't like it.

"I'm sorry," he said. "Are you getting ready to go out?"

"No." But she looked nervous, as if he'd caught her at something.

He had another, more unpleasant thought. She was entertaining someone in her bedroom, someone who would wait quietly in there until Dev dropped off the cup and left. If so, he'd better stick with handicapping the stock market, because his instincts regarding women sucked.

"Well," he said, "if I've come at a bad time, I can always—"

"That's okay." She stepped back from the door. "I'm touched that you went shopping for a cup so soon. It really wasn't necessary." As she closed the door behind him, her glance took in the red bag in his other hand. "Something smells good."

"Yeah, I saw this and thought of you." He handed her the bag. "And here's the cup."

"Thank you, Dev." She stood clutching both against her furry robe. "That's very thoughtful of you. I—"

"It smells different in here." An exotic fragrance totally unlike the cinnamon and cloves he remembered filled the apartment. While the cinnamon had made him feel cozy and had aroused him in a slow, sensuous way, this stuff attacked him at a gut level.

One whiff and he imagined a sex orgy—naked bodies, silk sheets, complicated positions and lots of warm massage oil.

"It's the patchouli blend I was talking about."

"So *that's* patchouli."

"I'm trying it out before we introduce it as the background fragrance for Heaven Scent this month. What do you think?"

It was sending him into sexual fantasyland. "It's okay."

"Maybe I need to try ylang-ylang, then. I want something very arousing, not just *okay.*"

If she used anything more arousing than this, she was liable to have people getting horizontal right there in the store, but he wasn't about to say that. He also wasn't sure if it was strictly the patchouli or seeing her in that furry bathrobe and bare feet. He wanted to know what was under the robe. He really, really wanted to know.

"Well, thank you for the cup and the—" she peered into the bag "—the candle. Mmm, cinnamon, my favorite."

"You're welcome." He stood there with his jacket still on, getting warmer by the minute as he waited for her to invite him to stay. The longer he waited, the more he suspected she had a guy stashed in the bedroom.

"Well, I suppose you have things to do," she said.

"Not much." His suspicions deepened. The patchouli, the makeup, the bare feet and the bathrobe all added up to funny business. He should just leave, because she obviously wanted him to. But, dammit, he was stuck with that funny feeling in his stomach and the feeling wouldn't let him just abandon the field without a struggle.

Besides, he wanted to see the damn cup to find out what Edna had come up with. "So," he said, "aren't you going to open the box?"

"Sure. Sure I am. Would you...like to take off your jacket?"

"Why not?" As he hung it on the moose head coat tree, he noticed what he'd been too preoccupied to figure out before. No other man's jacket hung there. People didn't run around in shirtsleeves on a February night in Chicago. So maybe there wasn't anybody hiding in Jamie's bedroom, after all. The knot in his stomach loosened.

She walked into her tiny living room and set the red bag on her coffee table. Then she looked at the square package more closely. "Wedding bells?"

He should have known a smart woman like Jamie wouldn't miss that, even though he had. "It was...the only paper they had on hand." Telling her the gift wrapping was free for wedding gifts would make him look really cheap. And no way was he confessing the murmurings of his soul on the subject of matrimony. Not until he'd had a chance to get used to the concept.

"It's pretty." She pried off the white ribbon and unfastened the tape carefully. "I should save it in case I need to wrap a wedding gift. It seems like one pops up every other week these days."

"I know what you mean. It's like this contagious disease."

She glanced at him, a smile on her wine-red lips. "You really are phobic, aren't you?"

"I might not be if my family would back off, but I hate being manipulated." The minute he spoke, he realized that he'd been resisting marriage because his family had been pushing it. How infantile was that? Besides, he'd manipulated the situation tonight to his advantage, so he was no better than his scheming relatives.

He massaged the bridge of his nose. "Okay, I have a confession to make. There's no guy with a broken computer who plans to call you about his questionnaire." He glanced at her, to see how she was taking the news. "And though I just told you I hate to be manipulated, I've been guilty of doing exactly that. I'd planned all along to come by with the cup, but I wanted to surprise you."

Holding the half-open package, she stared at him, her cheeks even pinker than the blush had made them. "You did? How come?"

"I, um..." He searched through his vocabulary and found it lacking. "I wasn't quite telling the truth last night."

She swallowed. "About what?"

"About not being attracted to you. I said that because I didn't think that you were attracted to—"

"I am."

His heart started galloping furiously. "You are?"

She nodded.

"That's...that's great." As he gazed at her standing there with the wedding bell paper in her hands, he had a feeling of inevitability. But that didn't mean he had to rush into anything.

She took a deep breath. "Well, would you like...coffee?"

"That would be good."

"Or...or wine? It's jug wine, though, and I'll bet you don't drink—"

"Sure I do. But coffee's good." He gestured toward the package in her hand. "Why don't you finish unwrapping that first?"

"All right." Her hands trembled as she took off the wrapping.

"Need some help?" He took a step toward her.

"That's okay. I have it." But she didn't. The cup tumbled out of the box.

Before it hit the floor and broke, Dev had a chance to see that it was a perfect match for the other one. Edna had done an outstanding job.

"Oh, no!" Jamie glanced down at the cup, then back at Dev. "Stay there," she said, holding up her hand, then pointing to her head. "We have history when it comes to picking up broken cups."

He crossed to her anyway. "I'll get you another one tomorrow."

"Oh, no, you won't." She dropped to her knees and began gathering broken pieces and putting them in the box. "I was half to blame before, and this was totally my fault."

"No, it wasn't." He crouched next to her, more careful this time so they wouldn't pull another Laurel and Hardy routine. "If I hadn't admitted I was attracted to you, you wouldn't have gotten nervous and dropped it."

She looked over at him. "I was hoping you couldn't tell."

"It's no crime," he said gently. "I'm nervous, too."

She broke eye contact and went back to picking up pieces of pottery from the floor. "I can't believe you're nervous, a guy like you, who's dated the cream of society."

"None of them could rattle off the first one hundred prime numbers. Faith told me you used to do that as a party trick, and you can even do it when you're toasted."

"Faith told me you dated one of the Wrigley heirs." She kept her attention focused on picking up the pottery shards. There were more this time than last.

"I have an idea." He took the box of broken pottery out of her hands.

Her gaze flew to his. "You do?"

"Yeah. Let's forget whatever Faith has told either of us about the other one." He set the box on the coffee table and sank to his knees in front of her. Then he reached out and cupped her cheek. Her skin was so soft. "What do you say?" he asked in a voice that had become thick with anticipation.

"I think…it's an outstanding idea."

"I was hoping you would." Leaning forward, he kissed those incredible wine-red lips.

IT WAS THE PATCHOULI OIL. And maybe the extra makeup she'd put on because it seemed to go with her outfit. Jamie couldn't come up with any other explanation for why the man who had hightailed it out of her apartment last night was on his knees kissing her as if he meant to keep it up all night.

But that was the message. A man who kissed this deeply and generously planned to have more than a cup of coffee before he left. Jamie decided, somewhere around the time that she started feeling dizzy, that she'd be a fool not to give it to him. She'd already grabbed the front of his sweater to pull him closer, so there was no point in trying to be coy now.

She might as well do as he'd suggested and put aside all that she knew about his past with glamorous society types. Instead she'd concentrate on his present, which included a nerdy, unsophisticated woman who by sheer good luck was wearing red leather under her bathrobe. And speaking of that bathrobe, he had his hands on the furry lapels, as if he wouldn't mind pulling them apart.

He lifted his mouth a whisper away from hers. "You drive me crazy," he murmured.

She'd never expected to hear that from him. She couldn't stop the shocked "I do?" from escaping.

"Yeah, you do." He slowly ran his hands up and down the lapels of her robe. "Jamie..."

Beneath the red leather, her heart thundered. "Mmm?"

"I want..."

She could barely breathe. "What, Dev?"

"Are you...do you have anything on besides...this?"

Untutored though she was, she came up with the right answer. ‘‘Maybe you should find out.’’ Then she released her hold on the front of his shirt and let her arms fall to her sides.

His breath caught as his fingers tightened on the lapels. ‘‘God, Jamie.’’ Then he delved into her willing mouth again.

But this time while he kissed her, he gently pulled the front of her robe open. She waited for his reaction with giddy anticipation. The red leather bra was outlined in gold studs and trimmed with fringe. It gave her cleavage for the first time in her life. The red leather thong was decorated to match and barely covered the essentials. Jamie had never worn anything that skimpy, not ever. And Dev was about to meet his fantasy.

After he'd parted the robe a few inches, he slipped a trembling hand inside. When he touched her leather-covered breast, he went completely still.

Gradually his mouth lifted. She opened her eyes to find him staring down at her in astonishment. Then he eased back on his heels, unfastened the tie of her robe, and pulled back the furry material. ‘‘Oh...my...God.’’

Maybe the patchouli oil had taken away her inhibitions, because instead of feeling self-conscious, she loved the way he was looking at her. For the first time in her life she felt seductive. ‘‘Like it?’’

He swallowed, his gaze riveted to her torso. He nodded. Then with obvious reluctance, he dragged his attention back to her face. He cleared his throat twice before getting the question out. ‘‘Why?’’

She settled for partial honesty. "Just…felt like it."

His voice was still hoarse. "I didn't know… didn't think that you…"

"Had fantasies?" Hers didn't include leather, but they certainly included him. So if she needed leather to get the guy, so be it.

He nodded again.

"I do."

"So do I."

She glanced down at the bulge in his jeans. She had caused that. Pride was followed by nearly uncontrollable desire. She'd always wanted him in the general sense. Now her needs were more specific.

His laugh was low and strained. "As you can see."

Slowly she lifted her gaze to his as fine tremors coursed through her. This was the point of no return. Slowly she stood and let the robe slide off her shoulders and fall in a fluffy mound around her ankles. "Then let's make our fantasies come true."

CHAPTER SEVEN

JAMIE WASN'T QUITE prepared for what came next. Without a word Dev got to his feet and swept her up into his arms. As he carried her down the hall, hesitating only slightly as he made sure he'd found her bedroom, she had barely enough time to remember that, one, she'd made her bed this morning and, two, she had a box of condoms in her top dresser drawer. She'd bought them after reading an article in *Cosmo* that said all single women should have a box on hand, because you never knew. And, sure enough, *Cosmo* had been right on the money.

Dev laid her on the bed and kissed her as if there was no tomorrow. Jamie didn't care if there was a tomorrow or not. All she needed was a tonight, and Dev's mouth on her lips, her throat, her leather-enhanced breasts. She'd left her bedside light on and was glad she had.

"I didn't bring anything." He lifted his head to gaze into her eyes. "So this is going to be all about you. Next time, we'll—"

"Next time?" She was stunned, thinking that tonight would be a one-shot deal and not caring if it was. But he was already planning a second go-round! Unbelievable.

"Of course there'll be a next time." His eyes glowed. "What kind of a guy do you think I am?"

My kind. But she didn't dare say that. "There's a box of condoms in the top drawer of my dresser, behind my panties."

His eyes widened.

"Are you shocked?"

"Not shocked." He combed back her hair with his fingers. "But you aren't anything like I thought," he said softly.

She decided that was a good thing. If she continued to surprise him, instead of being boring old nerdy Jamie, he might stick around for a while. She was going to mine that questionnaire for all it was worth.

He gazed at her for a moment longer. "Where did you say they were?"

"You weren't listening."

"Once I heard *box of condoms* my heart started pounding so loud I couldn't hear."

"Top dresser drawer," she murmured. "Behind my panties." And now she wished they were all black lace.

He leaned down and plunged her into heaven with another of his specialty kisses. "Don't go away," he whispered.

"Wouldn't dream of it." Not that she could have moved from the bed, boneless as she felt.

When he came back with the box, he was already starting to open it. He fumbled the job and dumped condoms on the floor. "To hell with it. That makes them easier to grab."

She nearly went up in flames. He didn't expect to stop with one.

He kept his attention firmly on her as he undressed, watching her as he kicked off his shoes and reached down to tug off his socks. The only time he broke the connection was for the split second when he pulled his sweater and T-shirt over his head.

She'd only seen him shirtless once, when she'd gone to his parents' house to meet Faith and he'd been playing basketball with his friends. She'd been so mesmerized by the sight of a seminaked, sweaty Dev that she'd walked into a lamppost on the way to the front door. He had the same effect on her now, but fortunately she didn't have to walk anywhere.

No, all she had to do was lie here and anticipate phase two, a journey into Dev territory she'd only imagined. And she had imagined, barely willing to admit to herself that she'd fantasized about him so intimately. Maybe that was why she was ready to take this step. He'd walked naked into her dreams a thousand times.

But the dream images had been indistinct. When Dev shoved down his jeans and briefs, he was so real she gulped. His penis, long and thick, jutted from a wild swirl of dark hair. He didn't seem to mind a bit that she was staring at him. In fact, when she lifted her gaze, he was staring back, his eyes filled with lust.

Slowly he came to her, his lips parted, his breathing ragged. "Leather," he murmured, easing down beside her and tracing the borders of her bra with one finger. "I still can't believe it."

She tingled every place he touched. The glove-soft leather against her skin aroused her even more. She'd thought of it as a male fantasy item, but wearing it was giving her the most incredible feeling, as if she'd been gently bound and offered up to him as a gift. Her feminist soul should be outraged at the concept. Instead she'd never felt more daring.

He cupped her breast. The slightest nudge from his hand and her nipple would slip out. "Do you wear this...a lot?"

She struggled to remember the English language. It shouldn't be so tough. She was a native speaker. "Some."

"I thought you liked cotton."

"I'm...experimenting."

"Lucky me." With that he gave that necessary little nudge that set her nipple free. "Mmm." Then he lowered his head and licked her like a lollipop.

She began to whimper and squirm. What he was doing was turning her on to an incredible degree. And there was something about that tiny leather triangle as it shifted around between her legs that drove her even closer to the edge of insanity.

Then his hand was there, stroking the small piece of leather. She was soon drenched, and the leather became slippery against her curls. Before long it was no trick for him to ease it aside. The swift glide of his fingers into her heat made her gasp.

Dear Lord, she was going to come immediately. She'd never had that reaction to a man. "Dev..."

He looked into her eyes and his breath caught. "I can't wait."

"Dev—"

"Hang on." He rolled away from her and grabbed a condom from the floor.

"Dev." She was bubbling and steaming, ready to boil over in a frothy, wild release.

He rolled to his back and grunted in frustration as he struggled with the wrapper. But his fingers were wet, for obvious reasons, and he had trouble tearing the package.

Too far gone to worry about protocol, she grabbed the package and ripped it open. "There."

"Thanks." Putting on the condom with a snap of latex, he pulled the leather thong out of the way, found his bearings and thrust deep. *"Sweet heaven."*

She dug her fingers into his tight buns and moaned. "Go."

His gaze swept over her, from her head to the spot where they were securely locked together. Then he looked into her eyes. "Yeah," he said softly.

He proceeded to take her on the shortest, wildest ride of her life. He pumped fast and with deadly accuracy, taking her the rest of the way in seconds while her cries escalated and her head thrashed from side to side. At the end, when she went crashing through the barrier, she was incoherent with pleasure.

As the ripples undulated through her, she was reduced to a litany of *Yes, yes, yes, yes. Oh, yes.*

DEV MAINTAINED HIS RHYTHM until her last tremor died away. He was a man in the grip of a fantasy, in bed with a woman he'd thought was an innocent nymph, a woman who'd turned out to be more seductive than even she knew.

Braced on his forearms, he let his hot gaze roam over her as he slowed the pace, fascinated by the effect of each thrust. He watched her change in expression and the shimmy of her breasts only partly cupped by red leather. He watched the slide of his penis until it disappeared within that riot of drenched red curls. He watched as his dark strands mingled with flame.

If only this fantasy could go on forever, but he was fast approaching his limits. He thought he could make her come again, though, and that was a prize worth going for. Shifting his weight to his left arm, he paused in midstroke and reached down to swirl his thumb over her trigger point. Sure enough, she began to quiver.

Looking into her eyes, he rubbed gently as he continued to thrust. "Can...you?"

"Mmm." Her green eyes darkened to jade.

"Yes?" He hoped she'd be able to come soon. His climax was bearing down on him like a 747 approaching the runway at O'Hare. Soon he'd have no choice but to land that sucker.

Her breath quickened and she nodded.

Ah, she felt so good. And he was too close, probably closer than she was. He might not last. Unless... It took a fair share of willpower, but he eased his penis free and slid down until his head was between her thighs. Her gasp of surprise pleased him. He liked being a step ahead.

No point in wasting time being hesitant, in case she might feel shy and try to stop him. He was on a mission and he took control, treating her to a thorough tongue bath. He loved his work. And from her response, she did, too. Before long she was making those wild climax noises and shuddering in his arms.

He let her play it out, and then he reclaimed his position. Locking his gaze with hers, he thrust deep inside her. Ah, yes. This would be something. This would be unreal. Yes. *Yes.* Spasms shook him from his scalp to the bottoms of his feet, taking away thought and speech. For long moments he hung above her, semiconscious, barely able to support himself on his braced arms as his body jerked with aftershocks.

Finally he was able to focus again, and he gazed down at her in wonder. Who would have thought that she'd be the one to give him the most incredible climax of his whole sexual life?

She cupped his face in both hands. ''Are you... okay?''

Still not up to speaking, he nodded.

''Would you...like some coffee, now?''

He smiled inside, but his muscles were still quivering too much for him to risk a real smile. After all that, she still wanted to be a good hostess. He could fall for this woman if he wasn't careful.

He licked his dry lips, tried to speak and had to clear his throat. Still, his voice sounded as if he'd been on the floor of the stock exchange all day. ''Anything you have to offer, girl, I'll take.''

JAMIE KISSED Dev goodbye at her door sometime after three in the morning. They'd already made plans for the next night. She went back to bed, trying to keep her promise to Dev that she'd get some sleep. But the bed was where they'd made love…three times. She lay in the dark, eyes wide, and remembered.

Every once in a while her brain shifted from all those hot memories and wandered into what-if territory. What if this was only a fling for Dev? What if it was more than a fling? What if Dev was on the rebound? What if he wasn't? But mostly her what-ifs centered around one question: what if she hadn't been trying out patchouli oil and leather lingerie?

Throwing back the covers, she climbed out of bed. After he'd left she'd put on her flannel granny gown. If she'd been wearing that under her white bathrobe, she never would have let him kiss her. You didn't kiss a guy like Dev wearing a flannel granny gown.

In the living room she turned on her computer instead of a light. All she needed was on the screen, anyway. She opened the Hot Commodity file, which now included Dev's questionnaire, and started to read. Grabbing the pen next to the computer, she started making notes. An hour later she went back to bed and dreamed of black lace and dangling ruby pendants.

THE NEXT MORNING as she boarded the bus for downtown, she seriously considered going in the back entrance and sneaking up to her office instead of meeting everyone for coffee. Everyone would include Dev. He'd already told her he'd be there. She wanted to see him so bad her teeth ached, but on the other hand, she would hardly be wearing leather to the office. When he came face-to-face with her ordinary self, he might reconsider.

Yet if she chickened out, she'd get the third degree from Faith. During the bus ride she came up with her only alternative. She wasn't sure she could pull it off, but she'd braved her way through the leather incident with outstanding results. She ought to be able to take the game a step further.

Faith, Dixie and Dev were already at the table when she walked in through the main entrance. When Faith waved, she waved back, but her heart was beating so fast she wondered if she'd pass out before she made it over to the table. Dev gave her one long, slow glance. Then he smiled.

One smile and she was a basket case. Maybe she couldn't complete the routine she had in mind, after all. But it seemed like a surefire way to keep him interested. She'd read his questionnaire answers. She knew what she had to do.

"How's everyone this morning?" she asked as she took off her scarf and coat to hang them over the back of the chair. Today Faith sat on one side of Dev and Dixie on the other, so Jamie ended up across from him. She'd chosen a black pantsuit with a snug fit, the best she could do under the circumstances. "Everyone sleep well?"

"Not really," Dev said.

"Poor baby." Faith patted his arm. "Worried about quarterly earnings already, I'll bet."

"I slept like a top," Dixie said. "Flannel sheets are God's gift to the single woman on a cold winter's night."

"I think something's wrong with the thermostat in my apartment." Jamie couldn't risk looking at Dev. "I was hot all night." She glanced up at Mr. Willis instead, who had appeared with her coffee. "Thank you so much."

"My pleasure." Mr. Willis's gaze circled the table. "Does anyone care for anything more?"

"A foot warmer for these long winter nights," Dixie said with a wink.

Mr. Willis blinked. "I beg your pardon?"

Dixie laughed. "Just kidding, Alfred." After he left she leaned forward. "I can't resist teasing him a little. I wonder if anything would loosen him up."

"I don't know, but that starched routine of his is great for business," Faith said. "People love to hear him talk." Then she turned to Jamie. "Get the super to fix that thermostat for you. Next thing you know, your utility bill will be through the roof."

Jamie flicked a glance in Dev's direction. "I will, but the heat was kind of nice. I put all my summer clothes in storage in the basement, though, and I don't want to drag them out. So just in case I can't get it fixed, I'm going to buy a couple of negligees from Sheer Delights this morning."

Dixie smiled, obviously pleased. "I never thought I'd see the day. Sugar, please don't tell me you want some ankle-length number that buttons up to your neck. Make Dixie happy and take home a sexy outfit for a change.''

Dixie was playing right into her hands. Jamie sighed, as if giving in to the inevitable. ''Oh, okay. If you insist. I'll try on that black lace set you've been raving about.''

''Oo, la, la!'' Dixie rolled her eyes. ''With your red hair, you'll look fabulous in that one.'' She pushed back her chair. ''Bring your coffee and come on up. I can't wait to see what you look like in it.''

''Why not?'' Jamie's pulse raced and she chanced one more look in Dev's direction. ''See you all later.''

Dev's blue eyes smoldered. ''You bet.''

As she left the table and followed Dixie to the stairs, she felt an uncharacteristic impulse to sway her hips as she walked. So she did, just a little. With luck, Dev was watching. With even more luck, he'd just swallowed his tongue.

DEV FOUND HIMSELF in a trap of his own making. As the days of anticipation and the nights of incredible pleasure went by, he knew Jamie was using the information on his questionnaire to spice up their encounters. More than once he'd started to tell her that he'd faked every last answer to confuse potential matchmakers. But he didn't have the heart, because she was...blossoming.

The night she'd made love to him wearing only the ruby pendant she'd temporarily borrowed from The Diamond Mine, she'd admitted having no idea how sensuous a piece of fine jewelry could feel when you were naked. He'd had a little trouble working around the cumbersome necklace, and it had nearly put his eye out during one particular maneuver. But Jamie had been so turned on by the concept that, in the end, he'd been turned on by it, too.

By now he'd forgotten half the things he'd said on the questionnaire, but Jamie had it permanently recorded on a computer disk and she seemed determined to work in every sexual preference she thought he had. He found himself longing for the simple woman in the jeans and sweatshirt, but Jamie apparently had left that woman in the dust.

Maybe it didn't matter. Once they got past whatever trappings she'd added for the evening's entertainment, they were down to two naked bodies and the most unbelievable sex he'd ever known. It was so good, in fact, that the M-word was running through his mind on a regular basis. He'd begun picturing how Jamie would look in white.

But her newfound spirit of adventure made him nervous. A woman in the midst of exploring her wild side might not be in the mood for commitment. Jamie had given no indication that this was more than a casual affair.

Well, that wasn't completely true. Through the recent Valentine uproar at The Red Doors, Jamie had seemed to use him as an anchor. He liked having her do that. She'd also admitted to Faith that they'd been dating, and Dev thought that was a major step.

Still, he didn't feel confident enough to think in

terms of happily ever after. Not yet. Maybe not for a long time. But Valentine's Day was on Friday and this was Tuesday. He needed to make plans, and they couldn't be a carbon copy of what they'd been doing so far—spending the night in her apartment and in her bed.

Any woman would expect something more elaborate from a guy she'd been seeing so often and so intimately. If she were the old Jamie, he could tell her to pack her comfy clothes and they'd head up to a secluded cabin in Wisconsin for the weekend. But this emerging Jamie would want a night on the town so she could wear a slinky dress and impossibly high heels. Maybe she'd put on the same red pair she'd worn with the red lace teddy the other night.

He didn't want to go out on the town, but he had to admit the thought of Jamie wearing red heels and lacy underwear got him very hot. He'd finally realized that she could do almost anything and make it sexy. Jamie was the secret ingredient.

He was falling for her, and he had to figure out what to do about that. He had to figure it out before Valentine's Day, too. Valentine's Day was a watershed occasion for any couple. People said and did things on Valentine's Day that could get them in a lot of trouble. If one person was thinking long-term relationship—as he was—and the other was thinking short-term sexual adventure—as Jamie might be—then Valentine's Day could be hideous.

But, for starters, he'd ask her to go to the Pump Room for dinner. No doubt the restaurant was already booked solid, but fortunately the Sherman name would get him a table. Normally he didn't like to pull rank, but this was an unusual situation. With an inward sigh he thought about the starched tux shirt he'd have to wear and the shiny dress shoes he'd never liked. But if Jamie wanted to dress up, then he'd dress up, too.

He climbed out of the cab wondering what she had in store for him tonight. They probably wouldn't just watch a movie and eat popcorn in bed, then enjoy some good old-fashioned sex. They wouldn't because he hadn't said anything on the damned questionnaire about liking to do that. She had no idea what the real Dev was all about, but he couldn't rain on her parade, not when she'd so recently begun having one.

She greeted him at her apartment door wearing a leopard-print sarong. The air reverberated with jungle drums, and when he kissed her, he nearly choked on the musky scent she'd poured on herself.

But she thought this was the perfume he loved, the magic potion that would drive him wild, and she was wearing it just for him. How could he not kiss her until they were both senseless? How could he not shove her against the wall with reckless abandon?

Access to her was easy—she'd worn nothing under the sarong. He paused only long enough to unzip his pants before rolling on a condom, grabbing her sleek bottom and lifting her into position.

In his frenzy to bury himself inside her he forgot the overpowering fragrance, forgot the jungle drums, forgot everything but stroking until he felt her climactic undulations caress his penis. Then he came in a burst of joyous energy.

When it was over, she collapsed against the wall and gulped for air. "I guess...it worked."

Still groggy from the force of his orgasm, he leaned his forehead against hers while he waited for his body to stop quivering. "What worked?"

"Jungle Goddess. I created it today."

"Ah." Vaguely he remembered the question on fragrance. He'd said something about loving an exotic, tribal perfume. For good measure, he'd added that he liked a woman who used a lot of it. In a minute, when he had his sea legs, he'd suggest they take a long, hot shower together. If he stayed with her constantly, she wouldn't have a chance to put that dreadful stuff on again tonight.

The drums continued their steady rhythm in the background. He'd probably mentioned the drums, too. The leopard-print sarong was nice, though. Much better than leather.

At last he could breathe normally again. And he remembered about the Pump Room. He lifted his head and gazed down at her. Her eyes were closed, and she looked very happy.

He wanted to keep making her happy. The Pump Room was a good idea. "Do you...have plans for Valentine's night?" he asked.

Her eyes flipped open immediately. "No."

He could tell from her expression that she'd been waiting for him to ask this, and he was a jerk for not bringing it up sooner. ''Will you spend it with me?''

''Of course.'' Little lights of joy danced in her eyes.

She should wear emeralds, he thought, and nothing so large and dangerous as that ruby pendant. A delicate little strand of emeralds settled into the curve of her throat would be perfect.

''Did you have something in mind?'' she asked.

''How about we start with dinner at the Pump Room? We'll have a long, decadent meal and then we'll hit a few nightclubs so I can show you off.''

She smiled. ''I'd better get a new dress.'' She looked as if she could hardly wait to start shopping.

He swallowed his disappointment. Jamie had obviously discovered her inner party girl. If her transformation happened to coincide with his longing to get away from all that and settle down in a cozy bungalow, it was his bad luck. If he wanted to be with Jamie, he'd have to go along.

But he didn't have to spend the rest of tonight choking on Jungle Goddess. He leaned down and feathered a kiss over her delicious mouth. ''How about a nice, long, hot, wet, slippery shower?''

''I'd love it,'' she murmured. ''Then we'll drink coffee out of our favorite blue cup.''

''And then we'll—''

''Yes.'' She smiled. ''We certainly will.''

CHAPTER EIGHT

ON WEDNESDAY MORNING Jamie asked Faith to help her pick out a dress for Valentine's night. The week before, Jamie had admitted that she was seeing Dev, and Faith had been ecstatic. Jamie had warned her they were only having fun, no strings. She warned herself the exact same thing all the time. But this Valentine's date seemed to take their relationship to a new level, so although she'd rather be dragged over hot coals than get dressed in another one of Dev's fantasy outfits and do the town, she'd suffer for his sake.

Faith suggested she and Jamie take a long lunch on Thursday and scour the stores. Faith reminded her that she was going away on Valentine's Day and could probably use a few new things herself. The next day, an hour into the shopping trip, Jamie was ready to call it quits. She wasn't satisfied with anything, and the price tags made her head swim. But she would do this for Dev.

Faith lounged in a chair by the triple mirrors in the fourth store they'd tried while Jamie tugged and pulled at the latest possibility, a black beaded outfit that glittered and outlined her figure well, but weighed a ton.

"It looks okay, but it feels yucky," she said.

"Hmm? What did you say?"

Jamie had an attack of conscience. "You're bored, and I'll bet you're tired, too. You've had a tough week, and I shouldn't be dragging you all over creation. And you haven't even bought anything for yourself yet! I'll take this one and be done with it."

"I'm not bored or tired. And that does look great on you."

"Faith, you were a million miles away."

"It's…the holiday, I guess. We've pinned our hopes on it, and thankfully the revised software and the wish list database are both pumping up our revenues. But I'll be glad when we can tally the bottom line and know where we stand."

"I know what you mean." Jamie felt doubly guilty now. She'd been so caught up in her affair with Dev that she'd barely had time to worry about the store's bottom line. Apparently, Faith had been doing enough worrying for both of them.

"So is that the dress you want?" Faith eyed it critically. "It looks wonderful on you. You wear designer clothes like a runway model."

Jamie checked the fit from the back. "A short runway model."

"Don't complain. I'd love to have a figure like yours."

"And I'd love to have cleavage like yours." Jamie laughed. "Come on. Let's buy this rag and go back to work."

Not long afterward, a garment bag containing the dress slung over her shoulder, Jamie walked beside Faith as they joined the stream of pedestrians on Michigan Avenue.

"You really like the dress?" Faith seemed to need reassurance that the shopping expedition had been a success.

"I like it." She sighed. "But I have to say, living up to Dev's answers on the questionnaire is wearing me out."

"So tell him that!"

"No."

"Why not? He's a big boy. Surely he will—"

"Faith, he's attracted to a woman who's into all that. If I tell him I'm not, I'm afraid he'll lose interest."

"Won't you have to tell him sometime?"

"I suppose." Jamie had given this a lot of thought. "But when I do, I have to be ready for the relationship to be over. I'm not ready yet."

"And it might not be over. He's not that superficial, Jamie."

"I don't think that's necessarily superficial. Aromatherapy has taught me that many unconscious factors go into creating an attraction between two people. He has a right to like certain things in a woman. And if that's not what I'm all about, then—"

"I think you're falling for him."

"No." The thought scared her silly. "No, I'm not. I won't let myself do that. It's too soon, anyway."

"Too soon? You've known the guy for twelve years!"

But not like this. "I just have to be careful, Faith. If I fall for him, and he doesn't feel the same, that could become very awkward for all three of us."

Faith shook her head. "Do you seriously think you have that much control over how you feel about him? Is there some little valve inside you that's either open or closed?"

"I can control it." Or so she'd told herself.

"If you say so."

"I can!" And all the while a voice within her was telling her that it was already too late. She was totally in love with Dev.

ALTHOUGH NOTHING SPECIFIC had been arranged, Dev assumed he'd go over to Jamie's Thursday night, because he'd been spending every night there recently. So when she left a message with Edna on Thursday afternoon saying she would be ice skating that night with some friends from her old job, he was taken aback. She hadn't invited him, and she hadn't suggested meeting him later, either.

He told himself it didn't matter. She had a right to make plans without him. But he went home from work feeling very left out.

He spent most of Thursday night in a blue funk and he didn't sleep more than a couple of hours. By Friday morning, as the sun rose on Valentine's Day, he'd come to an inevitable conclusion. Apparently there was only one way to handle this relentless ache in his heart every time he thought about Jamie. He would have to gather his courage and do what had to be done.

BOTH MALE AND FEMALE customers flooded The Red Doors on Friday, and Jamie was grateful. If only her personal life hadn't been in chaos, she could be even happier that the marketing strategy to bring women into the kiosks had succeeded beyond her fondest hopes. There'd been a nearly disastrous incident involving the Valentino diamond Faith had on display and even that had only briefly distracted Jamie from her personal affairs.

She was now back to being tied in knots thinking about Dev. She'd tried pulling back a little, had even taken a night off from seeing him to give them each what the relationship gurus called "a little space." There had been nothing *little* about it. She'd felt as if a galaxy separated them.

No matter how hard she'd tried to have fun with her friends, she'd thought of Dev constantly and regretted not spending the evening with him. That was a very bad sign. He'd probably watched some sports on TV and barely noticed they were apart.

Fortunately the crush of customers mobbing the boutiques and kiosks prevented her from dwelling constantly on her problems with Dev. She was in Heaven Scent helping to fill orders when Dixie came through the door.

Dixie looked unnerved as she walked over to the counter. "Sugar, can I talk to you a minute?"

"I'll be right there." Jamie quickly rang up the computer-generated purchase and handed it over to

Veronica. Dixie so seldom got rattled that Jamie was worried. "What's up?"

"Can you walk out to the mezzanine with me? I want to show you something."

"Sure." Even more concerned, Jamie followed her out of the boutique, thinking there was some trouble on the main floor. "Is there a problem at The Red Bean?"

"No. I wanted to show you something and I didn't want Veronica to see it." Dixie pulled a velvet jeweler's box out of her skirt pocket. Opening it, she showed Jamie the contents.

"What a gorgeous locket!" Looped on a delicate chain, the walnut-size heart was created with gold filigree. "Did you just buy it over at The Diamond Mine?"

"No. It came from there originally, but it was delivered to my desk, and it was from—" she paused and flushed bright red "—my secret admirer."

"Oh, *Dixie.*" Jamie grinned at her. "I do believe he's raising the stakes. And from the looks of that locket, by quite a tidy sum. Your secret admirer obviously has two nickels to rub together. Plus he also knows where to shop."

"Jamie, if you know who bought this for me, you'd better tell me right this very minute."

Jamie held up both hands. "I don't. I swear I don't. Who do you think sent it?"

"I haven't the foggiest, and it's killing me! Are you sure you don't know?"

"I don't. And if I knew, but I'd been sworn to

secrecy, I'd at least tell you that. But I'm just plain clueless. What about Faith?''

''I checked with her first. Apparently she wasn't in The Diamond Mine when this was bought. Stacy was.''

''Ah. Stacy of the last-minute elopement. How convenient for your secret admirer.'' Jamie gazed at the intricate locket. ''You have to admit that he has very good taste in jewelry.''

Dixie traced the heart's outline. ''It's pretty. Classy, even.''

''Have you tried it on?''

She glanced up and shook her head.

''Why not? Here, let me put it on for—''

''Nope.'' Dixie jerked the box out of reach. ''The note says if I wear it, my secret admirer will reveal himself. What if it turns out to be some toad? Then what?''

Jamie laughed. ''What if it turns out to be the handsome prince?''

''Come on, honey. I'm fifty-six years old. My chances of attracting a creepy toad are much higher.'' She closed the box with a snap. ''I'm not wearing it.''

''I think you should. If it turns out to be someone awful, you can handle him. I've seen that *Steel Magnolia* routine of yours.''

Dixie put the box back in her pocket.

''Come on, Dixie. Take a chance.''

''Easy for you to say. You know who your date is for Valentine's night.'' Dixie winked. ''Looking forward to it?''

"You bet." Jamie smiled with as much enthusiasm as she could dredge up. The closer she came to closing time, the more she felt anxiety churning in her stomach. She was in love with a man who thought she was someone else.

"Well, you go out and have a marvelous time, sugar. And now we'd both better get back to the salt mines."

"Right." Jamie turned and hurried into Heaven Scent. The day was going by fast—too fast. She didn't have time for a lunch break, but she wouldn't have been able to skate, anyway. After taking her skates home last night so that she could have them for the outing with her friends, she'd forgotten to bring them back to the office this morning.

Quitting time arrived before she knew it. As she rode home on the bus, romance-minded couples seemed to be everywhere. The whole world was falling in love.

She should never have let herself get so involved with Dev, she decided once she was home and struggling into the heavy black dress. They could have ended things with a one-night stand, but she'd been greedy. Now she'd pay for that greed with a broken heart, because she couldn't keep up this charade much longer.

Underneath the black dress she finally managed to zip, she wore a black lace underwire bra that did wonders for her cleavage and pinched her skin something fierce. The black garter and lace panties felt weird every time she sat down. In fact, sitting in a beaded dress wasn't something she wanted to spend much time doing, and yet she was supposed to eat dinner in it.

The whole makeup session was another pain in the rear. Every time she wiped the mascara over her lashes she'd sneeze, giving her little black fan-shaped smudges under her eyes. After several tries she got the makeup on, but she wasn't happy with the job.

She'd been on her feet all day and had to cram them into the four-inch black heels she'd bought yesterday to go with the dress. As she walked around her apartment, her feet hurt, her breasts felt squeezed by the underwire, her shoulders had already begun to ache from the weight of the dress, and she'd managed to smear her mascara *again.*

"I can't do this!" She kicked off the torture shoes so hard they flew across the room and bounced against the books in her bookcase. Then she reached for the zipper of the dress. The charade was over.

THE HIGH, STARCHED collar of Dev's tux shirt irritated his neck, but it was a small price to pay for giving Jamie a night to remember. A dozen red roses in a long floral box under his arm, he climbed the stairs to her apartment and tried not to think about how stiff the darn dress shoes were. He hoped he could dance in them without pain.

He arrived at her door feeling noble. He might not be doing what he wanted tonight, but they would be doing what she wanted. That was important, especially considering his recent decision regarding Jamie.

He pictured her primping in front of her bathroom mirror, checking to make sure her dress looked good from the back. Then all his thoughts came to a dead stop when he noticed the note taped to her door.

He had to read it twice. The first time the words kept jumping around on him.

> Dev—
>
> I can't make it tonight. I'm not the woman you thought I was. Unfortunately I'm the kind who would rather go skating than out on the town, so that's what I'm doing tonight. I'm sorry for misleading you.
>
> —Jamie

Fire raced through his veins. She'd ditched him for some guy she'd seen last night! Here he was, turning himself inside out to give her a special evening, and she didn't even want a special evening! She wanted to go skating.

Tossing the box of roses down beside her door, he ripped the note off and headed back to the main floor, taking the stairs two at a time. By God, he was not going to let her get away with this. She'd tied him up in knots with her fancy lovemaking, and now she thought she could simply walk away? Not likely!

He'd asked the cabbie to wait, anticipating that Jamie would be coming down with him. He hopped in the back seat. "Take me to the McCormick Tribune rink on Michigan."

The cabbie turned, and his glance flicked over

Dev's starched collar, black tie, dress coat and white silk scarf. Then he shrugged. "Okeydoke."

Dev tapped on the seat impatiently as the cab threaded its way through heavy Friday night traffic, made worse by the snow falling faster every minute. She'd gone skating. He even liked skating! If she'd only said something, they could be skating together right at this moment.

Then he thought of the questionnaire. Maybe she hadn't dared tell him who she really was. After all, he hadn't told her who he really was, either. Because of that, she'd gone skating with another man tonight, when she was supposed to be with him.

When the cabbie let him off near the rink, he could see right away that he'd have an audience. The rink was busy, filled with couples who'd chosen to spend a romantic evening gliding over the ice, despite, or perhaps because of, the falling snow.

He looked for Jamie among the couples and couldn't find her. Then he spotted a short skater with flaming hair circling the rink like an Olympian going for the gold. She was alone.

After watching her for a couple of minutes Dev decided she didn't have a date, after all. He didn't know if that was better or worse. She'd chosen to be alone instead of with him. That really hurt.

But hurt or not, he was going to straighten this out. Walking to the edge of the rink, he waited for her to come by. Even before he called her name, he could tell she'd seen him.

Her eyes widened and she veered away from the spot where he was standing.

He couldn't believe it. She didn't even want to talk to him. "Jamie!" he called, but he knew in advance she wouldn't stop.

He waited for her to come around again. Again she veered.

"Jamie!" He held out a hand, but she ignored him and sped off. This was ridiculous. He couldn't keep this up. People were starting to stare.

The next time she came around, he stepped out onto the ice. "Jamie, please come over here and—"

"Nope!" Her cheeks pink, she turned on the speed again.

"For God's sake, Jamie!" Frustration spurred him on, and he started after her. An attendant shouted something, but he paid no attention. Unfortunately his dress shoes weren't made for running, let alone running on ice. He made it about thirty yards before losing his footing and going down hard.

The attendant, a kid with peach fuzz on his chin, hurried over. "I'm sorry, sir, but we can't allow—"

"Dev! Are you all right?" Jamie sprayed ice as she whirled to a stop beside him.

He glared at her. "Physically I'm fine."

"Oh, good." She sighed in apparent relief and crouched beside him. "When I saw you take a tumble I was scared."

"I said I was physically okay. Mentally, however—"

"That's what concerns me, sir," the attendant said. "Anyone who would run on the ice wearing what you're wearing most likely has some sort of mental prob—"

"It's okay," Jamie said, glancing up at the kid. "This is Deverell Heathcliff Sherman the Fourth."

Dev groaned. "No, I'm not." He'd rather be an anonymous crazy guy.

"I'm sure his family donated a huge amount to help build this rink," Jamie added. "And he'll be leaving soon anyway, right, Dev?"

"Not without you."

The pink in her cheeks deepened. "Dev, we have nothing in common. It's better if—"

"We have more in common than you think." Dev glanced at the kid. "Could you give us a minute?"

Although the kid looked more than ready to eavesdrop, he backed away.

Jamie bent close to Dev. "Look at me. Look at you. We're polar opposites."

He grabbed hold of her scarf and pulled her closer. "The only difference between you and me is that I'm a man and you're a woman. And I think we've already worked through that obstacle."

Her eyes filled with distress. "But I wasn't being me!"

"And I wasn't being me," he said gently. "All my answers were lies, because I was afraid my questionnaire would be used to find me marriage prospects. I wanted to recognize them when they showed up."

"You *lied?* I don't believe it. Whenever I tried something from that questionnaire, you loved it.

You went bananas over the black lace, and the Jungle Goddess, and the leather—''

He tugged a little harder on her scarf, wanting her close enough so no one else could hear, and close enough to kiss those lips that didn't have a trace of lipstick on them. ''I went bananas over you,'' he murmured. ''I tolerated all the other stuff, because you were the one peddling it.''

''Tolerated? *Peddling?*'' She gave him a hard shove.

He skidded a couple of feet on the seat of his pants, but he kept a grip on her scarf, so she was pulled along with him, sliding on her knees.

She was breathing hard. ''This is ridiculous. Let go of my scarf.''

''Not yet. Listen, maybe I used the wrong words.''

''Duh. Do you think? You weren't *tolerating* anything, Mister Hot Commodity! You were into it, and don't try to tell me you weren't.''

''Some of the stuff, okay. But—''

She leaned closer and lowered her voice. ''At this very moment I'm wearing plain cotton panties and a sports bra. Don't you dare tell me you'd find that as sexy as black lace. Don't you dare.''

''I wouldn't dare. You might shove me clear across the rink. I can only take so much public humiliation.''

''Dev, be serious.''

''I am serious. I'm getting hot thinking of you in plain cotton panties and a sports bra.''

''I don't believe you.''

"If I didn't have this overcoat to disguise the evidence, you'd have to believe me."

A smile flickered in her eyes as she gazed at him. "You lied about everything?"

"Uh-huh. Told you the exact opposite of what I really like. What I really like is simplicity. Like when we got out of the shower Tuesday night. Just us. Nothing fancy."

"You're not just saying that, are you?"

"No, and I'll prove it." He pulled aside the flap of his dress coat.

"Dev."

"Take it easy. I won't flash the skaters." He reached into his slacks' pocket and pulled out the small velvet box he'd carried out of The Diamond Mine this afternoon. "Happy Valentine's Day, Jamie."

She stared at the box for a long, long time. Slowly she reached out and took it. "Dixie got a locket from a secret admirer today. I'll bet this is a locket, too."

He sat there, his butt getting cold and wet, and the snow falling faster and faster.

"I didn't expect a gift, you know," she said.

"This isn't a gift."

"Of course it is. It's a—" She gasped as she saw what was in the box.

"It goes with the wedding wrapping paper," he said. "I didn't know that back then. Well, I kind of knew it, but I didn't totally trust my instincts."

"Oh, Dev."

"Marry me, Jamie. I love you. I don't care what

you wear or don't wear. I can take any kind of perfume or no perfume. I just want you."

She started to cry, tears streaming down her face as she looked from the ring to him, then back at the ring, then back at him.

"Jamie, what does that mean?" His stomach pitched at the thought that she'd turn him down. "Is that a yes or a no?"

"It's a yes, you crazy man. I thought if this moment ever came I'd faint. Turns out I become a water faucet instead."

His throat closed with emotion. "So...are you saying that...you're in love with me, too?"

"I am so in love with you. I've been in love with you for a very long time. If you've only just fallen in love with me, you have some major catching up to do." Wrapping her arms around him, she pulled his face to her tear-stained one and gave him the saltiest kiss he'd ever tasted. Snow pelted them in the face.

He held her tight and wondered how long it would take for them to find somewhere warm so they could get naked and do this thing right. He'd probably been in love with her for a very long time, too, but he hadn't realized it until recently. Oh, well. She was just naturally smarter than he was. And she loved him, anyway.

After kissing him with enough enthusiasm to thoroughly convince him of that, she pulled back and gazed at him, her eyes still glittering with tears. "Happy Valentine's Day, Dev."

At the look in her eyes, he forgot the cold ice, the

heavy snowfall and the curious stares. He forgot about going somewhere warmer. ‘‘It sure is.’’ Then he went back to kissing her. He might not be a genius, but he knew that this would be a moment they’d tell their grandkids about. And you didn’t rush a moment like that.

[illegible] parents and the church [illegible] the [illegible] of [illegible] [illegible] [illegible] [illegible] [illegible] [illegible] [illegible] [illegible] [illegible] [illegible] would be [illegible] [illegible] [illegible] [illegible] and you didn't [illegible] such a [illegible] like that.

DIAMOND MINE

Stephanie Bond

To Brenda, of course.

And many thanks to childhood friend and jewelry guru Brigitte Blevins Waddell for her expert story advice.

PROLOGUE

Valentine's Day, 2002

FAITH SHERMAN checked her watch, then sighed and slid her empty wineglass across to the lady bartender at Mister's restaurant. "Dixie, what would you say about a man who stood you up on Valentine's Day?"

The attractive middle-aged blonde refilled Faith's glass and sent it back. "That he had better be embalmed."

Faith drank to that. The problem was, every time Officer Carter Grayson was late for a date, she was caught between frustration that he didn't care enough about her to be on time, and panic that he might have gotten his big self shot. She glanced toward the entrance to the restaurant for the millionth time, hating herself for willing him to appear. If Carter *had* been rushed to the hospital with his lifeblood pooling on the linoleum, it wasn't as if her name would be in his wallet as an emergency contact—their relationship was too new for that kind of familiarity. Her heart pinched. Too new, in fact, for this...*attachment* she'd developed for the unpredictable man who could make her laugh the way no man ever had.

"He's a thirty-seven-year-old cop, has never been married, and still rents an apartment," her brother Dev had pointed out over lunch yesterday. "I don't mean to burst your bubble, sis, but this guy doesn't sound like commitment material."

"What bubble?" she'd asked carefully. "I have no bubbles."

"Oh, really? You've got that look."

"What look?"

Dev had pointed to her lettuce wedge and tomato soup. "That hungry look. *You* are on a diet."

"Am not."

"Are, too."

"I am *not* on a diet," Faith had insisted. "I'm just...trying to eat more healthfully."

"Good," Dev had said with a wink. "Because you certainly don't need to lose weight, and especially not for a man, and especially not for *this* man, considering he disappears for days and he's late every time you go out."

"His job isn't exactly nine to five," she had argued.

"Does he wear a bulletproof vest?"

"What? I...he says it's too confining."

"There you go."

"Did I miss something?"

Dev had set down his fork and taken a long drink of coffee in preparation for his big-brother act. "Faith, if everyone had your big heart, *every* day would be Valentine's Day."

"The point to your flattery?"

"That you're...susceptible."

"Susceptible? You mean I'm a pushover."

"No." Then Dev had sighed. "Yes. Sis, I'm sure this Carter is a nice guy, but he's giving you signals."

"Signals?"

"The 'don't fall for me because I'm a player' signals."

"And you know this how?"

He'd grinned. "Because I wrote the manual."

True enough—Dev was the epitome of a happy bachelor.

"Look, sis, over the years I've given you good financial advice. All I'm saying now is don't get too invested in this guy if you're moving in opposite directions." Then he'd clasped her hand. "I don't want to see you get hurt."

Now Faith chewed on the last olive from the once full bowl on the bar meant for the martini drinkers—lots of heart-healthy mono-unsaturated fats, she rationalized—and mulled over her brother's well-intended warning.

Dev was right, at least about the financial advice. He had convinced her and her best friend, Jamie, to invest in a handful of start-up technology companies, and then to sell while the market was booming. In fact, last year on Valentine's Day, she, Dev and Jamie had been lifting a toast to their profits. It was the only decent Valentine's Day she'd ever spent because she'd caught the glimmer of something romantic pass between her best friend and her brother.

Then over a bottle of good wine, the girls had hatched a plan to someday launch an upscale boutique of lingerie, perfume and jewelry geared toward male customers. Even Dev had agreed the concept had merit. They'd been developing the idea further over the past year and Dev had been wonderfully supportive. His encouragement meant that much more because Faith trusted her brother's business instincts implicitly.

But were his instincts about men—specifically Carter—equally on target? Although she hadn't admitted it, Dev had managed to nail her feelings to the wall—she was dangerously close to falling in love with Carter Grayson, and that was without any encouragement on his part whatsoever. What if things went as she'd planned tonight and she wound up in his bed? And what if he turned out to be the powerful lover she fully expected him to be? If she was this miserably infatuated with only a few full-body kisses under her pillow, how wretchedly far gone would she be after a night in his arms?

Faith drank from her glass and noticed she'd managed to delay her decision to leave by a full ten minutes. She glanced at all the couples seated at the tables with their heads together above flickering candle votives, sharing forks of food from their plates. Champagne buckets and open ring boxes sat on a few tables, and smiles and touches prevailed. The whole world seemed to pair off on Valentine's Day.

She caught sight of herself in the bar mirror, with an empty bar stool on either side. *And as usual, the cheese stands alone.* She tingled with humiliation that she'd gone to the trouble of pinning up her dark hair. And shopping for a new dress the exact shade of her pale blue eyes. And searching for the perfect Valentine's card. And sliding a condom into her purse. She eyed the foil packet sardonically as she removed her cell phone to see if she'd somehow missed Carter's call.

No call. She worried her lip with her teeth as she weighed how "susceptible" she would appear if she called him.

"Don't do it."

She looked up into Dixie's knowing eyes.

"But he could be hurt," Faith murmured. "Or dead even." God, was that her voice sounding so pitiful?

The woman gave a disbelieving shrug and turned to serve another customer.

Faith squeezed her eyes shut. Dixie was right, of course. And so was Dev. She was being stupidly stubborn, holding on to the absurd fantasy of a magical Valentine's Day that would never be. She slipped the phone back into her purse and wondered briefly about the condom's shelf life.

And to think the day had started out so promising. She always dreaded the busiest jewelry retail day of the year, but this morning she'd been fueled by the anticipation of seeing Carter. He had to feel something for her—a man didn't ask just anyone to meet him on Valentine's Day evening, right? With Carter on her mind today, she'd lost count of how many engagement rings she'd sold. Zerrick's Jewelry had been jammed with men wearing anxious expressions as they peered into the glass cases. *How big is that one? How much does it cost? Do you have a financing plan? Do you have a*—gulp—*return policy?*

Over the course of the ten-hour day, she had tried on every engagement ring in stock and held it up to the light, moving her hand this way and that so they could imagine how it would look on their girlfriend's finger.

"Her hand isn't quite as big as yours," they would invariably say.

"Then the stone will look even larger," was her standard cheerful reply as she curled her fingers under.

She took another sip of wine and studied her left hand. Long and broad, as the rest of her, she acknowledged wryly. And completely devoid of rings. It was a running joke among her friends and family—Faith the gemologist, who was surrounded by cases of engagement rings day in and day out, didn't have a diamond ring of her own. Sure, she could buy herself any ring she wanted, but the only ring she wanted was the one that her husband-to-be would someday slip onto her finger. Was that romantic notion so far-flung?

Faith sighed. Maybe so, if she were willing to fall for a man who was a no-show on the most romantic day of the year.

She slid off the stool and tested her weight on feet that had gone a little numb from sitting. "I'd like to settle my tab," she said to the bartender, pulling on her long wool coat—one did not toy with Chicago weather in February.

Dixie waved her off. "It's on the house, hon. Happy Valentine's Day." She leaned forward and whispered, "The man's a fool." Then she handed Faith a stack of napkins and gave her arm a sympathetic pat. "For the ride home."

Faith swallowed hard and stuffed the napkins into her purse. This was definitely a night for Ben & Jerry's Karamel Sutra ice cream. She sniffed, lifted her chin, and headed for the door, thinking ahead to what was on television tonight. Her feet hurt and a headache was coming on, but she'd feel better once she got home and into her fuzzy yellow robe.

She was about ten feet from the entrance when the door opened and Carter Grayson breezed in, dressed in jeans, T-shirt and leather bomber jacket, his jet hair still damp and holding the lines of his comb. She registered the fact that he seemed to be uninjured, but her relief at his blatant well-being quickly turned to irritation. He was a lumberjack of a man, wide and tall, with the face of a mischievous boy. She had liked the look of him from the moment he'd walked into Zerrick's Jewelry following a robbery attempt just after Christmas. Allegedly, he had liked the look of her, too.

"Hey," he said with a smile that took her breath away. "Sorry I'm late. I lost track of time and—" He stopped and inspected her dress. "Wow, you look nice. What's the occasion?"

Faith blinked. "Dinner. With you."

He pursed his mouth and looked her over again, his gaze lingering on her strappy high heels. "Okay. Well, I thought we'd have a beer first, then get some ribs at Nuke's, but maybe we should see if we can get a table here instead.'' He took in the packed restaurant. ''Sure is busy for a weeknight.''

Pure, abject, unadulterated mortification bled through her. With fumbling fingers, she began to button her coat. ''That's because it's V-Valentine's Day.''

He looked back, eyebrows high, then realization dawned. ''Oh...right.''

She wanted to evaporate, and cursed herself for not leaving sooner. ''Good night, Carter.'' She flung the ends of her scarf around her neck, and walked out the door into the frigid temperatures. In her next-to-nothing shoes, her feet were instant blocks of ice. An arctic blast stung her eyes and dislodged one pin, then another, from her careful upswept do. She blinked back tears. Why had she even bothered? Walking to the curb, she held up her arm to hail a cab. Booted footsteps sounded behind her.

''Faith, wait!'' He touched her arm, but she pulled away. ''I'm sorry I kept you waiting. We can still have dinner.''

She swallowed hard, unable to look at him. What a *fool* she was. She had read far too much into their casual dates and occasional phone conversations. ''I'm going home.''

''I'll take you home.''

She opened her purse and withdrew her leather gloves. ''No. I don't want to see you anymore, Carter.''

Silence. Then, ''Let me make it up to you.''

A cab slowed and pulled in next to the curb. She

reached for the door handle and his warm hand closed over hers.

"Faith," he said softly, earnestly. "I'd like to see your pretty dress."

She swung her gaze up to his. Big mistake, because the intensity in his green eyes reminded her of everything she'd wanted to happen tonight—for them to take their fledgling relationship to the next level. But while she had been thinking Valentine's Day candlelight and romance, he had been thinking Thursday night beer and ribs. And worse, now he *knew* what she'd been hoping for. He *knew* she cared more.

She tugged open the cab door. "Goodbye, Carter."

He hovered behind her as she slid into the seat. "Faith, it doesn't have to end like this," he said, spanning the open door.

"Yes, it does."

"But why? I thought we had a good thing going."

She was glad his face was cast in shadows—it made him easier to resist. "It's my fault, Carter. I'm looking for something you're not prepared to offer."

He glanced around, as if whatever she was looking for might suddenly appear. "What's that?"

Faith wanted to shake him, but his cluelessness seemed dishearteningly sincere. He was lost to her, but maybe the next woman could benefit from her gross miscalculation. "What am I looking for? A *re-la-tion-ship.* A bona fide, old-fashioned, one-man, one-woman thing. Let's face it, Carter, you are *not* commitment material."

Her words must have sufficiently stunned or angered him, because he stepped back as she slammed the cab door closed. She gave the cabbie her address in a choked voice, dug in her purse for a napkin, and resisted the urge to look back as they drove away.

Carter Grayson stood watching the cab pull away, feeling as if he'd been hit by a double-decker bus. Faith Sherman was one hell of a looker and could hold her own at a pool table—not at all what he'd expected out of the daughter of one of the oldest, wealthiest families in Chicago. He'd thought they were having fun and maybe were headed for a good no-strings-attached roll in the hay.

Or two.

He had no idea she wanted…all that other stuff. Especially from him, a roughneck whose original art collection consisted of his niece's crayon drawings, and whose wardrobe was dictated by which pair of jeans happened to be clean.

You'd think that one of the guys at the precinct would've informed him today was Valentine's Day—a suspect holiday at best, but one that somehow had been elevated to the status of relationship benchmark. And apparently, he had failed. Horribly.

Carter sighed and rubbed his hand over his face. Perhaps he should have foregone police work and looked into soothsaying. It appeared he was never going to master this dating thing until he could learn to read a woman's mind. Still, dammit, he'd never been *dumped* before.

Out of the corner of his eyes, he spotted an object lying on the sidewalk where Faith had stepped into the cab. Had she dropped something? He squatted and a dry laugh escaped him. A condom?

Well, well, he and the lovely lady might have been entertaining some of the same thoughts, after all. He stood and slipped the packet into his jacket pocket, then stared in the direction she'd gone. For a split second, he was struck by the sensation that he'd just missed out on more than a night of excellent sex.

Carter rubbed at the sudden tightness in his chest and, to his relief, the feeling passed.

CHAPTER ONE

Saturday morning, February 1, 2003

FAITH FINGERED the brass nameplate on her desk: Faith Sherman, Owner And Manager, Diamond Mine Jewelry. "I owe you one, Dev," she said into the phone.

"So did Captain Stewart," Dev said. "That's why he promised to personally select a light-duty officer to handle the security for this Valentino diamond. He said a uniform would stop by the jewelry store this afternoon for instructions."

She hoped "light duty" didn't mean inexperienced, but beggars couldn't be choosers. And she couldn't very well expect the city of Chicago to take one of its finest officers off the street to baby-sit a pretty rock. "Thanks, Dev. I'll phone the insurance company to let them know we'll have an extra armed guard on the premises."

"Jamie said you have great coverage lined up to let the public know the stone will be on display. The crowds could be huge."

"Let's just hope that huge crowds lead to huge sales. We need a strong Valentine's Day showing."

Then she narrowed her eyes. "You and Jamie have been talking a lot lately."

"Um...listen, sis, there's a phone call on the other line that I need to take. See you for coffee in the morning?"

"Sure."

"Bye."

"Bye." Faith hung up the phone and smiled. Dev and her business partner, Jamie, had both been acting strange lately when she mentioned the other person's name. Maybe this Valentine's Day would be successful for *some*body. She leaned back in her desk chair and sighed. After last year's fiasco with Carter Grayson, she had written off all future emotional expectations for the most romantic day of the year. Instead, she was planning her first vacation since the opening of The Red Doors boutique at the beginning of November. This February 14, after she locked the doors on The Diamond Mine—the self-contained jewelry store that was her domain in the upscale mall—she was heading for the airport and a week of blissful solitude on Captiva Island, Florida. She would be far away from the chilly temperatures of Chicago, and the chilly reminder that, once again, she was alone on Valentine's Day.

Faith pushed to her feet and hugged herself. Almost a year later, it was still impossible to remember that evening waiting for Carter and to not feel overcome with humiliation. She hadn't seen him or talked to him since.

Not that she'd expected to after laying all of her expectations at his feet like that. Still, she had no regrets. She did wonder from time to time, though, about his safety considering his somewhat cavalier attitude about his own well-being.

But she had more pressing items on her plate at the moment, such as the next two-week sales period. The solvency of the entire mall hinged on the potential high-dollar-volume sales generated from the jewelry store. Bringing in the Valentino diamond had been her brainchild to help increase visibility and foot traffic. She hoped the gimmick worked, although she hated to resort to gimmicks at all—it smacked of The Gift Program, their copycat competition. But she would use whatever means necessary to get women into the store and registered on the "wish list" database. That database, combined with aggressive follow-up reminders to husbands and boyfriends, Faith firmly believed, was the key to their success.

She wanted the sales success for her partner Jamie's sake—she felt responsible for talking her friend into giving up her corporate systems engineering job to take a stab at a high-end retail concept. But, darn it, she wanted the sales success for herself, too, to prove to her family that she had inherited some of the Sherman business sense. Her father had agreed to rent them the bottom two floors of the Sherman Building—prime storefront property on Michigan Avenue—at a reduced rate. But D. H. Sherman had maintained his conviction that his children should earn their own way and, thus, had cautioned Faith that he wouldn't intervene if the business stumbled. Bottom line—The Red Doors needed to be making headway by the second quarter, and Valentine's Day would be the best indicator of their momentum.

Massaging her neck, cramped from poring over catalogs and financial statements, Faith walked over to the valet stand in her office and removed the slate-gray suit jacket hanging there. Thirty minutes until opening—just enough time to meet everyone downstairs for a cup of coffee.

As always, her spirits rose when she exited her office into the showroom of The Diamond Mine, a dazzling presentation of gold, silver, platinum and mixed-ore jewelry in state-of-the-art tiered display cases lined in splendid black. Grounded in luxurious red carpet, the room exuded masculinity, from its dark mahogany walls adorned with brushed nickel sconces, to the tall, black-leather chairs placed next to the cases for serious browsers, to the bass-rich jazz playing over Bose speakers, to the massive red door leading into the opulent surroundings from the mezzanine.

Despite its impressive size, the door was spring-loaded to glide open and closed. She stepped through and locked the door behind her, then paused to take in the realization of the dream she and Jamie and Dev had conceived nearly two years ago. One positive thing had come out of that last encounter with Carter Grayson—she had abandoned the destructive fantasy of life beginning when she found the right man and had immersed herself in their business plan. In less than a year, The Red Doors was open for business, introducing a new retailing concept of individual high-end shops under one roof. If you weren't a sexual being when you walked into The Red Doors, you certainly were by the time you walked out.

To her left and behind red door number one was the Heaven Scent boutique, a sumptuous sensual feast of perfumes and aromatherapy products—Jamie's domain. To her right and behind red door number three was the Sheer Delights boutique, a visual indulgence of lingerie and loungewear to satisfy every lover's desire. Dixie Merriweather was straightening a deep-red floor-length dressing gown on a curvaceous mannequin in the window. She smiled and waved at Faith. Faith waved back. "Coffee?" she mouthed.

"In a minute," Dixie mouthed back, and indicated she would join her downstairs.

Correction—*two* positive things had come out of the last encounter with Carter: Dixie, the beautiful blond, sociable middle-aged bartender who dispensed wine and wisdom had popped into Faith's mind when she and Jamie had sat down to define the type of woman they needed to run the lingerie store. Dixie was a smooth-talking Southern belle who knew how to flatter male customers without taking any guff. She was the men's mother, sister, aunt and teacher, and she could sell the sky, one blue patch at a time. Women customers loved her because she encouraged them to take risks and made them feel beautiful.

The Diamond Mine, behind red door number two, sat in the center. Faith liked to think of it as the crowning jewel of the posh establishment—not that she was biased.

With a satisfied nod, she turned and descended the circular staircase that swept up both sides from the ground floor and the main entry. More plush red carpet on the stairs stole the sound of her footsteps until she reached the gleaming black-and-white checkerboard marble tiles. The two-story foyer, open to the mezzanine level lay wide and bare except for a row of potted palms that led customers into an area beneath the shops. There, customers were treated to a sitting area of wide, comfy chairs, an immense fireplace, a shoeshine stand with complimentary newspapers, private booths housing computers for customers who preferred to shop online, and a coffee bar aptly named The Red Bean. The coffee bar was already renowned for its exceptional cherry-bark coffee and miniature croissants, and for Alfred Willis, chief server-slash-handyman-slash-concierge and all-around gentleman, affectionately known as Mr. Willis.

"Good morning, Mr. Willis."

The stately man turned and a smile lit his pleasant face. "Good morning to you, Miss Faith. What can I get for you this fine day?"

She shivered and slid onto a stool. "Something warm with a jolt."

"I know just the thing," he said, then poured something that smelled delicious from a carafe into a Red Doors's ceramic mug and set it in front of her. "There you are, madam."

Faith lifted the mug and inhaled. ‘‘Mmm, vanilla?’’

He nodded, pleased.

She drank deeply and closed her eyes. ‘‘Mr. Willis, this is divine.’’

He blushed to the roots of his salt-and-pepper hair—what little was left—and tugged at his immaculate tie. ‘‘My pleasure.’’

‘‘A man would warm you better,’’ Dixie said, winking at the gentleman and sliding onto the stool next to Faith.

Mr. Willis pursed his lips and Faith smiled. ‘‘Don’t mind Dixie, Mr. Willis.’’

He harrumphed and Dixie laughed teasingly at him, which only flustered him further. ‘‘I’ll have the morning blend with a shot of Baileys, Alfred.’’

Faith hid her smile in her cup as his jaw tightened. Maybe working in the lingerie store was starting to affect Dixie—she seemed to delight in tormenting the unflappable man.

‘‘You *know* we don’t serve libations here,’’ he said in a clipped tone.

The older woman sighed dramatically. ‘‘Okay, plain old cream then. I guess I’ll live.’’

Faith shook her head. Dixie looked more vibrant than any woman had a right to—knockout legs, snug orange sweater, radiant skin, and flashing brown eyes. Fifty-six never looked so good.

‘‘Where are Jamie and Dev this morning?’’

‘‘Dev’s already in his office and Jamie seems to be running late.’’ She arched an eyebrow. ‘‘They’re both off-schedule today. Hmm. Faith, have you lost weight?"

She laughed. "Not quite."

"Not that you need to," Dixie said. "You got the kind of curves a man likes to *ride,* honey."

Mr. Willis cleared his throat disapprovingly.

Dixie shot him a frown, then said, "Seriously, your clothes are getting loose."

"I joined a gym," Faith said. Her Christmas present to herself. Get out more, meet people, forget about Carter—wait...where *had* that come from?

"A gym? But you already run a hundred miles a week."

"I run two miles a day."

"Gawd—isn't that enough?"

"I'm just playing around with the dumbbells at the gym, toning up a little."

"Well, do me a favor and don't turn into a gym bunny, okay?"

Faith laughed. "No worry there as long as Ben & Jerry's stays in business." In truth, she hadn't been able to eat Karamel Sutra since she'd pigged out so excessively on it last year. She didn't even want to think about how many calories she'd consumed that night. Or how many napkins she'd gone through during her crying jag. The elderly cabbie had been so distraught that he'd walked her to her door and refused a tip.

Dixie sipped from her cup, made a face, then asked, "Got plans for Valentine's Day?"

A mouthful of coffee went down hard. "I'm going on vacation, remember?"

"Oh. Right. Florida. Alone?"

"Yes."

"Hmm."

Faith concentrated on her coffee. Dixie was probably remembering the pathetic picture she'd been last year, all dressed up and nowhere to come—er, *go.* She'd hoped against hope that she hadn't dropped that condom at the bar. If Dixie had found it and connected it to Faith, she hadn't said so. And while Dixie could be outrageous, she'd never teased Faith about that night, as if she sensed it was too sensitive a topic.

Faith finished her coffee in one drink. Why, all of a sudden, she was determined to relive the details of that night, she couldn't fathom. A year had passed. She'd embarked on a new career. She'd had other men…over for dinner. "I need to set up the cases," she said abruptly, and stood so quickly she nearly tripped over the stool. She ignored the sharp look Dixie gave her, thanked Mr. Willis for the coffee, and wheeled to go. At the last minute, she remembered her conversation with Dev and turned back.

"Oh, Mr. Willis, I'm expecting a police officer to stop by sometime today to discuss security for the Valentino diamond."

"Yes, Miss Faith. A man or a woman?"

"Actually, I'm not sure."

"I'll keep an eye out. Shall I call you when the officer arrives or send him or her on up to the jewelry store?"

"Send the officer on up."

CARTER GRAYSON stared at the piece of paper, then back to Captain Stewart. "You can't be serious."

"As an effing heart attack."

"Chief, this is a security guard job—I'm a lieutenant!"

"You're a *wounded* lieutenant who got that way because you didn't follow procedure."

Carter set his jaw. "I always follow procedure."

"Like wearing your bulletproof vest?"

He ground his teeth. "A bulletproof vest wouldn't have kept me from getting shot in the leg."

"I was making a point." His captain sat back in his chair. "Grayson, if you have some sort of problem, you could tell me and we'll get you some help."

"Problem, Sir?"

"You know—alcohol, drugs."

He scoffed. "I don't even take the painkillers the doctor gave me for my leg."

"Is it a woman?"

"I don't have a woman."

"Maybe that's your problem."

"Are you my captain or my mother?"

His captain shrugged. "Something's affecting your concentration. You refuse to take vacation time, you've been as cross as a damn bear with everyone around here, and considering the way the Dorsey Avenue bust went down, you've been about as reckless as one, too."

Carter bit down on the inside of his cheek until the metallic taste of blood filtered into his mouth.

First his friends and relatives, and now his co-workers—was this some kind of conspiracy?

His captain sighed and steepled his hands. "Look, Grayson, I know this assignment is a pissant job, but you could use some downtime. I can't put you back on the street until you're well, so it's this or desk duty."

Carter winced.

"Take it, son. Take a couple of weeks and work out whatever's messing with your mind. There's even a gym close to this place where you can finish your rehab."

Carter knew when to say when. He dropped into a chair with a defeated sigh, rubbed his throbbing leg, then reread the assignment sheet. "The Diamond Mine." He looked back up. "Never heard of it."

"New jewelry store down on Michigan Avenue in a swanky place called The Red Doors. Try not to touch anything."

CHAPTER TWO

Saturday afternoon, February 1, 2003

CARTER FUMED during the drive to Michigan Avenue, gripping the steering wheel of his SUV until his hands cramped. "Traffic's a freaking nightmare," he rumbled. "Where did all these people come from? Don't they have anything better to do on a Saturday than to clog the streets?"

In the passenger seat, his adopted yellow Labrador, Trudy, lifted her head and barked.

"I'm *not* talking to myself. I'm talking to *you*."

She cocked her head.

"What, are you in on this…this…this *citywide intervention* to force me to be a nicer person?"

She barked again.

"Yeah? Well, what if it's not my problem? Maybe everyone *else* has the problem—did you ever think of that? Using their pop-psych analysis to try to figure out why I'm not Mr. Sunshine all the time. I'm a *cop*—what the hell do they expect?"

Trudy laid her head on the console and telegraphed sympathy with her eyes.

"You know, my sister thinks I adopted you because I was lonely. I tried to explain that you just showed up at the station and followed me around until I had no choice but to take you home. She wouldn't listen. Like most females, she just jumped to her own damned conclusion."

Let's face it, Carter, you are not *commitment material.*

He cursed and wiped a hand over his mouth. Faith Sherman's last words were only haunting him because it was getting close to that time of year again when men were expected to prove their devotion by coughing up an expensive bauble or making a big production out of dinner or doing something really crazy like popping the question just so a woman could brag that her man outdid everyone else's man. He knew Valentine's Day was encroaching because he'd circled the damn date on his calendar, in red. Just in case he was involved in another promising situation, he didn't want to muck things up by asking the woman to do something on that day.

Not commitment material? He was just as much commitment material as most of the guys he knew—maybe even more so. He paid his rent on time. He picked up after himself...mostly. He rarely let the trash overflow onto the floor. He wouldn't mind sharing a television remote because he had two televisions in the living room—one for pro sports and one for college sports. The reason he left the commode lid up was so that Trudy could drink from the toilet bowl if she had the urge. He didn't snore...much. And he didn't care about most things enough to argue about them.

He was *too* commitment material—it just so happened he didn't want to be tied down to one woman. Responsibility. Monogamy.

And he flatly refused to believe that his mental state had suffered over the past several months because of her offhand dismissal. Okay, her dumping him had thrown him at first, but on mere principle, *not* because he felt anything special for her. After all, they hadn't even slept together—it was just a few casual dates of bowling and pool. She hadn't given him time to work his way up to darts. If things had still been going well after that, his next step would've been to think of some way to talk her into going to bed with him.

Of course, from the looks of her that night, she might have been willing to skip a few steps.

Still, in hindsight, it would have been a matter of time anyway before she noticed that he wasn't up to snuff for the daughter of D. H. Sherman. Better for things to have ended when they did in the unlikely event that he would have developed some kind of *feelings* for her. After all, hadn't she told him she was looking for a *re-la-tion-ship?*

Trudy barked, and he reached over to scratch her head. "You're the only woman I need in my life, old girl. I'll be in a better mood soon—I'm just in a slump, that's all." He flexed his left leg as much as the floorboard would allow. "And my leg is making me cranky."

Maybe Captain Stewart was right, maybe he did need a change of scenery for a few days. He slowed as the storefront came into view. The Red Doors.

He whistled low at the prime corner location, the elegant signage, the red awning over the enormous set of doors. This would definitely be a change from the bad neighborhoods and dark alleys he usually patrolled. Well-heeled men and women strolled the sidewalks of the high-end retail area, suits and dress coats prevailed.

He looked down at his jeans and leather jacket. "Think they'll let me in?"

Trudy seemed more optimistic than he felt. He pulled into the parking garage and surrendered his key and a twenty to a somber-looking attendant. "Watch my dog for a few minutes, will you, pal?"

The man looked uncertain, but took the money with a gloved hand and nodded.

Carter took a minute to look at his reflection in the side mirror. The ball cap was probably a bad idea. He yanked it off and ran his hand through his hair to displace the distinct flattened ridge. He hadn't cut his hair since he'd been on sick leave, and it was well below regulation length, flipping up on the ends. But it would have to do. He tossed the cap inside. "What's the quickest way to get to that Red Doors place?"

The man looked him up and down, then pointed mutely to the nearest exit sign.

"Much obliged."

The exit took him to a sidewalk that led to the entrance. The two immense doors opened into a small enclosed foyer, with a waist-high mahogany counter on the right, sporting a brass plaque that read Package Pickup. A few feet behind the counter, an elevator opened and a tall, older gentleman alighted carrying two wrapped packages.

"Yes, sir, how may I help you?"

"I'm looking for a place called The Diamond Mine."

One of the doors leading to the interior opened and an attractive middle-aged blonde stuck her head out. "Alfred, if Mrs. Bangs stops to pick up those packages, don't you *dare* let her shake them."

The stiff-backed man frowned hard. "I'm with a *customer.*"

The woman turned her gaze to Carter, and he got the feeling that she liked what she saw. Then she squinted. "Are you here about the security job?"

"As a matter of fact, I am."

The older man made an impatient noise. "I was just about to send him up to see Miss F—"

"Alfred," the woman said rather sharply. "I'll show the gentleman to the jewelry store." She turned a curving smile toward Carter. "Won't you follow me, Mr....?"

"Lieutenant Grayson of the Chicago P.D., ma'am."

She led him through the doors into a spacious lobby with checkerboard marble floors. "Lieutenant? My, my. Can you tell me the time, Lieutenant Grayson?"

He was busy taking in the lavish surroundings. "Sorry, ma'am. I've never gotten into the habit of wearing a watch."

She made a disappointed noise. "That's too bad. You just might be late for something important someday."

"TRY THIS ONE." Faith smiled at her customer, a paunchy man who had come in supposedly browsing for a gift for his wife, but had wound up looking at pinky rings for himself. She had learned rather quickly that adding a few men's items to the mostly female selection would be a boon. At the man's request, Faith held up a small mirror so he could see how the ring would look when he shook hands.

"It's not too pretentious?" he asked, biting his lip.

The showroom door opened and Faith glanced up. "Not—" Her voice disappeared in a squeak as her eyes sent a message to her brain that it wouldn't accept. *Carter?* She blinked and her heart stalled painfully. Impossible. Why would he be here?

He hadn't come to see her, judging from the look of surprise on his face that must have rivaled the look on hers. His lips parted and he stood with his hand on the doorknob, his gaze boring into hers. Time stood still as a dozen emotions collided within her. Hadn't she fantasized of this moment, of running into him unexpectedly?

"Hello," he would say.

"Hello," she would say, and then tilt her head. "I'm sorry, I can't seem to remember your name."

And he would say, "Funny, I can't seem to forget yours."

And they would—

"Miss?"

She jerked her attention back to her customer. "Yes?"

"I said, you don't think it's too pretentious?"

"Er, no." She looked back at Carter who was slowly walking toward her. She was torn between the crazy urge to run away and the crazier urge to run into his arms. "Would you excuse me for a moment, sir?" She stepped forward and into the curve of the U-shaped display case. Carter stopped opposite her. Faith was glad to have the two feet of glass barrier between them as she forced her mouth upward at the corners. "Hello, Carter." His face was thinner, his hair longer, his eyes greener.

He gave her a curt nod. "Hello, Faith. I didn't expect to find you working here."

She willed her racing vital signs to slow. "This is my place."

His eyebrows shot up. "Yours?"

"Yes. Mine and my partner's."

"Your partner?"

"My business partner, Jamie Ruskin. She's my best friend actually. You didn't meet Jamie… before."

"Oh."

She clasped her hands together. "So, are you looking for a gift?"

"Hmm? Oh, no." He laughed and scratched his temple. "Actually, my captain sent me here, something about security for a special rock?"

Faith gaped. "You?" Then she caught herself. "I mean, I thought he was sending someone expendable—I mean…someone on light duty.'' She swallowed and started again. ''I would think you'd be too high-ranking for…security work.''

The hint of a smile danced on his mouth. ''I thought the same thing.'' He shifted awkwardly, favoring his left leg. ''But I'm recuperating from an injury and I'm on light duty for a couple more weeks.''

She put her hands behind her back to keep from reaching out to him. ''You were wounded?''

''Nothing serious,'' he said, but she didn't quite believe him.

His gaze tracked hers, and they were silent. Seconds ticked off, and she thought her chest might burst from the breath she held. At last she exhaled. ''I don't think this arrangement would be a good idea.''

''You're right,'' he said, nodding.

''You'd probably be bored silly here, and, well… it could be awkward.''

''I'll explain to my captain that we're…acquainted. He'll find someone else.''

''Yes.'' She crossed her arms over her chest and felt more in control. She glanced around to make sure that her assistant, Stacy, was handling the customers, then looked back to Carter. Alarm was beginning to set in that he looked so good to her, even better than she remembered. ''So, how are you? Um, other than the wound, of course.''

''I'm great.''

Faith nodded. ''That's great.''

''You?''

"Oh, I'm great."

He looked around the showroom. "It looks like things are great."

"Yes. Things are…great."

He glanced back and rubbed his chin. "When you mentioned something about a partner, I thought maybe you'd gotten married."

She lifted one hand to toy with the initial pin on the lapel of her jacket. "No, I'm not married." She laughed. "I don't suppose *you're* married?"

"Me? No." He joined her laughter.

"I didn't think so."

After a few seconds Carter stopped laughing, but she didn't seem to notice. A slow burn started in his stomach that she was so amused by the idea of him settling down. *You are* not *commitment material.*

"But I am living with someone," he blurted.

She stopped laughing and her remarkable ice-blue eyes widened. "Really? That's…great."

Vindication barbed through his chest. So what if it wasn't true—Faith didn't have to know. "Yeah, we're really committed to each other."

"Oh."

In for a penny, in for a pound. "In fact," he said, peering into the cases around him, "I'm planning to pop the question on Valentine's Day."

"Really?"

He nodded. "Why wait around when you find the right woman?"

She smiled. "Why indeed. Congratulations."

He deflated a bit. What had he expected—that she would burst into flames of jealousy? "Er, thanks."

Across the showroom, a young woman lifted her hand. "Faith?"

Faith nodded, then looked back. "I need to get back to work, but it was good to see you, Carter. I hope everything goes well with the wedding."

Carter swallowed and tried to smile—even though it was all make-believe, the word *wedding* still hit him hard. He watched her walk away from him, tall and statuesque, with enough curves for a man to get his hands around. Her black, black hair, startling against her fair complexion, skimmed her shoulders. Her nose and cheekbones were model-perfect, her lips wide and berry-red. And those eyes...a man could grow old and never tire of looking into them. And now that he was faced with the thought of walking out of here and possibly never seeing her again, his big dumb feet wouldn't move. On the other hand, he couldn't think of a good reason to stay. Feeling much the way he did the night he'd watched her drive away in the cab, he turned and started toward the door, massaging his left thigh, which had begun to throb.

The customer that Faith had been attending when he had walked in was moving toward the door at the same time, but his body language was all wrong—walking too fast, seeming too intent on the exit. All of Carter's senses went on alert. He looked back to see Faith's gaze jump from the man back to the counter where he'd been seated.

"Sir," she said, her voice just short of panicked. "The ring! Stop!"

Instead the man made a run for the door. Carter

moved out of instinct, sprinting the few steps it took to overtake the man, then tackling him in front of the door. When they landed, white-hot pain ripped through Carter's leg, stealing his breath. He gritted his teeth and pushed himself to his good knee while wrestling the man's hands behind his back. "I'm a police officer. Be still, dammit, or I'll shoot you." He didn't even have his weapon on him, but the threat worked.

"Don't shoot," the man cried. "The ring's in my pocket. Take it back, please. Don't arrest me."

Carter held him down with one hand and felt in the man's jacket pocket with the other. He pulled out the ring and handed it to Faith, who stood nearby, white-faced. "Call the police," he said.

"Stacy is doing it right now," she said in a strained voice. "You're hurt."

He shook his head. "Nah." Truth be known, aside from his burning leg, he felt pretty darn good—it was the adrenaline rush. And it wasn't every day that a man got to be a hero in front of a girl he...didn't hate. "If you get up," he told the man, "I'll shoot you." With a bit of teeth grinding, Carter stood and took a few deep breaths until the worst of the pain subsided. He lowered his voice for Faith's ears only. "Tell me your security is better than yelling 'stop' as the thief runs out the door."

Faith nodded, but bit into her lip. "It is, but I'm starting to think it could use some tweaking considering the crowds the Valentino diamond might be bringing in."

"This Valentino diamond, that's the guard assignment?"

"Yes. I thought it would help increase foot traffic before Valentine's Day."

The disturbing sensation he felt when he thought he was walking out of her life was still fresh. He had an inexplicably perverse desire to spend more time with her, and the opportunity to do it was staring him in the face. Before he could consider the ramifications, he said, "Maybe I'll take that assignment, after all. I could review your general security measures while I'm at it." He attempted a casual shrug. "That is...if you think it wouldn't be too awkward."

She hesitated for what seemed like an eternity. He was on the verge of withdrawing his offer when she gave him a small smile. "I think it's clear that I—I mean, *we*—need someone like you around." She extended her hand as if to set the boundaries of their interaction. "You're hired, Lieutenant Grayson."

Carter shook her hand, but the jolt of awareness that shot through him when his fingers touched hers left him with the foreboding that this assignment could prove to be the most dangerous of his career.

CHAPTER THREE

Monday morning, February 3, 2003

"BREATHTAKING," Stacy murmured.

"Mmm-hmm." Faith looked from the spectacular twenty-seven-carat Valentino diamond safely tucked away under bulletproof glass to where Carter stood a few feet away. He was reviewing a procedure checklist with Ben Sills, the armed guard who'd delivered the stone and would be sharing security duties with Carter. Dressed in his navy uniform, Carter was an imposing figure, and reminiscent of the way he'd looked when she'd first met him after a robbery attempt at Zerrick's Jewelry where she used to work. She told herself her gaze kept straying to Carter because he was an unfamiliar presence in the store, but, in truth, for the past two days she hadn't been able to stop thinking about the fact that she'd apparently underestimated his capacity to settle down.

Why wait around when you find the right woman?

"Hey, listen to this," Stacy said, reading from a brochure. "The stone has a love legend. A man named Adrian Valentino bought a diamond mine to find the largest, most perfect diamond possible for his bride-to-be. When this twenty-seven-plus-carat diamond was discovered, he had it set aside for a pendant. But his true love died before they could be married. He claimed her spirit was in the stone, and remained unmarried so he could join her when he died. Says here that if you look into the diamond and the light is shining just so, you'll see their two hearts entwined.'' Stacy looked up. ''Spooky, huh?''

Faith made a noncommittal sound and pressed her fingers against a twinge in her temple. She'd barely been able to concentrate Saturday after Carter had left the store. Yesterday he'd shown up about an hour before the Valentino stone arrived, but, thankfully, she'd been able to attribute her nervousness to the brouhaha surrounding the diamond. They'd barely exchanged enough words to constitute a conversation, yet she'd gotten even less sleep last night than the previous one. She'd spent long, dark hours replaying his features in her mind, reliving her reaction to seeing him again...and obsessing over the woman who had captured his big heart.

She knew it was a ridiculous, juvenile, pathetic exercise, but the man evoked such a powerful physical response in her, she couldn't help but compare herself to the mystery woman. And some small part of her acknowledged that she had harbored a reunion fantasy about Carter—that they'd cross paths and something would...*spark* and they'd get a second chance at whatever might have been. Accepting that Carter was nearly engaged meant letting go of that fantasy and conceding that his limited interest in her had nothing to do with his aversion to commitment and everything to do with his aversion to committing to *her*.

"Earth calling Faith."

She blinked. "Hmm?"

Stacy angled her head. "I asked if you'd seen the hearts in the diamond."

"Er, no."

"Are you all right?"

"Of course."

"You seem...preoccupied. Are you worried about the crowds?"

"A little. I think I'm going to get some coffee before we open. Can I bring you anything?"

"No, thanks." Stacy bent to peer at the glass-encased stone.

Faith tried not to frown as she approached the two men, who seemed to be embroiled in yet another dispute. They had agreed on little since the stone had arrived yesterday. Ben Sills was almost as tall as Carter, but not as broad. And while his fair hair and coloring made him seem less...dangerous, he wasn't backing down from his line of reasoning.

"Gentlemen, is there a problem?"

Carter's body language eased a fraction. "No, Faith. No problem."

Ben Sills, lean and handsome in his own dark uniform of slacks and sport coat, gave her a pleasant smile. "Ms. Sherman, I was saying I think it would be better if Officer Grayson—"

"*Lieutenant* Grayson," Carter interjected.

The other guard conceded with a nod. "If *Lieutenant* Grayson doesn't wear a firearm."

Carter jammed his hands on his hips. "And I was saying that's bullshit."

"Mr. Sills," Faith said in a calm voice, "why do you object to Lieutenant Grayson wearing a firearm?"

The fairer man hesitated, then passed a wary glance over Carter's rigid bearing. "Would you excuse us for a moment, *Lieutenant?*"

Carter glowered, but stepped away several feet to stand in front of the entrance with his back to them, arms crossed.

"Ms. Sherman—"

"Please call me Faith."

The guard smiled amiably. "All right. Call me Ben." He stole a glimpse at Carter's back, then leaned close. "Faith, I've traveled with this diamond for six years, and the only times I've had trouble was when I had to work with a cowboy type like Grayson. It's not his fault—he's a seasoned cop, and he's overqualified for this job."

She murmured agreement.

"Unfortunately," he continued, "a man like Grayson can come across to the public as menacing, especially with a firearm at his side. I was put on this tour because I understand not only the security aspect of the job, but also the marketing aspect." He lifted his hands apologetically. "We only want you to get your money's worth. This diamond is supposed to be an accessible exhibit that people can enjoy."

Faith pressed her lips together. "But the contract required that I provide an additional armed guard."

"Didn't you add an armed guard by the main entrance?"

"Yes...at the lieutenant's suggestion."

"That will satisfy your obligation." He opened his sport coat to reveal a revolver in a shoulder holster. "Meanwhile, my firearm will be here *and* unobtrusive."

She smiled. "All this talk about guns makes me a little nervous."

"So you see my point?"

She sighed and nodded. "I'll talk to Lieutenant Grayson." Faith moved toward the showroom entrance where Carter stood. The other man was right—Carter looked like a thundercloud, dark and intimidating. She didn't remember him being so edgy before, but then again, she'd already determined she hadn't really known him. She walked up and turned on her most cheerful voice. "Join me for a cup of coffee downstairs?"

He turned, and she wondered when over the next two weeks she would become immune to this man's presence. Something hot flashed in his eyes, then disappeared. He was angry with the other guard. It was absurd to think that he harbored any anger toward her over the way she'd ended things. After all, if she hadn't gotten into the cab that night, he might never have met his live-in lover—the woman he wanted to marry. Besides, if he were angry about that night, wouldn't he have said something before now?

He studied her until her skin began to tingle. "Coffee? Sure," he said finally, then held open the red door for her to exit. As she walked under his extended arm, she caught the barest scent of his earthy cologne—evergreen and spice. He moved with the casual grace of a large animal, in command of every muscle, even the ones compromised by his injury.

"How is your leg?"

"Coming around."

"How did it happen?"

He shrugged. "Drug bust that went down wrong. Caught a stray bullet."

Faith shivered. He could just as easily have been killed. "Would you like to take the elevator?"

"Not for my leg, but I do need to double check the elevator's operation."

Yesterday he had double- and triple-checked every inch of the place—doors and windows, heating and air ducts, even the chimney. He had watched their opening and closing procedures, observed traffic patterns, and asked a hundred questions. Faith was grateful for his expertise, and had already enacted his recommendations. The man made her feel so safe, yet at the same time so vulnerable. This was the enigma, she told herself, that she had mistaken for infatuation when they had known each other before.

She led the way down the catwalk to the elevator, highly aware of his body moving next to hers. His size was no small part of her initial attraction to him—she wasn't a small woman, but felt diminutive standing next to Carter. He was beautifully proportioned, but everything about him was oversize: his shoulders, his limbs, his hands and feet. When he'd kissed her, she'd had the sensation of being absorbed into his body. And during their more heated kisses, she had felt the promise of his impressive arousal. She had shamelessly wanted to sleep with him, a feeling that she could call up even now because he was the only man who had ever made her feel so wanton.

"Faith."

She blinked. "Yes?"

He was holding the elevator door with his arm. "After you."

She walked in, feeling flushed and foolish. If she was going to have a successful sales period over the next couple of weeks, she was going to have to regain her focus. And the best way to remain focused would be to keep telling herself that the man simply wasn't available. Period. End of story.

The door closed behind them, as if sealing her resolve. Oblivious to her inner turmoil, Carter studied the metal ceiling plates, the button panel, and checked for a dial tone on the emergency phone. Satisfied, he pushed the ground-level button and assumed a wide stance, pelvis thrust forward, arms crossed. The man expanded to fit the space he occupied. They faced the closed door, his sleeve touching hers. His imposing proximity sent her nerves dancing as they descended to the lower floor.

"Um, Carter...about your gun. Maybe Ben is right."

He turned and lifted one black eyebrow. "Ben?"

Her cheeks warmed. "He has a point about not making the public uncomfortable."

"I'm only interested in making would-be thieves uncomfortable."

"And I appreciate your suggestion to add an armed guard at the main entrance. But after further consideration, I'd rather you not wear your sidearm in the showroom."

His mouth tightened, then he shrugged. "You're the boss."

Her chest rose at his offhand tone. Yes, she *was* the boss. Carter was obviously accustomed to having a woman around with an accommodating nature. She frowned. The more she thought about his live-in lover, the more she questioned the woman's good sense. In fact, she'd bet that the more she found out about the woman, the better she'd feel about dumping him. Faith fingered a lock of hair behind her ear and affected an equally casual tone. "So, Carter, tell me about your girlfriend."

Carter heard her words, but his brain took its sweet time to assimilate them. Oh, yeah—Faith thought he had a girlfriend. A *live-in* girlfriend. His tongue froze in his mouth as he cast about for credible details. "Um, she's…great." The elevator door slid open and he prayed she'd drop the subject.

"What's her name?" she asked as she stepped out.

He winced and followed her. "Um, Trudy." Hadn't he said his loyal Labrador was the only woman he needed in his life?

"How did you and Trudy meet?"

His mind raced. "She…came to the station."

"You work together?"

"No. She…was visiting."

"Oh."

Great—now Faith probably thought his girlfriend was a criminal. "I mean, she was lost."

"Oh."

Great—now Faith probably thought his girlfriend was dim. "I mean, she was new in town." He held open the interior door and stole a glance at her rear view as she walked through. She wore a short, flowered skirt with a flirty ruffle that stopped just above her knee. The woman had mouthwatering legs. Carter wet his lips and reminded himself he was supposed to behave like a man committed to another woman. The trouble was, his sex-deprived body didn't seem to want to play along.

"What does Trudy do for a living?"

He followed her across the polished checkerboard floor of the foyer. "She…works from my—our—place…fetching and…running around and…doing things."

"She runs errands for people?"

"Yes. She runs errands. For people."

"That's a very up-and-coming service industry."

It was? "Uh-huh."

Thank goodness they were at the coffee bar. He nodded to Mr. Willis, the token male in the establishment, and ordered a large black coffee. "None of that flavored stuff," Carter said, then added, "No offense."

"None taken," the man assured him, then handed

over one of the best cups of coffee Carter had ever tasted. Damn, going back to the sewer water at the station would be hell.

Faith ordered something exotic for herself, and an extra cup that he presumed she was taking back to the girl who worked in the jewelry store. As inconspicuously as possible, he observed Faith over the rim of his mug and watched her expression change as she interacted with Mr. Willis, a man she appeared to hold in high esteem. With a jerk of conscience, he wondered if she'd ever looked at him that way. When they'd dated a year ago, he'd been so wrapped up in curbing his desire for her, frankly he'd been afraid to watch her face too closely, afraid he might see something that would compel him to tell her what she wanted to hear to take her to bed. Now he had a sinking feeling that in his clumsy attempt to be a gentleman, he'd unintentionally neglected her.

They took the stairs back to the mezzanine where the three stores were located. He called upon his discipline training to keep from staring at her skirt as she ascended one step in front of him, but he simply couldn't resist the urge to devour her sway. Swish, swish, back and forth. His body hardened to the innocent rhythm, and he had to remind himself they were in a public place.

But it was a public place designed to pique the senses, he noted dryly as they walked past the perfume shop and inhaled some kind of citrusy scent that made him think of Faith and eating at the same time—a dangerous combination. On the other side of the jewelry store was a lingerie shop full of all kinds of temptations for a single man. While in there, he'd focused all his attention on the cash drop box to overlook the racks of sparkly, sheer, minuscule creations, and how they would look on tall, leggy Faith Sherman.

When they entered The Diamond Mine, he experienced a totally immature stab of disappointment that he would once again have to share her company. The disappointment was quickly followed by irritation when she handed the extra cup of coffee not to her young female employee, but to Sills—the guy who wanted him unarmed and emasculated, the guy who, instead of analyzing potential breaches in security, spent most of his time analyzing Faith's cleavage. The guy who was flirting with her right now.

Carter strode over, determined to think of a good excuse to interrupt. When he stopped in front of them, she was on the verge of sopping up a circle of coffee on the front of Sills's jacket.

''Faith,'' he said abruptly.

''Yes?''

''If you don't want me to wear my firearm, we should put it in the vault.''

She handed the napkin to Sills with an innocent smile, but the smile had disappeared by the time she turned and nodded. ''Good idea. Follow me, Carter.''

He narrowed his eyes at Sills, who frowned back, then trailed her and her swishy skirt to the short hallway that housed the vault. From her jacket pocket she removed a ring of keys and used two to unlock the outer door. The vault door itself had a keypad into which she punched a long series of numbers. When a tiny green light came on, she swung the door open and stepped inside.

Carter followed and was immediately assailed by the realization that being with Faith in a small space could become habit forming. The vault itself was moderately sized, about twelve feet square, but the walls were lined with deep metal shelves to hold the trays of jewelry removed from the display cases at night, leaving a pathway of about five feet down the center of the vault for maneuverability. Faith walked to a tall, black file cabinet—one of four—and used a key to open one of the drawers. "I think your gun will be safe in here."

Funny, but *he* wasn't feeling too safe in here. When she looked up at him, he was struck anew by the sheer openness of her expression—her bright eyes, dark eyebrows, clear skin, wide mouth. Hers was a morning face, glowing with the kind of fresh, natural beauty that a man wouldn't mind waking up to. Knowing he'd never see her in that sleep-tousled state made his gut clench. With a start, he realized that everything about Faith was understated—her gloriously simple straight hair, her elegant clothes, her scant jewelry.

"Is something wrong?" she asked, wide-eyed and irresistible.

He removed his weapon from its holster and settled it into the drawer. "I was just thinking it was interesting that you work around fancy jewels all the time, but you don't wear any."

Her gaze immediately dropped to her bare hands, and a little laugh escaped her. "I prefer jewelry that has sentimental value." She pulled back her left sleeve. "This watch was my mother's." She touched the pearl drops in her ears. "And my father gave me these when I graduated from college."

As if his hand had a mind of its own, it raised and fingered the silver initial pin on her lapel. "And this? You wear it every day, so the person who gave it to you must be special."

She swallowed. "He is."

Carter's heart quickened. "'He'?"

"My brother, Dev."

"Oh." Relief flooded him, and he dropped his hand reluctantly.

Faith studied her clasped hands, then looked up with a tentative expression in her eyes. "Carter, I've been waiting for the right time to bring this up, and I guess now is as good a time as any."

At the heightened color in her cheeks, hope bled into his chest. She was sorry for the way she had ended things between them.

"I'm sorry for the way I ended things between us."

In hindsight, she had misjudged him.

"In hindsight, I made a rather hasty judgment."

And she'd like to make it up to him.

"And I'd like to make it up to you, Carter."

She wanted to pick up where they'd left off, hours shy of making love.

His lips parted and his muscles poised to drag her to him for a long kiss. Blood raced to his belly in anticipation of her yielding curves being pressed against him.

A sudden smile lifted the corners of her red mouth, revealing a high dimple. "That's why I thought I'd let you know that not only do you qualify for a hefty employee discount at The Diamond Mine, but I will personally help you select an engagement ring for Trudy."

CHAPTER FOUR

Wednesday afternoon, February 5, 2003

"WHEN SHOPPING for a diamond," Faith recited for her apprehensive-looking client, Carter, "remember the four *C*s. Cut, clarity, color and carat." This wasn't the first time she had helped an angst-ridden man pick out an engagement ring, but it was the first time that the undertaking had filled *her* with angst. But she'd had to do *something* when they were in the vault the other day—having Carter around was wreaking havoc on her senses. Her brain simply hadn't accepted that he was unavailable, so what better way to drive the point home than to participate in his upcoming engagement?

As painful as it might be.

They were alone in the showroom. The Valentino diamond was locked away in the vault after another hard day of bringing in an amazing number of lookers, most of them women whom she and Stacy had persuaded to fill out a "wish list." Tonight the data processors would enter the information into the database and generate "hint" postcards to the designated gift-givers on the person's list. If the first three days were indicative of the kind of traffic they could expect over the next two weeks, The Diamond Mine would likely bring in some major revenue.

At least her business would benefit from Valentine's Day this year, even if her heart wouldn't.

From the vault she had set aside one small tray of exquisite engagement rings, most of them solitaire settings. Carter stood with mouth pursed, inspecting the dazzling display with a deer-in-the-headlight expression. His hands were sunk deep into his pockets, as if he were afraid to touch them. "By cut, you mean the shape?"

"Actually, the cut refers to how intricately the facets are arranged—how much the stone sparkles. But when most people say cut, they generally mean shape. And the shape does affect the way facets are cut." She pointed to an oval diamond in a gold setting. "This one is exquisitely cut, but it has a lower color rating than some of the others."

"Color?"

"The more clear, the better. Like this one." She held up an emerald-cut solitaire set in silver so he could look at it from the side.

He nodded. "I see."

She bit back a smile because she could tell he didn't see at all. "And then there's clarity, which simply refers to the tiny imperfections that occur naturally in nearly every diamond." She handed him a pear-shaped solitaire in a platinum setting and invited him to look through her jeweler's monocle. "This stone is of particularly good clarity."

He reluctantly pressed his eye to the magnifying device. "Uh-huh."

"And of course, there's the carat weight, which seems to be rather important to most brides." She forced a smile onto her face and handed him a round solitaire set in white gold. "Carat for carat, a round cut generally makes the most of the stone's weight. This one is about three-quarters of a carat."

"Hmm." His face was a study of pure bewilderment, but Faith had been down this road before.

"Maybe we should start with the setting—does she wear gold jewelry or silver?"

"I...never noticed."

"Okay. Would you say her style is more classic or more trendy?"

"Um, classic, I guess."

A starting point. "Has she ever mentioned a particular shape that she likes? Maybe admired a friend's ring?"

"Um, no."

"Is her wardrobe dressy or sporty?"

"Sporty." He coughed. "She likes baseball."

"Not bowling?" she teased.

A boyish grin split his face. "She's not as good a bowler as you are."

His comment shouldn't have cheered her so immensely. "Can you tell me anything else about her?"

"Um, she's small. Blond. Finicky eater."

Her cheer evaporated as a vision of a petite Barbie doll came to mind. "If she has small hands, any shape and size stone would look nice." She quelled the stab of jealousy and curled her own long fingers under.

He scratched his head and gave a dry laugh. "I didn't realize there was so much to consider."

Faith nodded. "It's an important decision. She'll wear this ring for the rest of her life." She'd delivered that line a thousand times, but she'd never been so personally invested in its claim.

"I would want my bride to have the best ring I could afford," he said slowly.

The money part was always sticky, and she didn't want to pry into his personal finances. "A general rule of thumb is to invest two months' salary in an engagement ring, but that's up to the individual."

He nodded, then laughed. "Two months of a cop's salary probably won't touch one of these babies." He turned over a price tag and blanched. "Or four months." He shoved his hand into his hair and shook his head. "I had no idea that women expect...all this."

"Don't forget the thirty-five percent employee discount," she murmured.

"That's very generous of you," he said, his tone suddenly quiet. "But I'd better give this some more thought."

Faith realized with a sinking heart that she would *give* him a ring for the woman he loved if it would put a smile back on his handsome face. And just like that, it hit her—she wasn't over Carter, not by a long shot. And even though he was lost to her, she couldn't bear to see him suffer.

"Carter." She reached forward and touched his hand. "When you really love someone, it's not about the ring."

He was silent for a few seconds, then put his other hand over hers, sandwiching her pale fingers between his strong, tanned ones. He lifted his gaze and smiled sadly. "Faith, don't tell me you wouldn't expect the man who proposed to you to come bearing a nice rock."

Her hand tingled between his. "That's exactly what I'm telling you," she whispered. "If a man I loved asked me to be his wife, I'd wear any ring he offered."

"You would?"

Her heart thudded in her chest. When she realized she was getting too caught up in a moment meant for another woman, she pulled her hand free. "Any woman would, and I suspect Trudy feels the same."

He looked down, then wet his lips and looked up again. "Faith."

The way he said her name stalled her heart. Throaty. Engorged with emotion. "Yes, Carter?"

His eyes seemed pained. "I—"

A rap on the door caught her attention, and his. Her partner Jamie walked in, laden with briefcase, purse, and accordion files. "I saw the light." Jamie's gaze went to Carter and she stopped. "I'm sorry, I didn't mean to interrupt—"

"You're not," Faith said quickly. "I'm helping Carter pick out a ring for his fiancé." She conjured up a smile. "He's going to propose on Valentine's Day." She had filled Jamie in on her history with Carter, with a disclaimer that he was almost engaged. But she had seen the knowing looks that Jamie and Dixie had traded over coffee. Best to nip their rampant speculation in the bud.

"Oh," Jamie said. "Congratulations, Lieutenant."

He shifted foot to foot, then nodded his thanks.

"Got big plans tonight?" Faith asked Jamie, to change the subject.

"Not really. I might meet Dev later."

Faith tried to suppress her smile. "Dev?"

"Yeah." Jamie's cheeks took on a telltale rosy tone. "Uh, want to join us?"

"No, thanks. Some other time."

Jamie looked relieved. "Okay, see you tomorrow."

Faith waved and murmured, "And they lived happily ever after." Those two were really becoming an item, and she couldn't be more pleased. She laughed and looked back to Carter to find his intense gaze fastened on to her. "I'm sorry, Carter—you were saying?"

But whatever had been in his eyes and on his mind before Jamie came in had fled. "Nothing," he said. "Nothing at all."

But she'd had the strangest feeling he'd been about to confide in her. Was the big man getting cold feet as the day of reckoning approached? A sliver of vindication pierced her that maybe she'd been right—maybe he *wasn't* commitment material.

But just as quickly as it came, the satisfaction disappeared. Because Carter Grayson, a man who was unable to commit, was just as lost to her as Carter Grayson, married man.

CHAPTER FIVE

Thursday evening, February 6, 2003

CARTER EXTENDED the leg press machine, grunting as the healing muscles in his thigh were taxed to exhaustion. He made it through two more repetitions by imagining Ben Sills's face on the receiving end of the weight plate. The man had tested his patience today, flirting shamelessly with Faith. And she hadn't held back, either, which was strange considering Mr. Traveling-Around-the-Country-with-a-Stupid-Rock didn't exactly strike him as commitment material.

He let the weights slam to the floor. The crashing noise covered the curse he released on an exhale. The anger that gripped him like a vise wasn't directed toward Faith or even toward that moron Sills—after all, he couldn't fault the man's taste. No, he was angry with himself.

For not jumping on the back of that cab a year ago to keep her from driving away.

For not calling her the next day and the next and the next and begging her forgiveness for being as dense as a tree where romance was concerned.

For concocting that preposterous story about living with someone in the hopes of making her jealous, then topping that lie with an even bigger whopper about planning to *propose* to the nonexistent woman.

And for not having the guts to follow through on his urge to confess his all-around idiocy and to do what he'd been aching to do since he'd walked through that damned red door—kiss Faith Sherman as she'd never been kissed before.

He sighed and wiped his face and neck with a white towel. Not that the most persuasive kissing in all of history would do him any good.

What am I looking for? A re-la-tion-ship. *A bona fide, old-fashioned, one-man, one-woman thing,* he recalled her saying.

And *that* was the reason he hadn't jumped on the back of the cab or called her the next day. *That* was the reason he'd lied about having a serious girlfriend. *That* was the reason he hadn't confessed his tall tale. Because Faith Sherman was holding out for a man who could promise her forever. And she'd likely prefer someone in her own social circle. He could promise only a few hot nights in bed, and his social circle included police department snitches. He knew himself and his short attention span well enough to know that even the powerful attraction he felt for her was not enough on which to build a long-term relationship. He had no business toying with a woman who had made her expectations perfectly clear. He didn't want to be responsible for someone else's happiness. He didn't want to be tied down. He'd lived in the same apartment for four years, and still paid his rent month to month. He didn't even own a watch, for heaven's sake!

No. Better to keep a lid on his libido until this assignment passed. Then he could forget about Faith and get back to his life. He flexed his leg and, satisfied at the diminished level of pain, pushed himself to his feet. A woman across the gym running on a treadmill caught his eye, but he had to look twice to be sure. *Faith?* Damnation, those were definitely her legs. He bit his tongue. The long, strong rest of her was outlined in damp, snug, brief clothing.

The lid to his libido developed a sudden vibration.

FAITH WISHED she had brought her own CD to listen to while she ran, but typically she could find something upbeat on the radio. Tonight, however, Chicago disc jockeys seemed to be gearing up for Valentine's Day by spinning every sad love song recorded in the past decade. Unrequited love. Broken hearts. Star-crossed lovers.

She'd come here hoping to forget about Carter for a couple of hours, to sweat him out of her system, or at least to exhaust herself until she was guaranteed a few hours' sleep tonight. He had been bad-tempered all day, snapping at Ben and even a couple of young boys who were roughhousing while in line to see the Valentino diamond. And when she had broached the subject of Trudy's ring again, hinting that they offered a generous financing plan, he'd glowered and said thanks but he didn't need her help, after all.

A shadow fell across her digital display. She

turned her head to tell the person she still had a mile to go, then almost lost her footing when she saw Carter standing there. She slowed the treadmill to a walk, and lowered her headphones to her neck. Her heart was pounding, but she couldn't rightfully blame it all on her aerobic workout—not when Carter was her every erotic dream come true in long, loose gray sweatpants, a white muscle shirt over toned, glistening skin. He had a towel slung around his neck, and his dark hair was wet and curly around his face and neck, his color was high from exertion. And he didn't exactly look happy to see her.

"Hello," she said, reaching for her own towel to wipe her neck and arms. Her gaze darted around—was one of the blond gym bunnies Trudy? The svelte woman on the stair machine? The stunner on the cross-country ski contraption?

"Hello," he said. "Fancy meeting you here."

He looked her up and down, and she was suddenly aware of how wet and clingy her clothing was. Resisting the urge to cover some bare skin with her hand towel, she maintained a slow walk on the treadmill. "Are you a member here?"

"Temporarily. My gym is near the station. But considering the proximity to your store, this location is more convenient to finish my rehab exercises."

"How's that going?"

"By the time I finish the security assignment, I should be ready to get back out on the street."

"That's good news. I'm sure your captain will be happy to have you back."

He made a noncommittal noise.

She looked around again. "Are you here alone?"

He frowned. "Hmm? Oh...yeah, I'm here alone. You?"

"Yes."

He leaned on the treadmill rail. "Thought maybe Ben Sills had tagged along."

She squinted. "Pardon me?"

"That cop wannabe was following you around the store today like a lapdog."

Piqued at his tone, she reached for her water bottle. "I know you and Ben don't get along, but for heaven's sake, Carter, you almost sound...jealous."

His shoulders pulled back. "Jealous? That's ridiculous. You and I aren't dating." He seesawed the towel back and forth on his neck. "Besides, I have...Trudy."

Hurt and embarrassment flooded her, but she was determined not to let on. "I meant jealous over guarding the diamond."

"Oh." He had the grace to look uncomfortable, then his eyebrows pulled together. "I just don't trust that guy. I think you should be careful around him."

Oh, that was rich, coming from the man who had hurt her more than even she had realized until the past few days. She might have laughed, if she hadn't felt so incensed. A year's worth of pent-up anger and frustration billowed in her chest, but she managed to keep her voice steady. "I appreciate your concern, Carter, but what Ben Sills does *for* me, *to* me or *with* me is really none of your business. Now, if you don't mind, I have plans later, and I'd like to finish my run." She returned her headphones to her ears, then increased the speed on the treadmill until she was back up to a run.

From his shadow, she knew he stood there for a full thirty seconds, but she refused to acknowledge him. She did, however, succumb to a flash of misery when his shadow disappeared. Short-lived, ill-suited, badly timed. No matter how one summed up their haphazard relationship, she and Carter simply weren't meant to be.

She ran one, then two more miles to boy-band love ballads in an attempt to purge her frustration. Then, afterward, she stretched to cool down. She didn't look for Carter, didn't see him, and didn't expect to. Feeling shaky and at loose ends, Faith piled on a coat, hat, gloves, scarf, and boots, then gathered her gym bag and headed home for her "plans"—a long, hot bath and an overdue cry.

CHAPTER SIX

Saturday, February 8, 2003

CARTER WAS THANKFUL for the Saturday crowd of people who'd heard about the massive Valentino diamond and wanted to take a gander at it. Constantly scanning the bodies queued up in serpentine fashion between black velvet ropes, and standing sentinel next to the glass case, helped pass the day without too many awkward encounters with Faith. Of course, she was busy in her own regard, maybe more so, handing out little cards to anyone willing to take a few minutes to create something called a ''wish list,'' and waiting on customers without a break in her smile or her step.

He'd replayed yesterday's events in his mind until he wished he could hit an erase button. He'd snapped at everyone in sight, including Faith when she hinted that she could arrange special financing for ''Trudy's'' ring. He'd felt like a louse for deceiving her, not to mention embarrassed and annoyed that she assumed he had no resources. Of course, why wouldn't she? He'd agreed to look at the rings only to be alone with her, then pretended the prices were out of his reach to get out of buying one! The truth was, he didn't earn an exorbitant salary, but he spent much less than he made, and he could have paid cash for any two rings on that tray, dammit, if he'd had a mind to.

So now on top of all her other opinions of him, she also thought he was poor—or cheap. And while that played into his plan of not becoming involved with Faith, it did not play well into his ego. He sank his hand into his pocket and fingered the small box that had burned a hole into his thigh all day. His mind kept saying that he might as well take care of an item of family business while he had access to a jeweler that he could trust. But his heart chimed in that revealing the box would go a long way in soothing his pride.

Last night at the gym...well, that had been a pure fuster-cluck all the way around. He suspected that Faith had gone out with Sills afterward because this morning the man kept hinting at what a "hot" date he'd had. The thought of the two of them together made him want to break something—especially since the guy was traveling on to Schenectady or somewhere after this gig was over. If Faith was suddenly hip to the idea of having a fling, why not have one with *him?*

Because, he reminded himself with a mental thump to the forehead, she thought he was on the verge of proposing to another woman! And wouldn't the box in his pocket only further cement his lie? His head hurt from chasing the same thoughts over and over. And he felt a distinct pain in the middle of his chest. He rubbed the skin over his breastbone with his knuckles. The only explanation he could think of was that he'd pulled a muscle in his chest last night at the gym.

A few straggling customers had kept the jewelry store open nearly an hour past closing time, so the rest of the mall sat dimly lit and quiet. Stacy waved to no one in particular on her way out, and Sills was busy unlocking the chains on the Valentino display case in preparation for rolling the diamond into the vault.

"I got this covered," Sills said to Carter. "You can go ahead and take off."

Carter glanced toward the vault where he could hear Faith humming to the music overhead. The man's message was clear: he wanted to be alone with Faith. Carter ground his teeth, but managed a passable smile. "I need to ask Faith a favor."

Sills frowned. "What kind of favor?"

"It's personal."

"Personal?" she asked, emerging to walk toward them.

He hesitated, then gave Sills a pointed look. The man scowled, then proceeded to roll the Valentino display case past them and into the vault.

Faith was looking at him expectantly. He shifted nervously, then withdrew the ring box from his pocket and set it on the counter in front of her.

"What's this?"

"My great-great-grandmother's ring. I was hoping you would appraise it for me. It isn't insured, and I was told it might be valuable."

She picked up the faded blue box and held it reverently. ''This looks like a Tiffany's box.''

He nodded. ''My great-great-grandfather purchased it from Tiffany's.''

She gently opened the box. ''Oh, my.''

Gratification buoyed him at the expression of wonderment on her face.

She looked up, and he noticed with a start that her eyes were also Tiffany's blue. ''Is this the original box?''

He nodded.

''Eighteen eighty-six?''

''That would be about right.''

Two spots of color bloomed on her cheeks. ''Carter, this ring could be *extremely* valuable.''

''I'll lock the vault for you, Faith,'' Ben said, walking up behind her. His smile was congenial as he held out his hand for her keys.

She looked at the ring, torn, then set the box down on the counter. ''No, that's my job. I'll be right back, Carter. Good night, Ben.''

Carter flashed a smug smile in Sills's direction, but the man was already moving toward the door. A warning bell went off in Carter's head—he'd seen that body language before. ''Sills, hold up,'' he said loudly, pushing away from the counter.

''The diamond's gone!'' Faith shouted from the vault.

Carter's body sprang into motion just as Sills turned and withdrew his revolver. ''Stop, Carter, or I'll put a plug in you.''

Carter's hand swept past his empty holster and he

realized the man had planned the heist all along. Carter reached down for Plan B, and heard Faith's gasp behind him.

"Stop, Grayson." Sills looked at him, but pointed the gun in Faith's direction. "Put your hands where I can see them, or I'll put a plug in *her.*"

Carter swallowed hard and lifted his hands. "Don't do this, man. One shot will bring the front-door security guard running."

He laughed. "I sent that guy home an hour ago, when the other shops closed. Not everyone is as conscientious as you are, Grayson. Or as suspicious."

Carter's head pounded from sheer frustration. "You'll never get away with this, Sills."

"Sure I will," the man said with a smile, then patted his jacket pocket where a sizable lump indicated he had stowed the priceless diamond there. "In fact, I just did." He looked back to Faith and made a rueful noise. "Don't bother trying to set off the silent alarm behind the counter. That's the advantage of being in the security business—I know how to disengage all those pesky little things." He gestured to the mounted cameras near the ceiling. "Same thing with the cameras." Then his glittery gaze landed on the blue ring box on the counter, and his smile widened. He extended his free hand and wiggled his fingers. "Faith, be a doll and bring me that ring."

Faith stared at the gun pointed to her chest—this wasn't happening. Her stomach rolled at the depth of Ben's betrayal to his company, and to her. It was her fault—she'd allowed the man to talk her into disarming Carter. And now he was going to take Carter's precious family heirloom because he'd overheard her say how valuable it might be. "No," she whispered, lifting her chin. "You can have anything and everything else in this store, but not that." A sob bubbled up in her throat. *"Please."*

"Faith," Sills said through clenched teeth, *"bring me that ring."*

"Give it to him," Carter said. "Just do what he says, Faith. *Now.*"

She pressed her lips together to stem her tears as she lifted the aged blue box from the counter and walked it toward him.

"That's close enough," he said when she was at arm's length. He snatched the box and dropped it into his jacket pocket. "Now, both of you, in the vault." He waved the gun, shooing them. "Hurry, I'm losing patience."

She exchanged glances with Carter who stood a few feet away. He nodded imperceptibly, but she knew he was wondering the same thing as she: was Sills going to take them to the vault and shoot them? The fact that he hadn't taken her key ring to lock them into the vault was not a good sign.

As she walked toward the vault, a thousand things ran through her mind. Words to loved ones unsaid. Good deeds undone. Exotic lands unvisited. She was too young to die. And the irony of dying with the man she was in love with—facing death had a way of erasing the ambiguity of her feelings—was too much to bear. And what about Carter? He was on the verge of starting a new phase of his life: marriage, probably children. He'd spent his career protecting others only to be taken out like this? Such a waste.

What could she do? She took a deep breath and forced herself to think. Her mind raced over the complicated security measures surrounding the vault. A red button on the outside panel would trigger an automatic lock that bypassed the keyed locks and activated when the door closed, but it was supposed to be for a manager's convenience and could only be disengaged from the outside with a lengthy security code. Still, if they could somehow manage to lock themselves inside, they could access an emergency phone to summon help.

She turned her head to glance at Carter, but he was darting his gaze all around, probably also trying to think of a way to save their hides. Would he remember the automatic lock button on the vault door amid all the information she'd given him during his intensive security review?

"Well, Faith," Carter said suddenly, "this hasn't exactly been a *red*-letter day."

"Shut up and keep moving," Sills said, prodding Carter with the gun.

But Faith's heart lifted—Carter remembered. Since she was walking in front, it would be up to her to press the red button without attracting undue attention. As they approached the vault door, she pretended to trip on the thick carpet, and fell forward, catching herself on the heavy door and managing to activate the lock.

"Get up!" Sills barked.

Carter helped her up and squeezed her hand. She looked into his eyes and squeezed back.

"Open the door and get in there, or I'm going to shoot you both right here."

Carter opened the door and she walked inside. Carter followed her and, to her dismay, Sills stepped in behind them. While keeping the revolver trained on them, he slid out a tray and scooped jewelry into his jacket pockets by the sparkling handfuls. After cleaning out a second tray, his pockets bulged. "Guess it's time to say goodbye."

"Just leave us in here and close the door, Sills," Carter said. "You haven't done anything really stupid yet."

She kept one eye on the door, still slightly ajar. If Sills pulled it closed behind them, all three of them would be in here for a while.

Sills angled his head. "I don't like you, Grayson. I didn't like you from the beginning, and my opinion of you didn't improve."

"If you kill a cop, they'll execute you," Faith said, trying to keep the tremble out of her voice but failing.

"Doll, they'll have to catch me first." He waved the gun back and forth between them. "You're mighty protective of your hired help. If I didn't know better, I'd say there was something going on between the two of you." Then his smile faded and he cocked the hammer. "Nice knowing you."

Carter dove into Sills and the men crashed against the heavy vault door, pushing it open. The gun fired into the ceiling and Faith hit the ground. When she realized she wasn't bleeding, she lifted her head. The men were still struggling. The gun was knocked to the floor, bounced, then slid under a wall of jewel-laden trays. Sills grunted, but managed to stay on his feet and leveraged to kick Carter in his bad thigh. Carter howled and pulled Sills down with him. They rolled over and over, crashing into the walls of trays. Jewels spilled out of Sills's pockets. Faith considered scrambling for the gun, but she was afraid she'd shoot herself or Carter in the process. So she pushed to a crouch and waited with her heart in her throat for an opening to get past them to run for help.

Then she remembered the vault emergency phone. After stumbling to the end of the vault, she yanked the red handset from its cradle. No dial tone—Sills had thought of everything.

But he had underestimated Carter's strength, even with his weakened leg. Emitting an animal-like roar, Carter put his large hands around the man's neck and squeezed. Sills turned red, then bluish, and Carter didn't seem to be letting up.

"Carter!" she shouted. "Don't kill him!"

He looked at her, then at Sills, and released the man abruptly, leaving him gurgling and coughing on the floor. As soon as Sills got in a couple of good breaths, Carter knocked him out cold with a right hook.

After all the commotion and the danger, the sound of the upbeat jazz music overhead was almost ludicrous. Faith sagged against the wall, weak with relief. Carter pushed to his feet, massaging his leg and taking in ragged breaths, then came to her. "Are you all right?"

She fell into his arms and buried her face against his chest. His arms came around her and he shushed her, stroking her hair and her back. She soaked up his warmth and his comfort and his strength. She never wanted to leave the security of his embrace, the sound of his heartbeat. He cleared his throat and loosened his hold first, and she reluctantly followed suit. He put his hand under her chin and looked into her eyes for several seconds, his expression soft and unreadable. His lips parted and she knew he was going to kiss her.

Sills moaned, and the moment was gone. Carter dropped his hand and sighed. "I guess I'd better take care of him."

She nodded, hiding her keen disappointment, and smoothed her hand down her neck. It was a rather silly to grieve for a missed kiss when they were lucky to be alive.

Carter lifted the unconscious Sills to a seated position, removed the man's jewel-filled jacket, and handed it to Faith. Then he grabbed Sills by the heels and dragged him out the vault door and into the showroom.

She held up the man's jacket by the collar, then stared at the dazzling jewelry and loose stones scattered and winking on the red carpeted floor of the vault. A splendid mess. The man had nearly gotten away with a fortune.

She reached into one of the pockets and withdrew the Tiffany's ring box. She lifted the lid, telling herself she wanted to make sure the precious ring was intact. It was, all one-plus carats of it, judging from her educated eye. The raised six-prong setting looked amazingly contemporary, but in 1886, situating the stone up and off the band so that light could pass through the facets was revolutionary, and unique to Tiffany's. If this ring was one of the six-prong originals, it would be worth a great deal. She bit her lip. With this astonishing ring at his disposal, no wonder Carter didn't want to buy Trudy a new one.

Faith looked over her shoulder, then slipped the ring from the box and onto her left ring finger. She expected it to stop at her knuckle, but it eased past comfortably, beautifully. She imagined the diamond danced with the fire of the many love stories it had represented over the past one hundred years. Her heart clenched. Trudy was a lucky, lucky girl.

Then she gave herself a mental kick and returned the heirloom to its box—there was way too much to do for her to be standing around pining for Carter and his ring. The police would need to be summoned, not to mention the company that owned the Valentino diamond, and the insurance company.

For peace of mind, she delved into one of the coat pockets until she felt the purple cloth used to wrap the Valentino diamond. She carefully unfolded the cloth and stared at the silver-dollar-size white diamond, brilliantly cut and virtually free of impurities, a nearly perfect specimen of nature. Filled with reverence, she tilted her hand to watch the light play over the stone. When she saw a shadow in the depths of the diamond, she stopped. She'd *thought* the stone was virtually free of impurities, and, indeed, it had appeared nearly flawless under her microscope. But there was definitely something suspended in the stone...a circle? No...a heart. No...she gulped...*two* hearts, overlapping. Stacy's recitation of the diamond's legend came back to her, but she shook her head. Impossible. She held the diamond closer, but whatever she'd seen—or thought she'd seen—was no longer visible.

Faith massaged her temple—she was starting to imagine things.

At the sound of Carter's telltale heavy footfalls approaching her in the vault, she rewrapped the Valentino diamond. Carter flung the vault door wide as if it weighed nothing, then strode inside and headed for the file cabinet. "I cuffed Sills and locked him in the bathroom, but I want my gun before I call for a black-and-white."

Faith looked over his shoulder. "Carter, the door!"

He turned. "What?"

It was like one of those bad dreams, where things move in slow motion. The heavy vault door bounced against its hinges and, with equal force, slammed shut with a vacuum seal.

Faith closed her eyes briefly. "Did you already call the police?"

"No, I told you—I wanted to get my gun first."

"Oh. No."

"What?"

"We can't get out."

A small laugh escaped him. "That isn't funny."

"Since I pressed that red button, the door can be opened only from the outside. With a code."

"Isn't there an alarm in here or something?"

"Deactivated."

"Phone?"

"Dead."

He pinched his nose with thumb and forefinger. "You mean we're stuck in here until someone finds us?"

"Yes."

"And when would that be?"

"My guess? Morning."

Carter turned in a small circle, his gaze bouncing all around the room, as if gauging the boundaries of his confinement. No other doors, no windows, no skylight, no escape. Then he swept her from head to toe with a helpless expression that mirrored what she was thinking.

How would they ever make it through the night, alone in this tiny space, without doing something they would both regret?

CHAPTER SEVEN

Saturday night, February 8, 2003

WITH A GRUNT Carter returned the last of the metal shelves to its place. He dragged his hand down his face as the reality of their predicament started to sink in. The phone line had been cut. He didn't have his radio. And the door could only be unlocked from the outside.

He really *was* going to have to spend the night in this vault with the woman who'd had his libido tied up in knots for an entire year.

"Find anything useful?" she asked.

"No." He didn't turn around—even standing as far away as possible, he could feel the pull of her on his body. "Were you planning to see anyone tonight?"

"What do you mean?"

"Someone who might be suspicious if you didn't show up, enough to raise an alarm?"

"No. I was going home to try to get to bed early."

He ground his teeth and turned. She'd extinguished half of the glaring lights, and sat leaning against a wall in the semidarkness. Her arms were crossed, in deference to the slight chill, and her long legs drawn up to the side. She had slipped off her high-heeled shoes and her modest skirt had climbed above her knees. She looked pale and tired and lovely. Every time he thought about Sills pointing a gun in her direction, nausea rose in his throat. ''Are you okay?''

She nodded, then shivered.

He hesitated, remembering their earlier embrace and how he hadn't wanted it to end, then walked over and gingerly lowered himself to sit next to her. His leg thudded with pain. When she moved an inch closer, he swallowed hard and draped his arm around her shoulder. She snuggled in close, the top of her head under his chin. He closed his eyes and gave in to the relief of having her near him and alive. His chest tightened involuntarily. Every day his job was to protect the innocent, but he'd never been so overwhelmed by the desire to safeguard one person. The silky slide of her hair against his skin, and the softness of her body against his chest, stirred his arousal and other emotions he couldn't identify.

''This was all my fault,'' they said at the same time.

She pulled back. Her eyes were luminous, as spectacular as any diamond ever mined. ''It was my fault for not trusting your instincts. You tried to warn me about Sills. And I was the one who insisted that you not wear your gun.''

One side of his mouth hitched as he leaned forward and lifted his pant leg to reveal a small, holstered pistol. ''As disarming as you are, sweetheart,

I'd never relinquish all of my defenses." Lot of good it did him though. With Sills's gun trained on Faith, he wouldn't have taken the chance that the man would have shot her as he went down. Carter shook his head. "No, it was my fault. I knew something wasn't right, and I still let him get the upper hand."

"Do you suppose he'll be okay locked in the bathroom all night?"

"After what he almost did to you, do you suppose I care?"

At the flash of surprise in her eyes, he checked himself; he was revealing too much about the strange goings-on in his head. This woman had her sights set on happily ever after, and she might misconstrue his...*concern* for something else entirely. He cleared his throat. "I see you gathered up the jewels. That's tampering with a crime scene, you know."

She smiled up at him. "Won't the D.A.'s office take the word of two eyewitnesses, one of whom is in uniform?"

He nodded to the defunct security camera in the corner. "They'll have to, considering Sills took pains not to be captured on tape."

"I picked up the jewelry on the floor and sorted it on the file cabinet, but I didn't take anything out of his jacket pockets...except the diamond—it looks fine." She smiled. "And your family ring."

His gaze went to the file cabinet and the blue ring box.

"I...wanted to make sure it was okay, too. And it is."

"Thanks."

She snapped her fingers. "That's it—Trudy!"

He frowned. "What about...Trudy?"

"When you don't come home, won't she call the station?"

Trudy would miss him all right, but would undoubtedly seek revenge by relieving herself in his favorite shoes. "She, um, won't think it's out of the ordinary if I don't come home."

She raised an eyebrow.

"I mean...she's pretty independent."

She nodded, but was clearly confused.

Such a statement *would* be confusing to a woman like Faith, who wanted an "old-fashioned, one-man, one-woman thing." He was quiet, loath to say anything else to enlarge his lies, even if it would make her think better of him. Then he perked up—his fabricated and flawed almost-engagement would be a buffer to keep his attraction for Faith at bay as the night wore on.

She smiled. "You must be excited about getting married."

He doubted that any man would use the word *excited,* but something told him not to say that out loud. "Who wouldn't be?"

She laughed, a sound that made his heart jerk. "Lots of men. My brother Dev, for one, although I have a feeling he's going to change his mind one of these days."

"Well," he said in a tight voice, "I guess if

someone like me who isn't commitment material can change, then there's hope for any man."

She was quiet for few seconds, then said, "I guess so. And after seeing your family heirloom, I can understand why you didn't want to buy a ring. I'm looking forward to appraising the piece—that is, if you still want me to." She pressed her lips together. "Of course I'll have it cleaned and sized for you, too."

"Sized?"

She looked down at her hands, then up again. "I couldn't help but notice the ring was above-average size, and if Trudy is as petite as you say, then it'll probably need to be cut down for her finger." She gave him a little smile and a shrug to match. "If you want to make it a complete surprise, just bring in one of her other rings and we can match the size. It'll only take a few minutes."

He studied the total sincerity shining in her eyes. She wanted his "proposal" to be perfect. Had she dreamed of a similar moment in her own life? She shifted her body to face him full-on, unwittingly enabling him to soak in her porcelain-doll beauty. He was struck by the irresistible urge to touch her. "Maybe I should wait until afterward. What if I have the ring sized and she says no?"

"She won't say no," she whispered.

He reached forward and cupped his hand around the cool skin of her neck, telling himself he would stop before things got out of hand. She rolled her shoulders in a shudder. *"Carter."*

And with the throaty murmur of his name on her

lips, his resolve melted. He pulled her to him for a gentle, searching kiss, all the while poised for her to retreat. When she didn't, he groaned and slanted his mouth against hers hungrily, marveling how quickly the memory of her taste, the contours of her mouth, came rocketing back to him—sweet, warm, eager. She nipped at his tongue and lips, and his body hardened in appreciation.

He lifted his mouth long enough to take a much-needed breath, then dropped kisses along the smooth column of her neck. She moaned and arched into him, plowing her hands into his hair, guiding his mouth along her skin, downward, downward, until he reached the limitation of her V-necked blouse. He dipped his tongued into the seam of her cleavage and was rewarded with a musical sigh. The light floral scent of the perfume she'd dabbed there sent his erection straining against its confinement. He shifted to give himself breathing room, and eased her shoulders down to the carpet. She was the picture of a woman ready to be taken—her dark hair splayed over the red carpet, her wet mouth parted, her eyes hooded and expectant, her breasts rising and falling with each half breath. Knowing his ability to think clearly was rapidly diminishing, Carter leaned over and fingered her hair back from her face.

"Faith," he murmured, "God knows I've tried to resist you, but I'm not superhuman." He hesitated, then plunged on. "I want to make love to you. Right here, right now."

Faith's mind spun with reasons to share her body with him, and reasons not to. She wanted to more than she thought possible, but the man's heart belonged to another woman. Still, this would be her one and only chance to experience Carter, to know whether they would be as good together as she'd imagined. They had unfinished business, and didn't she deserve to know everything about the man she loved before he was lost to her forever? Besides, she would be doing Trudy a favor—after Carter got her out of his system and took his vows, no doubt he'd be faithful to the end of his marriage.

"W-what about your leg?"

He gave her a pained smile. "It's not my leg that needs your sympathy at the moment."

She laughed in spite of the serious implications of her decision, wondering if he realized that his ability to make her laugh made him even more appealing. *Sexy, sexy man.* In the security of their accidental cocoon, the outside world and the consequences seemed far, far away. Faith lifted her hand to brush his warm cheek. "Yes, Carter, make love to me. Right here, right now."

He sank to meet her, and kissed her hard, releasing a pleased guttural sigh into her mouth. Her body flamed to life and she knew that no matter what happened, she'd rather live with regret than to miss out on being intimate with this man. His skillful tongue meshed with hers, teasing, hinting, promising. Her fingers found his shirt buttons and undid them, only to be frustrated by a T-shirt underneath.

He tore his mouth away from hers. "Let's get rid of these clothes." He shucked both shirts, then waited for her to do the same. Faith sat up, then slipped out of her suit jacket. Having his eyes upon her made her nervous, but brazen. She pulled the thin silk shell from her waistband and lifted it over her head. At the sight of her lacy shell-pink bra, his lips parted. She stopped, waiting. He pulled off his boots, then shed his pants and socks. His long, athletic-style briefs molded his straining erection.

Light-headed at the knowledge that his arousal was destined to fill her, she shimmied out of her skirt and panty hose, thinking if help arrived at this moment, their rescuers would simply have to wait outside until this adventure ended. When she'd removed all but her undergarments, she leaned back on her hands, arching her back for his benefit, reveling in a moment of pure feminine satisfaction that her bra and panties matched and were drop-jaw sexy. Carter emitted a low growl, then joined her on the springy carpet.

Music floated above them, soulful horns and a moody bass. They lay facing each other, rubbing sex against sex, creating a sensual friction. Heat and moisture pooled between her thighs and she longed for no barriers between their skin. He slid his hand into the waistband of her panties and massaged her hips, pressing his fingers into secret flesh. She gasped against his neck, and undulated alternately against his fingers and his monster erection. She slipped her hands inside his briefs and clutched at his hips in kind, then reached lower to stroke the sensitive origin of his manhood. His breathing became more ragged and he twitched in response to her touch.

"Does it hurt?" she asked, still concerned about his healing leg.

"No," he rasped, then pushed her panties down. She wriggled out of the lacy garment, then tugged at his briefs, undressing him as gently as possible. The wound on his leg was angry and jagged, and her heart squeezed at the pain he had endured. She lifted her gaze and took in the whole of him slowly enough to burn the impression into her mind. Clothed, Carter was an impressive physical specimen, but naked… She sighed in appreciation and curled her fingers around his thick, silky sex. He groaned like a wounded man, and oozed warm, slick fluid. "Go slow, Faith—I can't stand this much longer."

When he stroked the dark nest at the juncture of her thighs, she parted her knees shamelessly. He dipped his finger into her wet folds and murmured his pleasure at her readiness. She tensed at the thrilling currents that made her limbs loose and her heart gallop. He found the tiny lever of her desire and tormented it with his fingers until she clutched at his back. A delicious, climbing warmth collected in her muscles. She moaned as a wave of desire began to overtake her. He nipped at her ear and coaxed her to a shuddering climax against his hand.

"Carter, yes…yes…*Carter.*" She loved him for making her feel so abandoned.

She loved him, period.

She writhed against him, and he allowed her to recover slowly, kissing her neck and shoulders. Then he reached for his pants and removed a condom from his wallet. Even through her sensual haze, the irony of the foil packet being the same brand of which she still had a full box was not lost on her. He sheathed himself, then rolled onto his back, taking her with him to straddle his waist. Nervousness flashed through her that she could accommodate him satisfactorily, that she could please him as much as he'd pleased her. She dragged her fingernails down his chest, toying with his dark, flat nipples and the patch of black hair that narrowed before traveling over his flat stomach.

"I want to see you," he said, then reached up and lifted her breasts from the confinement of her bra cups without removing the flimsy garment. The globes of her breasts spilled over and her nipples jutted into the cool air. "Wonderful." He covered her breasts with his hands, groaning and prodding her lower back with his erection.

Electric jolts shot through her as he thumbed her nipples, tweaking them to full attention. She laid her head back and rolled her shoulders, feeling beautiful and appreciated. Wanting him to feel equally satisfied, she planted her hands on his chest and lifted her hips, then lowered herself onto the tip of his sex, teasing, testing.

He gasped and pulled her forward to take one of her nipples into his mouth, flicking the sensitive round with his tongue. She moaned and undulated down his shaft another inch before retreating, feeling like one long live wire, every nerve ending alive and pulsing.

After a few seconds of mutual sweet torture, a

muted growl tore from Carter's throat. He clasped her hips with both hands and impaled her with his entire length. The sudden and complete fullness stole the breath from her lungs, and for a few seconds she was unable to move. He was still, his teeth clenched, allowing her to adjust. When she could no longer be still, she began to move up and down, releasing him, then taking him into her body again with exaggerated slowness.

They locked gazes, and her doubts about whether her technique felt as amazing to him as it did to her were erased when he breathed her name with reverence. She smiled, feeling heady with sexual control, but her smugness dissolved when she felt another orgasm begin to flower in her womb. At his urging, her rhythm increased.

"Come on, sweetheart, let me hear you." He tensed beneath her.

The sweet but searing hum deep inside her surged in intensity...unbearable ecstasy.

"Hurry, sweetheart...hurry."

The sound of his hoarse urgency sent her over the edge. She cried out his name and contracted around his rigid maleness, but realized pure fulfillment when his muscles bunched and he climaxed with her. "Faith...Faith...Faith."

Once the spasms had subsided, she lowered herself to his chest, weak with satisfaction. His arms came around her back, stroking her shoulder blades to ward off the room's chill. When questions and qualms threatened to descend, she banished them to the far corners of her mind. They were together now, and now was all that mattered. At least for now. With her cheek pressed against the coarse hair on his chest, she listened to his heartbeat and breathing return to normal. After a few minutes she thought he had dozed, but he began to stroke her hair. "That was...amazing."

She was afraid to speak because suddenly she was feeling "susceptible." She'd promised herself she wouldn't expect his feelings to change suddenly just because they were good together...just because they shared a powerful physical connection...just because she cared enough for both of them. But a small part of her had hoped that he would undergo some sort of transformation, that he would realize he couldn't truly love one woman and have this kind of experience with another woman.

Could he? He'd said that Trudy was "independent." Was she somewhere tonight expressing her own independence? Did they have an open relationship? She swallowed hard, giving in to a few seconds of panic that she might have misjudged his character so terribly.

She pushed up and gingerly disengaged their bodies. He grunted, but he didn't protest when she pulled away. She shivered in the cold air and crawled around, gathering her clothes. Her knees stung and she realized with mortification that she had carpet burns. She breathed deeply, trying to calm her pulse. She wasn't a coed; their lovemaking aftermath needn't be a dramatic episode. They were consenting adults who'd practiced safe sex. They would simply get dressed and maybe try to sleep and wait for help to arrive in the morning and…pretend as if nothing had happened.

She stood on wobbly legs to don her lacy underwear, but the sight of Carter, big and bare, rising up to reach for his clothes sent a dizzying array of emotions to her empty stomach: desire, satisfaction, sadness. She turned her back to him and stepped into the pink panties, but her gaze landed on the blue ring box from Tiffany's sitting on the file cabinet. As she adjusted the scalloped waistband of her frilly underthings, Faith added guilt to the disturbing emotional soup.

Yes, they would simply pretend as if nothing had happened.

CHAPTER EIGHT

Monday afternoon, February 10, 2003

"AND THEN WHAT HAPPENED?" the wide-eyed newspaper reporter asked. He was young, and a feature on the bungled burglary of the Valentino diamond would be a great human-interest scoop for the week of Valentine's Day.

Faith shifted on the stool at The Red Bean, took a drink from her coffee mug, and let Jamie take over. She was tired of repeating the details, but her friend was still caught up in the drama.

Jamie leaned forward and paused for effect. "*Then* when I came in early Sunday to tackle some paperwork and found the lights on and the door open to The Diamond Mine, I knew something was wrong. I called the police and when Faith didn't answer her home phone, I called her brother. When the police arrived, we opened the vault to find Faith and Lieutenant Grayson alive and well, thank God."

Poor Jamie—she had been frightened out of her wits. Faith smiled into her coffee. It was a good thing that Dev had been there to comfort her.

"Ms. Sherman, what was it like to spend the night in a locked vault?"

Faith felt Jamie's curious gaze on her as well as the man's. Her friend had done everything but come out and ask her if she and Carter had "done it." Had Jamie picked up on the faint scent of sex in the air and seen her rug-burned knees, or was it perhaps the telltale look of remorse on her face? Regardless, Faith had decided to keep mum about her tryst with Carter.

"The temperature was a little cold, but I knew we were safe, so I didn't worry."

The man pushed up his glasses. "How did you keep warm?"

Faith hesitated and glanced at Jamie, who had one red eyebrow arched. "We, um, tried to move around as much as possible."

"Calisthenics?"

"Er, yes."

"And the Valentino diamond was in the vault with you all night?"

"That's right."

"Tell me about the legend surrounding the stone."

Faith repeated the story from the brochure.

"And have you ever seen the two hearts that are supposedly suspended in the Valentino diamond?"

She ran her finger around the rim of her cup, suddenly ill at ease. "Well...I did see a shadow in the stone...that resembled...two hearts intertwined."

"You never told me," Jamie said, her tone mildly accusing.

"It was right after the robbery," Faith said. "In the vault, when I was making sure the diamond was okay.'' She smiled sheepishly. ''More likely it was my imagination, or a trick of the light.'' Or her emotional state.

The reporter was scribbling away. ''Where is the diamond now?''

''Understandably, the company that owns the Valentino diamond took it back for a full inspection.''

Of course that meant that Carter was no longer needed, which was best, considering what had happened between them. Amid the hoopla and milling uniforms Sunday, she had performed some online research, phoned a couple of trusted gemologist associates, and determined that his family heirloom was indeed an original Tiffany's six-prong setting, and worth the hefty sum that she'd surmised. She'd delivered the good news and returned the ring to him, expertly cleaned and polished, before he left that afternoon. The moment had been awkward, so she'd thanked him for...everything, and shaken his hand.

''Good luck on Friday,'' she'd said.

He'd frowned. ''Friday?''

''Valentine's Day,'' she'd reminded him.

''Oh. Right.''

''Ms. Sherman?''

She jerked her attention back to the moment and to the reporter. ''I'm sorry—what were you saying?''

''I asked what happened to the jewel thief.''

''Ben Sills is in jail, waiting to be arraigned. Apparently he'd been waiting for an opportunity to steal the diamond. Chicago afforded him access to an international airport—the police found fake identification and a plane ticket to South America on him."

"I understand he's being charged with attempted armed robbery and attempted murder."

"That's right."

He frowned. "That's not a very romantic wrap-up. I don't suppose you and—" he consulted his pad "—Lieutenant Grayson fell in love while you were in the vault all night?" He grinned, hopeful.

Faith bristled and refused to look in Jamie's direction. "*No,* I don't suppose we did."

The man's shoulders fell. "Too bad. Would've made for a happier ending to the story."

CARTER STRUGGLED to keep the frustration out of his voice. "But, Captain, my doctor just released me to return to work." He shook a sheet of yellow paper as if the man on the other end of the phone could see it. "I have the release form in my hand."

"Good for you, Grayson. But I'm not about to put you back out on the street until we've had a chance to talk."

Carter winced. With the security assignment at The Diamond Mine scrubbed, he was looking at an endless, mindless stack of paperwork on a light-duty desk. "Fine, Chief. I'll come by the station to see you tomorrow."

"Can't. I'll be in city council meetings tomorrow and Wednesday. Make it Thursday—" papers rattled in the background "—at four, but don't be late.

I'm taking off early to buy my wife something nice for Valentine's Day.'' The older man sighed. ''I plain forgot last year, and I thought she was going to shoot me with my own gun.''

Carter frowned into the phone. ''I know that feeling.''

''Well, what can I say, son? Some things are worth the trouble. See you Thursday, Lieutenant. Oh, and stay out of jewelry vaults.'' The man belly-laughed and disconnected the call.

Carter dropped the phone into its cradle and walked to the kitchen for a beer. The robbery attempt had been all over the news, with much being made about the fact that he and Faith had been locked in the vault all night together. The guys at the station had been ribbing him mercilessly.

On the way to the kitchen, he heard his next-door neighbor's stereo blast on. A teeny-bopper song thumped through the walls at decibels loud enough to send Trudy under the table. Carter pounded on the wall. ''Turn down the music, dammit! Other people live here, you know!''

In answer, the volume was turned up a notch. Carter gritted his teeth and considered citing them for disturbing the peace, but next month it would simply be a new renter with a louder stereo and probably even worse taste in music. He cracked open a beer and looked at Trudy, hunched under the table with her head on the floor and her paws crossed over her nose.

''You know,'' he said, pointing his finger, ''we should buy a house.''

Trudy lifted her head.

Carter shrugged. "Why not? I can't rent forever and, frankly, this place is a dump." He crouched to rub her ears. "Maybe a little backyard so you won't have to wait on me to come home to do your business."

She licked his hand, and the tightness in his chest eased a tiny bit. He didn't miss Faith—really, he didn't. It was only the proximity in the vault and robbery scare that had thrown their emotions into overdrive. And so what if he'd replayed their lovemaking over and over in his mind? He hadn't slept with a woman in months; it was a natural response.

Although he never remembered it being quite so...memorable.

He pulled out a chair at the table and fingered the blue Tiffany's ring box he'd set next to the salt and pepper shakers and Tabasco sauce. After another swallow of beer, he opened the box and stared at the diamond his great-great-grandfather had bought for his great-great-grandmother as a token of their undying love. The great joke of the Grayson family was that the ring had fallen to him, a confirmed bachelor. A stunning, rare stone, and no finger to put it on. He knew he'd be hard-pressed to find a woman who would truly appreciate its heritage. Unless it was someone like Faith. And the irony was that every time he looked at the ring, he pictured it on Faith's hand.

He pulled a hand down his face. How scary was that? Faith made no bones about the fact that she was looking for a lifelong commitment, and as much as he admired her and was physically attracted to her—okay, that last part was an understatement—could he truly promise her forever? Forever was a long time to a man who didn't even own a watch.

Let's face it, Carter, you are not *commitment material.*

Faith was right. And if he waited for this...*attachment* to wear off, everything would be fine. He had the perfect excuse not to call her again—she thought he was going to marry another woman.

He propped his legs on the corner of the table and tipped up his beer for another swallow. Yep, everything was going to be just...*fine.*

CHAPTER NINE

Wednesday, February 12, 2003

Dear Ms. Sherman,

As a token of our incalculable appreciation for preventing the loss of the priceless Valentino diamond, enclosed is a cashier's check to be allocated in whatever manner you deem appropriate among your security staff. And as soon as the diamond is ready for public viewing again, we would very much like for The Diamond Mine to be our first host.

THE LETTER WAS SIGNED by an executive of the company that owned the diamond, a name Faith recognized from her many conference calls with the company and its insurers. She unfolded the check and lifted her eyebrows. *Nice.*

And rightfully Carter's, every last cent. Jamie, she knew, would agree.

She picked up the phone to call directory assistance for Carter's home number, but the likelihood of his live-in lady answering the phone changed her mind. The last thing she wanted was a sweet, little voice to go with her visualization of the Barbie doll.

Having the check couriered to his home was a possibility. She sat back in her chair and pursed her mouth. But seeing him face-to-face would give her a chance to clear the air about what had happened between them. After all, she wouldn't want him to think that she was pining for him. And she wouldn't want him to carry a guilty conscience down the aisle. The night in the vault was an impulsive mistake, and she had already put it out of her mind.

Or so she would tell him.

In truth, she had thought of little else, to the point that she had to force herself to concentrate at work. Her assistant, Stacy, was starting to suspect something was wrong. Jamie and Dev called her what seemed like every fifteen minutes to "check in." And Dixie had developed the most annoying habit of handing her a napkin every time they passed in the halls.

Then another option occurred to her: she could hand deliver the check to Carter at the station. She pulled out the phone book, dialed the main number for the Chicago Police Department, then asked to be transferred to Carter's precinct. When she asked for Lieutenant Grayson, she was told he was expected in tomorrow, around four. She thanked the person and hung up, her heart tripping faster at the mere thought of seeing him again.

She had it bad.

But she would play it cool. She was planning to take off tomorrow afternoon, anyway, to help Jamie pick out a dress for Valentine's Day dinner with Dev—at least she had someone to be happy for. In spite of their differences, her brother and her best friend made a great couple, and there was no one she'd rather have for a sister-in-law than Jamie.

And she still had a tiny bit of shopping to do for her trip to Captiva. When she had booked the trip, she couldn't have known she'd have so much more motivation to leave town, but now she was doubly glad she'd have somewhere to escape to when she closed the store on Friday.

But first, she had to bluff her way through her final meeting with Carter. And this time he'd never suspect that she cared more than he did.

"I'M GOING AWAY," Faith said.

"Why?"

"Because, Carter, I'm looking for something you're not prepared to offer."

He watched helplessly as she climbed into the cab. His feet were cemented to the ground. Don't go, *he wanted to shout.* Give me a chance. *But his tongue was glued to the roof of his mouth.*

"Goodbye, Carter." Slam.

"Goodbye, Carter." Slam.

"Goodbye, Carter." Slam.

Rain started to fall, first in droplets, then in large wet slices.

Slowly, Carter blinked himself awake to find Trudy licking his face as if it were a salt block. He moved, and his muscles protested. Arrggghh, he'd fallen asleep on the couch...again. He was beginning to think he might never get another good night's sleep. The woman was haunting him, day *and* night.

Trudy licked him again. He winced and wiped his cheek. "All right, I'm awake." He gingerly sat up and stretched his cramped neck and arms. Trudy picked up her leash from the floor and held it in her mouth.

"I'm looking more and more forward to that backyard," he said.

She wagged her tail, as though in agreement.

He pushed himself to his feet and walked to the kitchen, washed his face and hands at the sink, and toweled off. He shrugged into a heavy coat, and when he walked back through his apartment, Trudy was sitting by the front door waiting. He had to smile—as much trouble as the mutt was, she was worth it.

What can I say, son? Some things are worth the trouble, his captain had said.

He rubbed at the tightness behind his breastbone, but was starting to suspect that whatever was in there wasn't going anywhere anytime soon. Sure, he had feelings for Faith…but love?

He hooked Trudy's leash to her collar and opened the door to a leaden day, bitterly cold and with the promise of snow. He walked across the parking lot to the common area set aside for a dog walk, and strolled behind Trudy a few feet while she went through her normal routine of sniffing and stopping, sniffing and stopping.

Love. Someone should come up with a euphemism for the word that didn't have such momentous expectations attached to it. Even if he did love Faith right now, he could never foresee living up to her expectations for the future.

He squinted as the light of truth glared back at him. Dammit, he *did* love Faith right now. And if he were honest with himself, he had been well on his way to falling in love with her last year when she dumped his ass for being such a moron. He'd taken the breezy bachelor bit too far, showing up late and taking her to places more suited to hanging out with his buds than romancing the classiest woman he'd ever known. And being so clueless as to forget Valentine's Day? *He* would have dumped his ass.

He puffed out his cheeks in a purifying exhale. But just as one weight lifted from his shoulders, another one settled upon him like a yoke. Okay, he'd admitted to himself that, for reasons still not completely known to him, Faith Sherman was the woman he wanted in his life. Everything was better when she walked into a room, when she smiled, when she laughed. She was sexy as hell, and the earth had moved when she'd climaxed in his arms, but this...*love* was more than a physical connection. It was emotional. Risky. And stuck in his heart like a wedge.

Now what?

He rubbed his hand over his unshaven jaw. He'd painted himself into a tight corner with his lies. If he came clean with Faith, he was going to look pretty ridiculous. After she stopped laughing, she'd probably tell him to get lost for good. But he had to try—he certainly couldn't go through another year like the last one, pretending he didn't miss her, didn't need her. Failure, he could live with, but regret…regret was a far colder prospect.

Romance wasn't his strong suit, but even he knew his only chance to convince Faith that he *was* commitment material where she was concerned was to come up with something…memorable.

He jammed his hands into his pockets against the biting wind and looked to the sky. He could usually tell by the position of the sun what time of the day it was, but today the sun was a no-show. For all he knew, it could be 10:00 a.m. or 2:00 p.m. Damn, he had to get his act together.

"Trudy, let's go," he called, jiggling the leash. "I need to go shopping—for a watch."

CHAPTER TEN

Thursday afternoon, February 13, 2003

FAITH WALKED into the police station on rubbery knees and stomped the snow off her boots. The weatherman had predicted snow all week. There'd been a light snow on Wednesday but this morning the flakes were falling pretty thickly. She prayed the weather would improve by tomorrow, not just for the sake of Valentine's Day sales, but so her flight to Florida wouldn't be canceled. Although she'd given up on her fantasy of someday having a magical Valentine's Day, she couldn't bear the thought of spending it in Chicago, alone. Again.

While Carter proposed to another woman.

Her nerves danced as she stepped up to the information desk and asked for Lieutenant Grayson. She'd been a wreck all day just thinking about seeing him again. Guilt plagued her—poor Jamie had thought she was bored watching her try on dresses for her big date with Dev, but she had covered up by saying she was just worrying about whether their Valentine's sales had been what they'd hoped for.

She had arrived early, but someone was kind enough to take her to Carter's desk and told her to have a seat while she waited. His work area was small, but neat, although a layer of dust had settled over everything, presumably in his absence. She pulled out his chair and sat, feeling a sense of loss that they hadn't gotten to know each other better. She scoured the pictures on his desk with no small amount of curiosity. They were group photos of older people and small children—his extended family? It seemed likely, considering the resemblances. Curiously, there wasn't a single shot of a beautiful, petite blonde, or a picture of Carter and his girlfriend together.

A bump at her knee startled her, then she smiled down at a beautiful Labrador retriever carrying a baseball in her mouth. "Hello, there," Faith cooed, and reached down to scratch her ears. "Where did you come from?"

The dog dropped the ball at her feet, and Faith dutifully rolled it into an empty corner. The Lab scooped it up and brought it back, again and again. When she showed no signs of tiring, Faith laughed and turned to a female officer sitting nearby. "Do you know whose dog this is?"

The woman scoffed. "That stray wandered into the station a few months ago and pestered us all to death." She turned and yelled across the room, jerking her thumb toward the Lab. "Hey, Jimmy! Do you know who wound up taking the mutt home?"

A man turned from his computer keyboard and craned his neck. "Oh, that mutt? I think Grayson took pity on her, didn't he?"

Faith smiled. "Carter Grayson?"

"Go figure," the woman said. "Maybe he's a softy under all that machismo."

Hmm. Just one more thing she didn't know about him. For some reason, Carter didn't strike her as a man who'd take on a pet, and certainly not one with the energy level of this Labrador. She scratched the dog's ears again and noticed her nametag: Trudy. Well, that explained a lot. "He must have given her to his girlfriend."

The woman stopped and squinted. "Girlfriend? Are you sure we're talking about the same Carter Grayson? Honey, that man hasn't had a girlfriend since the Reagan administration." She laughed. "Hey, Jimmy, this lady thinks that Grayson has a *girlfriend*."

Jimmy slapped the top of his desk. "That's a good one. I've never met a man so commitment-phobic. Whatever gave you the idea that Carter has a girlfriend?"

Faith opened her mouth to explain, then closed it again. Either Carter was extremely private about his personal life around his co-workers, or...

How did you and Trudy meet?

She...came to the station.

What does Trudy do for a living?

She...works from my—our—place...fetching and...running around.... She's small. Blond. Finicky eater.... She likes baseball.

Trudy, the small, blond Labrador dropped the baseball at her feet.

She'd been played for a fool.

Cold mortification swept over her. Carter had invented a fictional girlfriend to avoid a serious entanglement with her? Talk about embellishment—the bit about the family heirloom had been especially convincing. Her throat constricted, and her heart shuddered. She'd fallen in love with a man who had no intention of ever settling down.

"Are you okay?" the woman officer asked.

"Yes," she murmured. "I'm fine. But I can't wait for Lieutenant Grayson after all. I'll...leave him a note."

"Okay. He's talking to the captain. He should be out soon."

CARTER SHUT THE DOOR to Captain Stewart's office, feeling better than he could remember, maybe in a year's time. He was filled with the satisfaction of a person getting his life in order for...the next phase. He'd be returning to his beat on Monday, and, meanwhile, somehow he was going to set things right with Faith. Ask her out. Take her to proper restaurants. Learn to dance, and romance her a little. Or a lot. Meet her family and introduce her to Trudy. Make love to her as often as she would let him.

He rounded the corner to his desk area, whistling under his breath.

"Careful, Grayson," Marie Shippel said. "Somebody might think you were *happy* or something."

"Shippel, even you can't ruin my good mood." He pulled out the bottom drawer, withdrew his bulletproof vest, and knocked off the dust.

"Hey, Grayson," Jimmy said, holding up a bulging manila envelope. "Good news—that jewelry store perp didn't deactivate the camera in the vault, after all.''

His head jerked up. ''Huh?''

''Yeah—the one in the showroom was fried, but the one in the vault was on a different circuit. The D.A. should have all the proof he needs.''

He strode over and snatched the envelope. ''Have you seen this?''

''There went his good mood,'' Marie muttered.

Jimmy frowned. ''No, I haven't seen it.''

''Has anyone else?''

The man pulled back. ''I don't think so. Why?''

Carter sighed, and took a deep breath. ''No reason. I'll take care of the tape.'' The thought of someone other than him seeing Faith like that… God, he really loved her. And the sooner he told her, the better. He looked around. ''Have either of you seen Trudy?''

''If you're talking about that fine-looking woman who was here waiting, she's gone.''

''I'm talking about my dog.'' He stopped. ''What woman?''

''Tall and curvy,'' Jimmy Peak offered. ''Knockout legs.''

His heart jumped. ''Faith?''

Marie shrugged. ''Didn't leave her name. But she seemed to have some kind of strange idea that you had a *girlfriend,* Carter. What's up with that?''

Panic infused his chest. ''What did you tell her?''

The woman gave him a deadpan stare. ''The truth—that you haven't had a girlfriend since I've worked here, and I'm about to retire.''

His heart dropped to his stomach. ‘‘What did *she* say?’’

Another shrug. ‘‘That she was going to leave you a note.’’

Trudy came loping around the corner with a baseball in her mouth, and an envelope attached to her collar. Carter fumbled with the envelope and pulled out a check—a *sizable* check. There was a handwritten note.

> Carter,
> The company that owns the Valentino diamond sent this reward money, and I wanted you to have it. Was nice meeting ‘‘Trudy.’’ Have a good life.
>
> Faith

Carter groaned and buried his head in his hands. *No, no, no!* He looked up. ‘‘Marie, when did she leave?’’

‘‘About ten minutes ago.’’ Then the woman made a rueful noise. ‘‘But if you ask me, from the look on her face when she walked out, she’s looong gone.’’

CHAPTER ELEVEN

Friday, February 14, 2003

"ELOPED?" Faith put down the phone, counted to ten, then put it back to her ear. "Stacy, this is the busiest selling day of the year. You *can't* have eloped."

"But I did!" Stacy squealed. "Ted and I are in Vegas! I'm sorry if it leaves you in a bind, Faith, but Ted proposed last night and suggested that we catch a flight before the airports closed and... Oh, Faith, I'm so happy!"

At the sound of pure joy in the girl's voice, she closed her eyes. In spite of her predicament, Faith smiled. "Of course you are. We'll manage. Congratulations, and have a wonderful honeymoon."

"We will! I'll be back next week."

Faith hung up the phone and sighed. Nothing stood in the way of true love, not even the livelihood of The Red Doors. Well, she'd just have to make do on her own today. Actually, with a blanket of snow on the ground, and more on the way, business might not be as busy as she'd hoped.

Resolute to be on her game today, she gulped her coffee to offset a miserable evening and a sleepless night. After leaving the police station, she'd holed up in a multiplex cinema, watching no less than three movies.

Not that she could recite the plot of any of them. She'd sat in the back, eating buttered popcorn—high fiber—and peanut M&M's—lots of folic acid—crying like a newborn into a stack of napkins. She was determined to shed enough saline to wash Carter Grayson out of her system once and for all. It wasn't that he'd turned out to be a bald-faced liar that hurt her so much—if the man was that unsavory, she didn't want him. It was that she'd so misjudged the man. If she was so susceptible to that kind of con, then she must be even more desperate and pathetic than she realized. A bad apple, she could recover from. But bad judgment ran deep.

She still tingled with humiliation when she thought about the great lengths he'd gone to, to fabricate such an elaborate lie. None of it made any sense. She leaned over and reached into her purse, withdrawing a small envelope she'd kept in her bedside drawer for a year and pulled out today. The valentine she'd bought for Carter last year, when she'd thought they were on the verge of taking their relationship to the next level.

She slid her finger under the envelope flap and withdrew the card.

"I think we're on to something here. Let's see where it takes us."

She ran her fingers over the raised words. Carter would never know how much courage it had taken for her to buy that card.

A knock on the locked door interrupted her musings. She dropped the ill-fated card into the trash can and walked out of her office. Dixie stood on the other side of the door, waving.

Faith straightened her shoulders and schooled her face into a pleasant expression. No one could know what a fool he'd made of her. She'd take her shame to her grave.

She walked to the door and unlocked it.

Dixie stepped inside, looked at her, and squinted. "Oh, no. You've got that look."

Faith blinked. "What look? I'm *not* dieting."

"No, but I've seen that look before—last year on Valentine's Day." Dixie shook her finger. "Honey, you have to stop letting that man break your heart. It's redundant."

Faith gaped. "I don't know what you mean."

Dixie frowned. "There are too many secrets around here."

"What are you talking about?"

Dixie held up a long gold chain from which dangled a heart-shaped locket. "This, for one. Recognize it?"

"Yes, it's one of our pieces."

"Aha! Who bought it?"

"Don't you know who gave it to you?"

Dixie puffed up like an irritated hen. "No, I don't. It just...appeared."

She pressed her lips together to hide a smile. "From your secret admirer?"

"Yes, and if you don't tell me who it is, I'm going to tell everyone that you and your cop did more to keep warm in the vault than jumping jacks."

Faith balked. "You wouldn't."

"I might."

"You wouldn't."

Dixie sighed, exasperated. "No, I wouldn't. But I simply *have* to know who bought this piece of jewelry for me."

"Let me check the computer."

A few minutes later she had pulled up all sales to date for the locket. "Hmm, four sold, three at Christmas, and one a week ago."

"That's it! Who bought it?"

Faith tapped a few more keys. "It was a cash sale, and the buyer is listed as 'unknown.'"

"Don't you remember the customer?"

"No. It says here that Stacy made the sale."

Dixie looked around. "Where is she?"

Faith smiled sadly. "She eloped last night."

"Eloped? Good grief, I've never heard of anything so irresponsible in my life. What was that girl thinking?"

"That she was in love, I suppose."

"Well, if she was in love last night, she would have still been in love in a few weeks, the time it would take to plan a proper church wedding."

Faith laughed. "That surprises me coming from you."

"Honey, I've known a lot of men in my life, but I only married one. I can't believe there'll ever be another man like my Lou, God rest his soul." She sniffed. "*Eloped.* I don't know what the world is coming to.'' She shook her head, and started back toward the front door. ''You're not still planning to catch a flight out of here tonight in this weather?''

''I'm counting on it.''

Dixie made a clucking noise, then opened the door.

''Maybe he'll reveal himself today.''

Dixie stopped. ''Who?''

''Your secret admirer.''

The woman's brows pulled together. ''That's what I'm afraid of.'' Then she chuckled at herself, gave a little finger wave and walked out the door with a sway to her hips.

Faith smiled. Stacy and Ted, Jamie and Dev, Dixie and her secret admirer. Love was definitely in the air.

Apparently, she was immune to the airborne contagion.

She sighed, turned the sign to Open, and prepared to help a lot of men make the women in their life happy.

Sales were good. In fact, sales were very good, and expedited, much to her delight, by the ''wish list'' hint cards that had been mailed as the database was updated. The men seemed grateful to have their choices narrowed, with the comfort of knowing their loved one would be pleased with any selection on the card. Mr. Willis and a hastily arranged temp came up to help her handle odd jobs, gift-wrapping and such. Despite the accumulating snow, she was continually busy showing pieces and carrying them to the register. She restocked trays of engagement rings several times. And answered the usual questions ad nauseam.

"How big is that one?"

"How much does it cost?"

"Do you have a financing plan?"

"Do you have a return policy?"

And she tried on ring after ring after ring after ring. An hour after closing time, she was down to one customer, and getting antsy that she would miss her flight if she didn't leave soon.

"This is a lovely choice," she said to the college-age man, and held out her hand for him to examine the solitaire.

"Her hand isn't quite as big as yours."

"Then the stone will look even larger," she said by rote, curling her fingers under.

After a great deal of hemming and hawing, the young man said, "Okay, I'll take that one."

Faith had never checked out a customer so fast. She gave Mr. Willis a grateful smile and hug, said goodbye to him and the temp, and locked the door behind them. The other shops had already closed, and the mall was quiet, seemingly more so because the outside was blanketed by nearly a foot of snow. A snowplow drove by, and behind it, a line of taxicabs and sport utility vehicles. The scant flakes falling now were fat and feathery, but she feared the damage had already been done.

She returned to the store, and carried trays to the vault. She stared at the area on the carpet where she and Carter had made love, and vowed to set a file cabinet in that spot. After the jewelry was secure, she ran a tape on the register and prepared the day's deposit for the drop box with a measure of satisfaction and relief. Sales had been even better than she'd expected, but enough to keep them running in the black until they built a more stable clientele? She didn't know. But those worries would have to wait.

She picked up her phone and dialed the airline. "I'd like to check the status of Flight 401, the 9:00 p.m. flight from Chicago to Fort Myers." *Please, please, please.*

Clicking noises sounded in the background. "I'm sorry, ma'am, that flight has been canceled. I can get you on a flight tomorrow afternoon."

She closed her eyes. Could she not escape the perpetual loneliness of Valentine's Day? "Do you have flights going *any*where south out of Chicago tonight?"

More clicking. "No, ma'am. Inbound flights only into O'Hare until further notice."

She sighed. "Thank you."

She hung up the phone and calmly talked herself out of tears. There was nothing to be done but go home and mark her least favorite holiday with a pint of Ben & Jerry's Karamel Sutra ice cream.

It was becoming an unfortunate tradition.

She pushed herself to her feet and put on her coat, boots, hat and scarf. Trudging to the front entrance, she turned off lights as she went. She nodded to the new armed security guard—she'd hired a security firm to provide bonded, licensed guards around the clock.

The man unlocked the main entrance to let her

out, and then bid her good-night. She pulled on her mittens, turned, and stared. She blinked, trying to absorb the scene in front of her: white carriage, driver, horses, man.

The man.

"Carter?" Her voice was muffled by the thick scarf she'd wrapped around her head.

He stood at the curb, dressed in a suit and tie and dress coat, holding a dozen snow-covered red roses and wearing an anxious expression. "It's me, all right."

She gestured to the carriage as gracefully as one could in twenty pounds of clothing. "What's all this?"

He gave her a tentative smile. "If you'll let me, I'd like to make up for last year."

Her heart was running like a racehorse, but she crossed her arms. "Why would I let you?"

He ran a finger around his dress-shirt collar. "Because."

"Because?"

"Because...I love you, Faith."

She stood watching snow gather on his newly shorn dark head, and curbed the urge to run and fling herself into his arms. "Funny—I thought you were on the verge of proposing to another woman."

He withdrew his wallet, handed the driver a bill and said something to him. The man took the bill and shook the reins, urging the horses forward. The clip-clop of their hooves hitting the snow-covered pavement carried in the moisture-laden air.

Carter stepped closer until he was only an arm's length away. ''I told him to drive around the block.''

She lifted her chin. ''You were about to explain yourself, I think.''

He nodded. ''I'm an ass.''

''Yes, you are.''

''And a moron.''

''Uh-huh.''

''And I don't deserve you.''

''No, you don't.''

''But I'm begging you to give me another chance.''

She studied her mittens for several seconds, recalling all too clearly the humiliation she'd experienced at the station. ''Why did you lie to me?''

He sighed, his breath frosty in the cool air. ''When you walked out on me last year, the last thing you said was that I wasn't commitment material.''

''You're not.''

''I wasn't.''

''You are now?''

''I think so.''

''You were saying?''

''I was saying that your words stuck with me, bothered me. When I saw you again, I wanted to make you think you were wrong about me, and I said the first thing that came to mind—that I was in a serious relationship.'' He grimaced. ''Then we started working together, and you offered to help pick out a ring, and I had to keep lying to maintain my other lies. It was stupid.''

"You made love to me under false pretenses."

"I'm sorry. You don't know how sorry."

She angled her head. "No, I don't."

He closed his eyes briefly. "I know you don't believe me, but that night in the vault changed my life. The day you were at the station, I had decided to come clean with you about everything and see if you still had feelings for me."

"Who said I ever had feelings for you?"

He balked. "Nobody."

She pointed to the roses. "Are those mine?"

"Yes." He shook them off, then handed them to her. "And there's something else I'd like for you to have." He withdrew a familiar blue ring box from his pocket, and her heart lodged in her throat.

"Carter."

He got down on one knee a little awkwardly due to his wounded leg and the thick carpet of snow. She bit back a smile.

"Faith, this ring was meant for you. I love you, and I don't want to waste any more time. Marry me, Faith. Or at least...*think* about marrying me."

Tears filled her eyes, and her heart was ready to explode. She took a deep breath and said, "I can't, Carter."

His shoulders fell and he looked down.

"Unless..."

He looked up. "Unless?"

"Unless you give me your heart, willingly and completely."

"It's yours for as long as it's beating," he said

earnestly. "Take all of me, all I have. Do you like dogs?"

"Yes."

"Good. I can't live like this anymore, Faith."

"Like what?"

"Without you."

She cleared her throat. "You mentioned a ring?"

He took the ring out of the box and held it up, dazzling under the streetlights. "Marry me, Faith."

She struggled with her mitten for what seemed an eternity before she managed to get it off, then extended her shaking hand. "Yes, Carter, I'll *think* about marrying you."

His face lit up with a grin. He slid the ring onto her finger, a perfect fit. It was as if she *were* meant to have this ring.

He tried to stand, but apparently kneeling in the snow on the sidewalk had compromised his muscle control. She reached out and helped him to his feet after a bit of slipping and sliding. They laughed, and her heart was near bursting. He pulled down her scarf and kissed her soundly, holding her face between his hands. He wrapped his arms around her and rocked back and forth. She wanted to remember this moment forever, to pass along to the child or grandchild who would someday inherit the ring.

At the sound of the carriage approaching, they pulled apart and held hands until the driver stopped.

"Shall we?" Carter asked, then helped her into the carriage seat.

Faith couldn't stop smiling, couldn't believe the turn her life had taken. Her heart was bursting with inexpressible joy. She settled into the seat and allowed Carter to spread a blanket over her knees. The carriage rolled forward, along the nearly deserted Michigan Avenue. The snow muffled any sounds of traffic and gave the streetlights glowing halos.

What a perfectly magical night. What a perfectly magical Valentine's Day. The snow was falling faster now, and her cheeks were frosty cold. He put his arm around her, and she snuggled into his warmth. But she felt something on the seat under her hip and reached down to withdraw a bulky manila envelope that felt like it contained a videotape. "What's this?"

He patted her hand. "Something to watch on our honeymoon."

She pursed her mouth, intrigued, but was distracted by another thought that flashed into her head. "Oh, Carter, don't let me forget to call a newspaper reporter first thing tomorrow."

He kissed her temple. "Sure. Why?"

Faith leaned against his shoulder and sighed. "Something about a happy ending to a story."

SHEER DELIGHTS

Leslie Kelly

To Jim & Lena Kelly. Thanks for raising such a wonderful son. And Mom, thanks for letting me "borrow" your big Italian family for this story.

And finally, to Vicki & Steph.
This has truly been an honor.

PROLOGUE

December 23, 2002

"NO. FOR THE LAST TIME, I am *not* buying your wife thong underwear for Christmas."

Joe Santori didn't go so far as to shake his finger in his brother Tony's face, but he shot him a glare that said their argument was over. Tony had been needling him for twenty minutes about what Joe should purchase for his wife. Joe had drawn her name in the annual Santori family Secret Santa exchange.

"Come on, it's not like I'm asking you to kill somebody. Just get her something hot—maybe a teddy—to make her start thinking that way again." His brother frowned like a kid who'd had his favorite toy taken away. Tony, the oldest of the six Santori children, had been dubbed "the little prince" by their mother on the day of his birth, and had taken the title to heart. He wasn't used to being told no. Joe mentally snickered. Apparently, lately, Tony's wife had been the one saying it.

"Please? I'll pay for it and I'll throw in an extra hundred bucks. Do it 'cause I'm your big brother, huh, Joey?"

"You're sick," Joe said as he reached for his beer. They sat at a table at the crowded pizzeria their parents owned. All around them, people called out greetings and holiday best wishes at an ear-deafening level. He leaned closer to the table to make himself heard. "Why don't you just buy them for her yourself?"

Tony groaned. "Because then I'll be a sex-craved pervert who doesn't respect the ordeal she's gone through." Tony seemed to shrink in his seat as he continued. "I'll hear all about the worst pregnancy ever, the thirty-hour labor and the four months of being enslaved by my demanding, colicky son. And I'll add another month of celibacy to my sentence."

Joe hid a grin. Tony Santori—the Mack truck of the Holy Name High School football team a few years ago—was completely whipped by a woman who stood no taller than his chin.

No thanks. None of that for him. No matter how hard his family pushed brown-eyed beauties in his path to try to rope him into marriage, Joe was staying free and clear. Not that he had anything against brown-eyed beauties. Hey, he'd gone out with two different ones in the past few weeks. But he didn't like the hearth-and-homey women his mother, grandmothers and sister-in-law kept coming up with.

No hearth. No home. No wife and ring and hapless husband who couldn't get laid for months because he'd been, one, stupid enough to get his wife pregnant and, two, nutless enough to agree to no sex because his wife didn't feel sexy after the pregnancy.

No thank you, not for Joe Santori.

"So, you want me to be the one who's the sex pervert?" Joe asked. "How's Mama gonna like that, me giving Gloria a wrapped present with hooker drawers inside?"

Tony tsked. "It's a secret exchange, Joe."

Joe shot him an incredulous look. "And you haven't realized after all these years that Mama decides who everybody draws?"

Judging by Tony's wide-eyed look, no, he hadn't known. Joe loved the little—*big*—prince dearly. But he was often damn glad the gene pool had spat out the bulky and slow progeny first, leaving the lean and sharp genes for him—son number two.

Finally, feeling sorry for the poor, horny bastard, Joe muttered, "How about I get her a gift certificate to some store that sells that kind of stuff? Would that work?"

Tony's face lit up like a starving dog who'd been thrown a bone. Then he frowned. "But don't get one from a department store or somethin'. She'll spend it on the baby."

"Ladies' store only," Joe agreed.

"But a kinda skanky ladies' store, okay? If it's a nice one, she'll buy some white boob-high granny underwear or nursing bras or something." His brother visibly shuddered.

Dear God, please get me out of this conversation without hearing any more details I really don't wanna know.

"Fine, Tony. I'll do it."

And that was how Joe found himself eighteen

hours later at a brand-new Michigan Avenue shopping complex, The Red Doors. Some of Joe's workers, who'd come into the office today to pick up their holiday bonuses, had mentioned the place. Not skanky in any way, its boutique, Sheer Delights, reportedly sold only the sultriest lingerie. He doubted he'd see any granny underwear or nursing bras. Not that he'd ever seen any on a woman before, thank heaven. That'd be enough to make any bachelor turn celibate.

Joe had to admit the complex was a good idea. The Red Doors was a one-stop center where women could shop for themselves in the boutiques, but also where men could shop for the women in their lives. Its unique hook was the computer system where guys could enter their wife's or girlfriend's measurements, coloring and preferences, and come up with the ideal gift. Either jewelry, lotions and perfumes, or, as in the case of Sheer Delights, lingerie. It was probably especially successful with men who got palpitations at the thought of entering a lingerie store and confronting all kinds of scary undergarments.

Inside, he asked about the gift certificate and was told that since the center had only been open a short time, he'd have to wait while they found some. In the meantime, he was invited to look around, and was especially encouraged to check out the private computer kiosks.

Following the instructions of the perky salesgirl, Joe made his way through the huge bottom floor of the complex. He passed a comfortable-looking coffee shop area, complete with juice bar and attentive staff.

Toward the back, beneath the sweeping staircase that led shoppers up to the three boutiques, he found several closet-size kiosks with louvered doors. Inside a vacant one was a desk with a computer terminal. He pulled up the program as if he were really shopping. "What would I like to purchase? Jewelry? Nah, let's cut right to it and see some silk and lace," he muttered out loud.

When the computer asked him to enter the coloring of the woman for whom he was buying, he paused. "Not Gloria." No way was he going to put his sister-in-law's information in here. The thought gave him the heebie-jeebies. Instead he started entering details off the top of his head. "Long, straight, light brown hair," he said as he chose. He added more preferences: midnight-blue eyes, heart-shaped face. "Tiny cleft in her chin." What could he say? He liked a bit of stubbornness in a woman.

When it came to body shape, there was no contest. None of that model-thin type for him. He liked curvy women. Very curvy women. With particular emphasis on the *northern* curves, as politically incorrect as it might be to admit it.

After he'd finished, he leaned back in his chair to wait, wondering if he was about to see Julie Roberts's head on Marilyn Monroe's body. "This'll never work," he said with a sigh.

The screen flashed dark, then a murky shape began to emerge from the blackness of the computer monitor. The hair, the chin, that face, those eyes—not to mention the figure.

She was his fantasy woman come to life.

"Unreal," he whispered.

Joe sat up straight in his chair and leaned closer to the screen. Reaching out his hand, he traced the figure of the woman with the tip of his finger. He'd seen her before. In his dreams. This was the woman he'd had erotic fantasies about since he was old enough to know what erotic meant.

"Who are you?" She couldn't be real. She was a computer-generated image put together out of the checklist he'd pulled from his subconscious and entered into the program.

She still awed him, though. Only about the size of a doll on the screen, she was perfect in every detail. From the highlights in her long golden-streaked brown hair to the depth of blue in her eyes. It was matched by the sapphire-blue teddy she wore, which clung to high, full breasts, complete with nearly visible dark nipples. Her tiny waist was accented by the curve of her hips and the slim, creamy legs.

Joe's heart raced. Sweat broke out on his brow. He stared at her for a long time. "Oh, wow, lady, do I wish you existed."

Several minutes later, when he finally managed to pull himself away to collect his gift certificate, Joe somehow found himself making another unexpected purchase.

A sapphire-blue teddy.

CHAPTER ONE

Seven weeks later

"OH, MR. SANTORI, back again, I see. How did your lady friend like the pink ensemble?"

Joe cringed as Dixie, the attractive, middle-aged sales manager of The Red Doors, greeted him on his arrival at the complex Monday afternoon. He'd hoped to sneak past the pickup counter in the front vestibule unnoticed. "Just fine, thanks."

Not pausing to chat, he pushed through the interior red doors into the main downstairs area of the center. He knew this place like the back of his hand. It had become his favorite shopping spot in the past seven weeks. The fact that he shopped for a ghost woman...well, nobody else had to know that, did they?

Besides, he planned to stop. He really did. Today was it, his last visit. He had several pieces of tagged, unworn lingerie hanging in his closet at home already—lingerie he'd purchased for the woman who existed only in his mind and on the computer screens at The Red Doors. Should his mother ever come over and find them, he'd never hear the end of it.

So, today was the last time, dammit. He had to get over this wacky need to come look at his computer dream woman before every real woman in his life—and in his little black book—got tired of waiting for him to call! Valentine's Day was four days away and phantom women didn't make for the best hot dates on the one night of the year a guy was guaranteed to get laid.

With a nod to the gentleman who ran the café area of the center, he ducked into one of the private computer rooms, sat and began keying in his familiar list. Long, straight, light brown hair, heart-shaped face, midnight-blue eyes, tiny cleft. And this time… "White negligee" he typed.

Then, there she was…clad all in sheer, diaphanous white like the wickedest, sultriest bride ever born.

"You're not buying this," he told himself, knowing he was going to max out his credit card if he kept investing in expensive lingerie for a phantom woman.

Bullshit. Of course he was buying it, as he'd bought so many other things from Sheer Delights in the past seven weeks.

He sometimes thought he was single-handedly keeping the place in the black. Though, judging by the number of shoppers he generally saw both in the downstairs coffee bar and computer area, and in the upstairs mezzanine where the three boutiques were located, they'd probably do okay without him.

Before he could convince himself to get up and leave, he heard a noise from the next kiosk. Though the screening rooms offered privacy from prying eyes, with their six-foot-high walls and swinging louvered doors, they certainly weren't soundproof.

And someone next door was making some noise.

"Ooohhh."

His eyes widened at the woman's long, low moan.

"Oooh, my!"

Joe grinned. Obviously somebody was going for it in the next room. Perhaps a couple getting a little carried away while doing some Valentine's Day shopping?

"Oh, my God!"

Wow, he must have been totally engrossed by his fantasy woman if the couple next door had progressed to the "Oh, my God" stage without him hearing anything. He had to hand it to them. Whoever the lovers were, they had to be pretty ballsy to go at it in a public dressing room in the middle of a Monday afternoon.

They definitely didn't need an audience, and Joe sure as heck wasn't a voyeur, so it was time to go. Before he could stop himself, though, he clicked on the order button for the white negligee, then exited the shopping system. The neatly wrapped nightie would be waiting for him at the pickup counter on the way out. He'd have to endure a knowing smile from one of the salesgirls, all of whom quite naturally assumed he was an incurable romantic since he came in so often to buy his lady friend such lovely things.

Somehow, it seemed slightly less pathetic to buy the stuff than to drift in here every week, moon over his cyber dream girl, then leave without spending a dime. He told himself he might actually find the right woman someday—way in the future—and have use for the secret stash in his bedroom closet. More likely he'd end up bringing it all back. Or, even *more* likely, considering how embarrassing it would be to return a bunch of unworn lingerie, he'd donate it to charity.

Grabbing his leather jacket off the back of his chair, he slipped out of the kiosk, trying to be quiet. Hopefully the amorous ones hadn't even realized anyone had been next door. He'd stepped past the louvered doors when he heard the woman's voice again. "Oh, please, no."

Joe paused. If the next words were, "Don't stop," he'd just walk on by. If they weren't....

He decided to stick around to make sure the lady was okay.

After a moment of silence Joe heard a tiny sound, like the plaintive whimper of a kitten. The sound grew louder, both in volume and in emotional despair. Then she began to repeat one word, over and over. "No, no, no."

Okay, enough was enough. The lady had said no and, dammit, she'd obviously meant it. Not even hesitating, Joe turned on his heel, pushed open the doors and stepped inside.

A woman sat at the terminal. Joe cast a quick glance around the tiny room. No man, no lover. She was here alone. Had he imagined the moans? "Excuse me, miss, are you all right?"

She turned to face him, enabling him to see her

clearly for the first time. Joe's heart skipped one beat, then another.

You're dreaming, Joe.

He had to be. This woman couldn't be here. She didn't exist. Not her, with the long, straight, light brown hair, heart-shaped face, midnight-blue eyes, and tiny cleft in her quivering chin.

One detail convinced him he wasn't home asleep in his bed, having another erotic dream.

The utterly heartbroken tears coursing down her cheeks.

MEG O'ROURKE'S DAY had started normally enough. Typical mid-winter projects at the parochial school where she taught second grade. Excited seven-year-olds wanting to make valentines instead of read. A trio of workmen whistling at her from a construction site when she'd walked to work from her apartment.

Huh? Workmen didn't whistle at Meg O'Rourke. She made sure of that, wearing dull, shapeless skirts and thick sweaters. She had mastered the art of remaining nondescript, with her loose clothes, plus her long, boring brown hair pulled into a simple clip at the back of her neck, and very little makeup on her face. It was hard enough being a teacher at a restrictive school in the neighborhood where she'd grown up and everybody—but *everybody*—knew her and her folks. She wanted no more attention to her physical appearance than she already got.

Meg had come to accept the way she looked. It hadn't been easy, particularly since the changes had started when she was only eleven years old, practically still playing with dolls! Her mother had glowed, her father had glowered, the neighborhood boys had snickered and her friends had whispered about her.

All because Meg O'Rourke was built like a brick shithouse.

She hated that expression, but it was pretty accurate. She was *way* more curvy than was fashionable. Big bust, teeny waist, full, round hips and long legs. If she hadn't been a good Irish-Catholic girl from a respectable ethnic Chicago neighborhood, she probably could have made a fortune as an exotic dancer. Well, if she could dance, which she could not. Except the Electric Slide, because, really, what woman who'd gone to the weddings of at least ten girlfriends in the past few years couldn't do that one?

Anyway, life was tough enough with overprotective parents living blocks away, a dour-faced priest as a boss, and her own embarrassment about her, um, assets. So the attention from the workers, combined with last week's flirtatious attitude from the guy who owned the neighborhood deli, and the request for a date from the uncle of one of her students, had been real surprises.

This morning, her friend and co-worker, Jenny, had clued her in. Jenny's boyfriend swore he'd seen Meg posing, nearly naked, in pictures at some new lingerie shop in The Red Doors.

At first she'd laughed. She'd never posed naked in her life. Though she wouldn't admit it to Jenny, she'd never *been* completely naked in front of anyone in her entire adult life. Her one and only sexual relationship, back at her small, strict college, had been more of a back seat groping kind of thing. Clothes were never completely removed because campus security could come by with flashlights at any time.

Looking back, she didn't care. Bad sex was probably better with clothes on. Good sex might be worth total nudity, though at the rate she was going, she'd probably never find out. Not only was her phone *not* ringing off the hook with potential dates, but her entire block provided a perimeter of protection better than any birth-control device known to man. "Peter and Paul Street," she sometimes muttered. "More like Peter *Repel* street."

She couldn't have coffee with a man without her mother finding out and grilling her about weddings and babies.

So she completely ignored the possibility that anybody could have mistaken her for a lingerie model. Jenny had insisted it was true, however, and convinced her to investigate. Which is why she'd come here to the shop as soon as school let out today.

She wished she hadn't. Sitting in the tiny cubicle, staring at an image of herself on a computer terminal dressed in the kind of black leather hootchie-mama outfit she'd never imagined really existed, she wished she'd never heard of The Red Doors.

She especially wished she hadn't when a big, gorgeous man burst into the room, looking ready to do battle. She turned to stare at him, trying to blink away the tears.

"This room is occupied," she managed to whisper, though her throat was thick and tight. The guy would have to be completely blind not to see she was crying. Before she could ask him to leave, however, she saw him quickly scan the tiny space.

She quickly swung her chair back around, banging on the keyboard to close the image on the computer screen before he saw it. "F what?" she muttered under her breath, unable to remember the instructions. Instead of getting rid of the provocative picture, though, she only succeeded in enlarging it. She accidentally zoomed in so the top of her head was cut off, and her breasts filled the screen in pin-up girl proportions.

Meg was not a stranger to computers. But frustration, anger, and a heaping helping of humiliation combined to make her brain freeze. She kept banging keys, but couldn't erase the image. "Control Alt this, you rotten, miserable piece of..."

"I think it's locked up," he said softly.

Meg mentally ordered a bolt of lightning to shoot through the ceiling and strike her down as she remembered the stranger in the room with her. He hadn't left. Swiveling around on the rolling chair again, she looked up at him and waited for what would inevitably come next. As the man's eyes widened in recognition of the black-leather-clad temptress on the computer screen, Meg wrapped her arms tightly around her body. She held her breath, anticipating the slimy come-on, the flirtatious remark, the gawking or the leer.

The stranger did none of these. He immediately turned his attention away from the screen and stepped closer, allowing the doors to swing shut behind him. "You're alone."

She nodded. The guy was drool-worthy with his thick, chestnut-brown hair, heavily lashed, dark eyes and lean face, but couldn't be too bright if he thought somebody was hiding in here. There was certainly no place in this teensy closet-size space where anyone else could be. "Obviously."

"I heard…that is, I thought…"

She realized he must have heard her moaning and bawling like a baby in here. "You were trying to help me?"

He nodded. "I heard you saying no, and I thought someone was, well, making unwanted advances."

Making unwanted advances. She almost laughed. It sounded like something her mother would have said, or one of the old ladies down in the neighborhood. Definitely the term did not suit this gloriously masculine man, whose body seemed to suck up every inch of space in the small kiosk.

The guy appeared tall, especially standing above her while she sat in the chair. Eye-level with his waist, she noted the faded, tight jeans, and a soft, broken-in, brown leather bomber jacket. The jacket, which probably didn't do much to keep out the Chicago cold, hugged broad shoulders and thick arms. So in some respects, it probably was effective at providing warmth in the winter—at least for all the ladies in his vicinity. Just the look of him could certainly be enough to make even the most happily married woman feel suddenly hot. And his jeans… the worn, strained denim did sinful things to the leanest hips and flattest stomach she'd ever seen on a man.

Swallowing hard, she continued to study him.

His dark hair brushed his collar and was matched in shade by his rich, brown eyes. He had the kind of chin that warned of stubbornness and the kind of mouth that could drive a woman crazy wanting to taste it. Even a woman like Meg.

So this is what instant attraction feels like.

She'd never felt it before. But she was a fast learner and—*wham, bang*—she suddenly knew what it was to look at a strange man and suddenly be filled with the most wickedly erotic longings she'd ever felt. How funny to feel them here and now, beside the humiliatingly bright, glowing image of her dominatrix-wannabe image on the computer screen.

It wasn't fair. A man had finally made her feel breathless, wondering and achy…and any moment now she was going to have to kick him and run. If he looked at the screen again and came up with one sexist, suggestive remark, she'd have to do bodily injury. On that amazing body. Yep, downright unfair.

He didn't look. Not one sneaky peek.

Instead, he crouched next to her chair and took her hand. Its coldness must have startled him, because he gently rubbed her numb fingers between both his hands. ''Are you okay?''

She nodded, still watching closely, waiting for the eyes to shift, for the mouth to lift in a smirk or an appreciative leer. *Come on, you're male. Just do it and put me out of my misery. Stop trying to pretend you're a concerned, nice guy.*

But as the silent moment stretched out, without the slightest attempt by the man to look at her nearly naked body, Meg began to relax. ''Yeah,'' she said, pulling her fingers free of his. ''I'm...a little confused, that's all.''

''Can I help?''

She stared at his face, liking the gentleness in his brown eyes. ''Think you could shrink me, tuck me into your pocket and get me out of this place without anybody seeing me?''

He thought about it. ''Nope. But I guarantee I can walk by your side, lead you out of here without anybody saying one word to you.'' Standing, he extended his hand, palm up, silently asking her to trust in him. And though he was a perfect stranger, for some reason, Meg did.

She took his hand and let him help her up. Still reeling from the discovery that her picture was, indeed, being used to model the most seductive lingerie she'd ever seen, she felt shaky and weak. He immediately slid his hand to her waist to steady her. ''You can do this.''

''I'll bet somebody said the same thing to Lady Godiva.''

He glanced at her concealing bulky sweater and

ankle-length skirt, which covered most of her chunky black boots. ''I don't think anybody's gonna mistake you for her.'' Glancing at her long ponytail, he grinned. ''I hear she was a blonde.''

Amazingly, Meg felt a tiny answering grin on her lips.

''Ready?''

Taking a deep breath for courage, she nodded. ''Let's go.''

''Oh, wait, I almost forgot,'' he said, letting go of her hand for a moment. Meg watched as he glanced down at the keyboard—never at the screen—and pushed a few buttons.

The image disappeared.

And even though she didn't know his name, Meg fell a little in love with him right then and there.

They pushed through the doors, but hadn't gone another step when the stranger paused. ''Head up, honey. Don't you let anybody make you feel ashamed.'' He lifted her chin with one finger.

His touch was soft, his skin rough and warm. She shivered slightly, though the store was well heated against the cold February day. ''What, are you some kind of superhero or something? Going around saving damsels in—'' *hootchie-mama lingerie?* ''—distress?''

''Just a man who doesn't like seeing a woman cry.''

Without another word, he led her through the crowded area. No one pointed. No one stared. Not one man leered. The place was crowded with shoppers, all of whom seemed to be having a good time in the new complex. If she hadn't been feeling so anxious to get out before anyone recognized her, Meg might have enjoyed checking the place out. Maybe curling up in one of the overstuffed chairs near the huge free-standing fireplace beside the coffee bar and warming up with some gourmet espresso.

She immediately nixed that idea. The waiters had probably all seen her in thongs and push-up bras.

As they exited the building, the man never left her side. Only in the vestibule did he look in another direction, keeping his head down and turning away as they passed the pickup counter. The attractive, middle-aged saleswoman was busy with someone else and didn't spare them a glance as they walked out the red front doors into the cold and sunny day.

"Okay, safe and sound."

"I can't thank you enough," she murmured.

"It was nothing."

"No, it wasn't. I'd probably still be sitting in there, afraid to come out, if it weren't for you. Some night watchman doing his rounds would have thought I'd hidden in there to rob the place when I finally got up the nerve to try to sneak out during the middle of the night."

He chuckled. "You had nothing to be ashamed of."

Meg mentally snorted. *Except the half-naked pictures on the computer screens.* "I'm in your debt."

"No, you're not. But you do have me curious."

She raised a wary brow. "Curious?"

"Yeah." He leaned close, glancing around as if

to ensure he wouldn't be overheard. "Answer one question for me and we're even. How could anyone not know they were a lingerie model?"

Judging by her widened eyes, Joe realized he'd hit the nail right on the head. He didn't know how it was possible, but her shock had been legitimate. The woman had had no idea her image was being used to model seductive lingerie in a public store.

Aside from her astounding confirmation, Joe still hadn't quite wrapped his mind around the fact that he was here, talking comfortably in broad daylight on a public street, with the object of his deepest fantasies. She wasn't supposed to exist.

But she did. And she was as perfect in person as she'd been in his dreams.

"I don't understand it myself," she admitted, biting helplessly on the corner of a full lower lip.

Joe watched, amazed at the creamy smoothness of her face, those blue eyes, the tiny cleft in her chin. He suspected she had a killer smile. And he really wanted to see it. "Someone told you about the pictures, I guess? You came to The Red Doors to see for yourself?"

She turned and glanced at the store they'd just left. "Yes. Listen, I should probably go. I've got to figure out what I'm going to do. Thanks again for your help."

"Wait," he said softly. "You don't look up to going anywhere yet. Why don't we go across the street and have a cup of coffee?" Her eyes widened, clearly showing her uncertainty. "Please?"

After a long pause she said, "How can I refuse

my knight in shining leather?'' He held his breath until she finally nodded. ''Okay, one cup. Then I really have to leave.''

We'll see about that.

CHAPTER TWO

TEN MINUTES LATER they were seated in a private booth in a quiet restaurant. The place was nearly deserted since it was too late for lunch and too early for dinner. She seemed to relax.

"So," she said after the waitress had ambled away, "I guess we've reached the introduction stage. My name's Meg O'Rourke."

"Meg," he repeated, liking the way her name tasted in his mouth. "It's nice to meet you, Meg."

"What should I call you, other than my hero?"

He shrugged, uncomfortable with the praise. He'd done what any man would do when confronted with a woman in tears. Well, okay, not exactly true. Probably most guys facing a crying woman would run like hell, stand there looking stupid, or go to the nearest roadside stand and buy her flowers.

Joe considered himself a step above the average guy when it came to how to treat women. Probably because his mama had threatened all five of her boys with a frying pan if she ever caught them being nasty to'da leedle girls—particularly their baby sister, affectionately dubbed the demon child of D'Angelo Street. "I'm Joe Santori."

"Santori... There's a great Italian restaurant called Santori's not far from my neighborhood."

He shrugged. "My parents own it."

She gave him a genuinely delighted smile, the one he'd wanted to see earlier. It was every bit as brilliant and sunny as he'd imagined it would be. But even he couldn't have predicted the tiny little dimple in her right cheek. That dimple grabbed the breath right out of his lungs and took a piece of his pounding heart right along with it.

Wow. What a smile.

"I've only been there a few times, but it's number one on my take-out list," she continued. "The last time I was there..." She bit the corner of her lip, shaking her head as she primly crossed her hands on the table in front of her.

"What? What happened the last time?"

She countered with a question of her own. "Your mother, she runs the place, right? Is she a dark-haired woman who wears a huge pin made out of various kinds of dried pasta on the collar of her dress?"

Joe nodded warily, wondering what his infamous mother had done this time. "Uh-huh. What'd she do?"

Meg giggled. "She, uh, made me stand up straight, walked all around me, then told me it was God's plan for me to have lots of babies and feed them the way nature intended."

He groaned and sank down in his seat.

"I wasn't offended. Believe me, I've heard it often enough from my mother and all her friends in the neighborhood.''

''I'm surprised she didn't insist you meet one of her sons. There are six kids in my family—five of us male—and only one married. Unfortunately, I'm second on the totem pole, so I'm the one in her matchmaking crosshairs right now.''

Meg laughed, the sound deep and throaty. It wasn't like her earlier girlish giggle. This laugh was full and rich, intoxicatingly feminine and mysterious. ''Oh, she tried. Are you her boy Joey who owns dat'a construction comp'ny buildin' the twenny story 'partment building for the millionaires?''

He shook his head. ''It's ten stories. And I'm just a contractor. Should I get up and leave now or would sinking under the table in total humiliation be sufficient?''

''I take it you've been embarrassed by her before?''

He shuddered. ''You have no idea.''

''I might. My family's the same way. My father fully expected me to come back to live under his roof after I finished college. When I insisted on my own apartment a few blocks away, he got all the young single cops at the local police precinct to check up on me every day. I think he was offering a dowry.''

Joe almost snorted. As if any man would need anything more than the woman herself.

''Some days I'm tempted to have a wild, public affair to shut them all up,'' she muttered.

He raised a brow. ''Oh? Any candidates in the

picture?'' *Say no. Say you're single. Say you're unattached and ready and I'll give you the wildest, most public affair you've ever dreamed of.*

''The only males I encounter on a daily basis are the seven-year-olds in my class, their mostly married fathers, and the hundred-and-fifty-year-old priest who runs St. Luke's.''

''You teach?''

She nodded. ''Second grade. And if you think it's bad having your mother trying to set you up with women who come into your family restaurant, get a load of my life. The mother of one of my students informed me last week that all the boys in my class are suddenly falling and getting hurt because they want a get-better hug. It seems they've been discussing the softness of my *pillows.*''

It took a second to sink in, then he let out a loud bark of laughter. ''Starting young.''

She sighed heavily. ''Males. It's a wonder we made it out of the Dark Ages.''

Their waitress brought their drinks, and Joe watched Meg sip carefully at her hot espresso. ''Better?''

She nodded. ''Much. I don't know whether I was colder from the wind or from the shock.''

''So you were really shocked seeing yourself?''

She raised a brow. ''Uh, yeah. Wouldn't you be? How would you feel if you found out women all over Chicago were ogling your half-naked body? Coming on to you? Whispering about you and catcalling as you walked by?''

He grinned. "You really want me to answer that?"

She rolled her eyes and took another sip from her cup. "Spoken like a true guy."

"Well, I am a guy," he explained in self-defense. "But you're not, and obviously you didn't have a man's reaction."

"Being flattered?" she asked.

More like horny. "I guess."

"No," she said quietly, her eyes growing suspiciously glassy again. "I don't think I'd say I'm feeling flattered. I'm humiliated. Shocked." She took a deep breath. "And very angry."

"If you didn't give permission, I'd say that's grounds for a lawsuit against the store," Joe said. "One of my brothers is an attorney. If you want, I can pass you his card."

"Thanks, I'll think about it. Right now I'm just trying to make sense of it. I don't understand how they could have gotten hold of my picture to begin with."

"You've never posed? Never been approached to model for Sheer Delights?"

From across the table, he watched the color drain out of Meg's face. She went pale suddenly, and her mouth opened once, then closed, then opened again in shock. "What did you say?"

"I asked if you were ever approached to model for them."

She shook her head, still appearing dazed. "No, the other part. The name. Did you say Sheer Delights? I thought the place was called The Red Doors."

"The complex is. But the three shops upstairs all have different names. There's a scent and lotion one, a jewelry one, and the lingerie shop, which is called Sheer Delights."

She sat back heavily in her seat, staring at him in complete disbelief. He saw her gaze shift quickly around the room, as if her thoughts were darting in all different directions. Finally, she smacked her hand flat on the table and growled, "That rotten, miserable, pissant little toad."

His fantasy woman had a temper. He suddenly liked her even better.

"I'll kill him."

Okay. He got the picture. She had posed for some photos. Probably in private. Probably for a boyfriend—an ex-boyfriend—who'd then sold them for a quick buck.

He hated to think of it. Of Meg, dressed in provocative lingerie for some guy who hadn't valued her enough to respect her privacy. Whoever the toad was, he'd not only been tacky enough to sell the pictures, he had to be pretty stupid to have let her slip through his fingers in the first place.

He had to hide a smirk of satisfaction, though, as he wondered what the jerk would think about being publicly called "little" by his ex. Every man's worst nightmare after a breakup.

Finally, seeing the way her fingers clenched convulsively on the table, he reached over and touched her hand. "It's okay, honey. He's a total loser, but at least you're rid of him."

"Rid of him? I'll never be rid of him. The louse is probably sitting at my mother's kitchen table right now, eating banana bread and telling her how much he loves the family."

Uh-oh. Maybe not such a definite breakup, after all. "He stayed friendly with your parents?"

Bad sign. The one time one of his ex-girlfriends had remained friendly with his family, he'd almost caved under pressure and gone back to her. Luckily, the Santori clan eventually got wise to her. When she heard Joe had gone to a Cubs game with someone else, she put sugar in his gas tank. That was why he now had a locking gas cap on his truck, but, thankfully, no ex-girlfriend hovering around the restaurant, making nice with his outraged mother, who held on to a grudge the way a toddler held on to his blankie.

"What a snake," she muttered, hardly paying him any attention, even though he was holding her cold, shaking hand. "I'll get you for this, Georgie."

"Georgie?" Joe's concern immediately dropped a notch. With a name like Georgie, how much competition could the ex be?

"As if it wasn't bad enough the time he broke a window playing baseball in the backyard, then leaned my pogo stick against the sill so Dad would think it was me."

Pogo stick? He somehow had a hard time picturing a grown woman on a pogo stick, particularly a woman as, uh, blessed as Meg. The sudden mental image was enough to make him shift in his seat as a rush of pure male heat dropped from his brain to his lap. *Meg. Jumping on a pogo stick. Dressed in the pink push-up bra and tap pants.*

He reached for his coffee, wishing he'd asked for ice water instead.

"Or the time he snitched one of my training bras out of my drawer and took it to school, selling peeks of it to the boys in the pew in the back of the church during mass."

He sucked in his bottom lip to prevent a grin. She probably wouldn't appreciate his amusement. Finally he ventured, "I take it Georgie's not an ex-boyfriend?"

"I wouldn't even categorize him as a human being." She sighed heavily. "He's my low-life, scum-sucking cousin, known throughout the neighborhood we grew up in as Georgie the Goat."

A cousin? With naughty pictures? *Kinky.* "Um, your cousin took pictures of you in lingerie without you knowing it?"

She sighed. "Oh, I knew it. I posed for them." As his brow rose, she rushed to explain. "But I was *not* in lingerie. I was wearing a perfectly respectable one-piece bathing suit. Blue to match the blue screen behind me. He said the suit wouldn't show up in the actual program. I didn't think he meant *literally.*"

"If Georgie's such a...scum-sucking lowlife... why'd you pose for him?"

Instead of answering, she bit her lip and moved her hand up to tug on her long, thick ponytail, which rested on her shoulder, then trailed down her body until it ended near the tabletop. She ran her fingers through the ends of her hair, staring at it, looking deep in thought. "I have the worst hair in the world."

The subject change came outta nowhere. "It's beautiful."

She shook her head and frowned. "It's straight, flat, never holds a curl. Completely boring. But I can't bring myself to cut it off." She pushed the hair behind her back, looking him in the eye. "My grandmother had really long hair and she used to love to brush mine. We'd talk for hours, me sitting on the floor in front of her while she brushed and braided and fussed. And she'd tell me how much I was like her. She'd laugh and whisper about how everyone saw the sweet-faced girl on the outside, but deep down there was a wicked Irish temper and a hint of stubbornness in both of us." She reached for her cup. "She died four years ago, right after I finished college."

"I'm sorry," he murmured, wondering how on earth they'd gone from her in lingerie, to her hair, to her late grandmother. "My grandparents were a big part of our lives growing up. It was hard losing both my grandfathers."

"It's sad, isn't it? With people waiting until later in life to marry and have children these days, many kids have lost out on that special bond. Some of my students never even knew their grandparents."

He hadn't thought of it before, but he agreed with her. Joe suddenly found himself wondering if maybe his mother was a little justified in pushing her children for marriage and grandchildren. After all, Joe was thirty and still nowhere near settling down. "Yeah, I guess you're right."

They fell into a companionable silence for a full minute, each sipping their drinks. Then she said, "You must wonder why I started talking about my ponytail. You see, Georgie hit me in my most vulnerable spot—my Achilles' hair, you might say."

The light dawned. "He said he was photographing your hair?"

She nodded. "You got it. He is something of a whiz with computers." Sipping again, she muttered into her cup, "Probably because cyber people can't discover what a toad he is."

One day, he'd like to meet her cousin Georgie. He'd like to say hello by introducing his fist to the amphibian's jaw.

"Anyway, the family's really happy he's doing well for himself. When he came to me and told me he'd been hired by a store to develop an interactive computer program to model different looks, I thought he meant a hair salon. I thought it was *Shear* Delights, with an *e-a,* not an *e-e.* I pictured cutting shears, not barely there, take-me-big-guy, sheer clothing!"

Joe couldn't stop a chuckle. She didn't take offense, her full lips breaking into a grin herself at her own foolishness.

"So, uh, your weaselly cousin appealed to your vanity, let you think you were modeling for a hair salon..."

"And I was so flattered someone would think this

long, boring mess was good enough for a salon, I said yes."

Unable to help it anymore, he reached out and pushed a long wisp of shiny brown hair off the side of her face. "If this conversation continues, it goes on without the negative comments. You have beautiful hair."

Her cheeks grew pink and she glanced away, obviously embarrassed. "Thank you. You really are a nice guy, aren't you?"

Not too nice. A nice guy would probably have found a way to admit he'd been ogling her on a computer screen for weeks.

But he sensed she wasn't ready to deal with that just yet.

Neither was he. Sitting here, getting to know her, getting caught up in her smile and the flashes of saucy wit, he found himself regretting ever looking at her on the computer. He felt dirty, like a teenage kid caught sneaking peeks into the girls' locker room.

She deserved a lot better. Not that he was going to tell her yet. He had the feeling something terrific was about to happen. He hoped so, anyway, and wasn't going to ruin things right off the bat with a stupid admission that would only embarrass her and do nothing to make him feel better.

"Anyway, I let this photographer friend of his take scads of digital pictures. Just me—smiling, not smiling, pouting, whatever—with my hair down. Georgie said his wonderful new 'smart' program would start there and create all kinds of different looks for customers at the boutique.'' She snorted and rolled her eyes. ''Can you believe it? I even asked him to let me know when the place opened, so I could go and get some ideas for new hairstyles for myself!''

Georgie really was a louse. He had known all along what she thought. ''With cousins like that, who needs—''

''Enemas,'' she interjected sourly.

The bawdy humor struck him as intensely funny coming from her prim, sweet lips, and he laughed out loud. ''So what will you do now? I assume Georgie had you sign over all rights, permission, etcetera, never pointing out the spelling of the word 'sheer'?''

She nodded, lowering her head. He suspected she was trying to hide newly forming tears.

''Honey, we'll deal with it. I'm sure the owners of the store are reasonable business people. If you meet with them, explain what happened...''

''I don't want to see anyone in there yet,'' she replied, her tone vehement. ''I can't set foot in there right now. It's bad enough walking down the street, wondering how many men have seen me like... that.''

Joe swallowed—hard. Now was definitely not the time to come clean. ''Okay, give it a day or two, then try approaching them. If you want, I'll come with you.''

''Why would you do that?'' She tilted her head, staring at him, as if trying to figure him out like a challenging puzzle. "Why would you go out of your way to help a woman you don't even know?"

He met her stare, saw the confusion on her lovely face, and told her the God's honest truth. "Because I knew you were somebody pretty special from the moment I laid eyes on you."

MEG WAS SO CHARMED and captivated by her newfound hero, she nearly forgot about her date. That wasn't surprising since she didn't have them very often. The last time she'd been out with a man, aside from this afternoon with Joe—which really didn't constitute a date since he'd merely been playing Good Samaritan—had been at least six months ago. So it wasn't any wonder that as they sipped coffee, chatting and laughing the afternoon away, she forgot all about her plans. She'd promised to go out with Ted Fairlane, the single uncle of one of the boys at school. She finally remembered while making a wisecrack to Joe about the humiliation of seeing herself clad in a black leather teddy.

Teddy. Ted! "Oh, my gosh, I have to get out of here. I have an appointment I forgot all about. Thanks so much again for everything." She jumped up to leave so fast Joe probably thought the coffee had given her stomach cramps.

"Wait," he said, taking her hand. The contact sent warmth shooting up her arm. He slowly smiled, telling her without words that he felt the spark between them, too. She concentrated on not melting into a puddle on the tile floor.

What is it about this guy? Why did the slightest

touch, the curve of his smile, the way his eyes scrunched up at the corners when he laughed, make her feel warm and comfortable, yet blazing hot, at the same time? She supposed it was that liking/lusting thing all over again. The liking had deepened through their long conversation. The lusting had been huge to begin with.

"It's almost dinnertime," he continued. "We have a good table. Let's just stay and eat."

She wished she could. Oh, how she wished it! For the first time in nearly forever, she'd spent hours with a man and felt completely comfortable, despite her extreme reaction to him. Her fierce physical attraction probably should have scared her. It oozed through her veins, making her achy and aware, making her want things she'd never wanted, and picture things she'd never done.

She'd watched the way he held his cup, noted the strength of his hands, and wondered what those roughened fingertips would feel like against the more sensitive parts of her body. As she'd watched his tongue slip out to lick away a spot of coffee on his lips, she'd been able to think of nothing but kissing him.

Serious attraction combined with serious liking. How rare was that? And it was even rarer to find a man who was incredible to look at, smart and funny. He had a great laugh, a quick wit, and the same kind of insight into growing up in an ethnic Chicago family as Meg. From the sound of it, Irish grandmothers and Italian grandmothers had a lot in common. Hers would probably have liked him very much.

Not to mention that she'd never once had to wonder if her father had set this up, if he'd turn out to be the nephew of her mother's best friend, or if he'd been one of the neighborhood boys who'd paid for a peek at her training bra during one of Father Pat's interminable sermons back in the sixth grade.

Joe Santori was just about perfect.

"Stay, Meg. Please?"

It was darned tempting. And if she had Ted's work number with her, she would have gone for it. She didn't have the number, though. So what it came down to was upbringing. Nice girls did *not* stand up nice men. It simply wasn't...nice. She shook her head. "I can't." Lowering her lashes, she glanced away. "Another time?"

"No question about it."

She nearly wrenched her shoulder rushing to get a pen out of her purse to write down her number for him.

She just prayed he'd call.

CHAPTER THREE

AS SHE GREETED Ted at the door of her apartment an hour later, Meg couldn't help making comparisons. Ted was good-looking enough, but here in her doorway she found herself not liking his dirty-blond hair and hazel eyes as much as she had last week when he'd asked her out. Suddenly her preference was mahogany-brown hair and dark-chocolate eyes.

"Hello, Ted," she said, grabbing her purse and coat off the chair beside the door.

He appeared startled that she made no effort to invite him in, but gentlemanly held out his arm. "Hi, Meg." He cast a glance at her long skirt and heavy sweater. "You look...warm."

"Cold evening," she replied, forcing a note of cheer into her voice. She really wasn't looking forward to this date, not one bit. She'd rather have gone on sipping coffee and eventually having dinner with Joe. She wondered where he'd gone tonight, if he had a date, too. If there was a steady woman in his life. *Get real. A guy who looks like that probably has ten steady women in his life.*

Her neighbor, Mrs. Monahan, stepped out of her apartment door just as they passed it. She stared at

Ted, then gave Meg a knowing smile. "Have a nice evening."

"Tell my mother I said hello," Meg muttered under her breath. Meg knew the woman would be back inside on the phone to her mother ten seconds after they exited the building. *Meg has a date. Pass it on.*

Her mother would probably have been happier living in the days of multi party lines. Ten families on one phone line would allow for quicker dissemination of information about her poor unmarried daughter's love life.

When they got into Ted's low-slung, two-seater sports car, Meg found herself tugging at the turtleneck of her sweater. They were close together, very close. The front seats nearly touched, as did their legs—which made it rather difficult to shift hers out of the way when Ted casually dropped his hand onto her thigh. "This'll be fun," he said, giving her a squeeze through the heavy cotton of her skirt.

She shifted like a contortionist. Leaning the top of her body closer to him, by necessity, she tried to swivel her hips and shift her knees closer to the passenger side door, out of groping range. Bad move. He seemed to take it as a sign that she wanted to get closer. She'd jumped right into the hot seat and had no one but herself to blame when he dropped his arm across her shoulders. "Cozy."

Icky.

She knew that thought wasn't nice. And it probably wasn't fair. But she couldn't help comparing the man she was with tonight with the one she'd been with this afternoon.

"We'll go to a great place on Taylor, okay?"

"Perfect." Taylor Avenue was loaded with good restaurants. More important, it was close. She'd be out of this car and able to maintain some needed distance within minutes.

It was just her lousy luck that he parked outside Santori's. "Uh, here?"

"Sure. You said the other day you loved pizza, and this place has the greatest pizza in Chicago."

Giving him a weak smile, she let him help her out of the car and lead her inside. As it had been the last time she was here, the restaurant was brightly lit and loud. Not dark, romantic and cozy as were many of the Italian places on this block, Santori's had found its niche by making its patrons feel as if they'd walked right into the kitchen of a big Italian family. Everybody knew everybody. People socialized across the aisles and in the waiting area. A glass window separated the dining room from a dark-haired man flipping pizza crusts into the air, to the delight of clapping children.

The owner, Rosa Santori, greeted many people by name. "Ah, you come back finally, eh?" she said when she saw Meg. Then she glanced at the man at her side and wrinkled her nose. Given everything Meg had learned from Joe about his mother earlier, she held her breath waiting for the woman's comment. "You I have seen here before, too." Her eyes narrowed. "You must really like'a the pizza."

Ted gave her a forced-looking smile as they walked to their table. "I guess they pay close attention to their customers."

As they dodged tray-laden waiters and hearty diners, Meg couldn't help glancing all around the room. She studied the faces of the people seated in the booths and aisle tables, looking for one in particular. No Joe. Thank goodness.

The first sign that there was going to be trouble occurred right after Meg sat in the cozy booth. Instead of sitting across from her, Ted slid in next to her, until his leg scrunched up against hers. She moved away. Considering the wood-paneled wall to her right, however, she couldn't go far. In the end, it didn't matter, anyway, since he followed her.

Please tell me I'm not on a date with a weasel.

"Don't you think it would be easier to talk if we sit across from each other?" She stuck out her elbow to discourage him from coming any closer.

"I was thinking of you. I didn't want you to be cold," he replied. "The door keeps opening and it's so windy out."

Sure. He was thinking of her, trying to be polite. She believed that about as much as she believed she'd ever be able to wear a strapless dress without a bra.

Then he proceeded to order—for them both. Telling herself he was merely being a gentleman, Meg decided not to mention that she'd really wanted to try out Santori's lasagna. Or that she hated mushrooms. She could always pick them off.

"Thank you," she said to their waitress when the woman placed a glass of warm, rich Chianti in front of her.

"To really getting to know one another," Ted

said, lifting his glass. Then he leaned closer. "Sexy little secrets and all."

Secrets? Sexy ones? A feeling of dread rose in her chest, then fell to her stomach. She somehow had the feeling Ted had recently done some shopping on Michigan Avenue. "Secrets?"

He nodded, then put his hand back on her leg. "Uh-uh. Some of us have some very naughty secrets, don't we? Like the kind of things we enjoy wearing under our clothes?"

For the first time in her life, Meg O'Rourke prayed her date was a transvestite who liked to wear women's underwear.

But somehow she doubted it.

MEG'S FACE was the first thing Joe saw when he entered his family's restaurant Monday night. He'd come over after returning to The Red Doors to pick up the negligee, not wanting to leave the store hanging. He froze in the doorway, letting in a gust of wind, earning a glare from his mother. The bouncer pulled the door shut and returned to his post as Joe stood there staring.

She had a date. Meg was here with another guy, looking cozy and friendly with a blond dork in one of the booths. She sipped her wine. She smiled. Her golden-brown hair shimmered in the soft light of the candle on the table in front of her. She looked so damn beautiful his heart rolled a little in his chest.

He almost turned and walked out the door, not wanting her to see him for some reason. Then he paused, looking at her again. After only one afternoon in her company, Joe felt able to gauge her mood. Her smile was forced, her body tense, and her face was pale. Her elbow was extended out to her side as if she planned to get up and do a Russian wedding dance. Or else slam it into her date's gut if he leaned too close one more time.

She's in trouble.

Instinct moved his feet. His mother's hand on his arm stopped them. "Joey, you wait right here," she scolded, lowering her voice to a husky whisper. "This man, he was in here three times last week with different women. He deserves what's coming. The girl, she can take care of herself."

Staring at his mother, he didn't ask how she knew who he'd focused all his attention on. His mother knew everything. She often said Santori women were born with the second sight. The one time he'd dared to remind her she'd been born an Antonelli, she'd thunked him in the head with a plastic soup ladle.

"Just you watch," she said.

So he did. He watched as Meg bent her head low over the table, reaching her arm beneath it. Then she said something to her date and began to slide down in her seat. He realized she was going under only when her butt hit the black-and-white-tiled floor. "What is she...?"

His mother merely smiled and nodded her approval. "She tells him she dropped something under the table."

"Why?" He realized why when he saw her boot-clad feet stick out, one after the other, from under the opposite side of the booth. Her feet were followed by ankles. Then curvy calves covered in sheer, silky hose. As she shimmied out, her skirt was shimmying *up*. Her curvy legs were revealed inch by heart-stopping inch.

She gradually gained the attention of other people in the room. Many stopped chattering and eating to watch the sexiest pair of women's legs this side of a *Playboy* centerfold emerge like a breech birth from beneath booth number seven. Then her hips, upper body and head popped out. She breathed a visible sigh of relief as she stood.

Damn, he wished he was close enough to hear what she said as she turned back to speak to her date. Or what the guy, who looked very surprised, said in return. He *was* close enough, however, to see where the guy's hand went.

Right under her skirt.

This time, his mother's restraining hand on his arm wasn't enough. He strode toward their table in time to hear Meg snarl, "Yeah? Well, I think you'd look awful hot and sexy in this!" Then she swung around, grabbed a plate of half-eaten spaghetti off a nearby table, which was thankfully empty and waiting for the busboy, and dumped it all over her date's head.

The entire place grew so silent you could hear a heart beating. Joe froze where he stood, watching as the man rose from his seat. Long sauce-laden pieces of pasta dangled from his hair into his eyes and plopped on the shoulders of his pansy-ass crew-neck sweater. Joe almost felt sorry for the pathetic S.O.B., who looked around and realized he was the focus of every person in the place. Remembering the guy's Russian hands and Roman fingers, however, he saved his pity for someone who maybe deserved it—like the cleaning person who was gonna have to try to get the red stains out of the sweater and tan pants.

Meg didn't stick around to hear her date's response. Instead she whirled on her heel and stalked toward the exit, never shifting her gaze away from the front door. She passed within five feet of him and still didn't see Joe. Judging by the fire in her eyes, she wasn't seeing anything but red.

As she reached the door and put her hand on the knob, someone began to clap. He only realized it was his mother when he heard her low laughter. Others in the dining room took up the applause. Finally hearing it, she glanced over her shoulder, obviously mortified as she realized what she'd just done in front of this audience of people.

Her eyes widened as they met Joe's. The color drained from her face before she turned and walked outside without a word.

"*Now* you go after her," his mother said, giving him a little shove of encouragement.

As if he'd needed any encouragement. Joe immediately zigzagged between the tables, not stopping to say hi to the many regulars who greeted him. He didn't spare another glance for the spaghetti man, figuring he'd crawled back into his booth to try to clean himself up with some napkins.

He caught up with her a few yards down the sidewalk. "Meg, wait." Catching her arm, he forced her to stop and look at him. "Honey, are you okay?"

Her lips were quivering, her eyes glassy and her cheeks reddened. Such a physical state could have been caused by the cold as well as the embarrassment.

Then she sniffed.

Aw, man, she's gonna cry again.

But he was wrong. She didn't start to cry. Instead, her lips widened into a tiny smile. A giggle spilled out. The giggle turned into a snorty chuckle, then an outright belly laugh. "Oh, God, Joe, did you see his face?" She leaned against a light post, bending over as she gave in to her laughter.

"I saw." He made no attempt to hide his grin. "I just wish whoever was sitting at that table had had the spinach pasta. The green woulda gone well with Mama Santori's famous red gravy in his hair."

She airily waved her hand. "Nah. Too Christmassy. This week's Valentine's Day, so I think the red was perfect."

He couldn't argue the logic. He simply delighted in her amusement. The dimple still slew him and he had a feeling the sound of her laughter would echo in his mind for a very long time to come.

"My mother would tell me I earned myself an extra year in purgatory. But you know what? It was worth it!"

"If it's any consolation, my mother, who's probably a lot like yours, told me the guy's a dog. He's here with different women all the time."

She shook her head in disgust. "The creep. He

saw me at The Red Doors. That's why he asked me out. He seemed to believe I'm a good little teacher by day and a wicked floozy by night."

Joe really wished he'd gone ahead and smashed the guy's face into red spaghetti, to match his hair and clothes. Anyone who'd spent more than five minutes in this woman's company should have recognized the goodness shining in her eyes and the sweetness of her smile. Absolutely the only thing mildly wicked about her was her sense of humor. And, perhaps, a bit of temper.

Two of the things he liked best about a woman.

She fisted her hands and put them on her hips, looking disgruntled. "My first date in six months and it blows up, not just in my face, but in front of dozens of strangers."

"Six months? You've gotta be kidding me. You been living in the nunnery next to that school of yours?"

"I'm not so good in the dating department," she replied, looking embarrassed. "It doesn't help that everybody knows my parents and any man I go out with has to duck and weave to get past my nosy neighbors."

"Note to self—study up on ducking and weaving. Anything else I should remember?"

"Yes," she said with a grin, obviously realizing what he meant—that he planned to be one of her dates. "At least feed me dinner before doing something to make me dump a plateful of pasta on your head."

He reached for the collar of her coat, buttoning it

to protect her from the wind whipping down the street. She'd rushed out of the restaurant so quickly, she'd barely pulled it on over her shoulders. After he finished, he held her shoulders, making sure she knew he meant what he was about to say. "Meg, I can't promise to never make you mad. But I will never *intentionally* say or do anything to hurt you."

She stared at him intently, gauging his sincerity. "No, I don't think you would."

She shivered. Probably from the cold. Or, possibly, because she felt the same certainty Joe did that something kind of incredible was happening here.

But what?

Seeing her clutch her coat tighter, Joe realized she must be cold. "Okay, let's get you something to eat." He offered his arm to lead her back to the restaurant.

Her eyes widened. "I can't go back inside."

"Sure you can. I've got an in with the owners." He took her arm. "Come on, we'll go in through the kitchen door."

She didn't move. "I can't show my face in there again. All those people saw what I did. Besides, he's still inside. His car's right over there."

"Well, then, he's eating pizza cursed with my mother's evil eye." Seeing her reluctance, he improvised. "Look, I'm parked in the alley behind the building. You wait for me there, I'll go in and snag us a pizza. We can sit in my truck and eat it, okay?"

He wondered for a minute if she'd agree, or if she was still feeling too uncertain because of the emotional ups and downs of her day. Seeing what she'd seen on the computer screen today had really hurt her. When she got over her amusement at the vision of her lecherous date with pasta hanging off his ears, she'd probably begin feeling very vulnerable again.

"What do you say, Meg? Do you want me to take you home? Or do you want to have dinner with me?" He held out his hand, waiting, letting her make the choice. If she said she wanted to go, he'd take her. If she wanted to go alone, he'd get her a cab…then follow it to make sure she got into her place safe and sound. But he really hoped she wanted to stay with him.

When she slipped her hand into his, he had his answer. He smiled gently. "Pepperoni?"

"And *no* mushrooms," she replied vehemently.

"Great." Leading her to his truck, which was parked within feet of the back door of Santori's, he locked her safely inside. "I'll be back in five minutes."

Sneaking in through the back door, he waved to his brother Tony, who was the only Santori child to follow their parents into the business. Sure, they'd all waited and bussed tables during high school, but only Tony wanted to run the restaurant when their parents were ready to retire. Joe was happy with the small construction company he'd built with his own two hands. His brother Lucas enjoyed swimming like a shark through the chum-filled waters of the legal system as a hot-shot attorney. The twins, Nick and Mark, had parlayed their enjoyment of pounding the crap out of people into careers in the military and law enforcement, respectively. Charlotte, the baby of the family, was unsure what she wanted to do with her life. But at twenty-two, just finishing college, she had time. Besides, she still had a *lot* of growing up to do.

Looking at Tony, he pointed to their father, who was tossing a pie crust into the air, then pressed an index finger across his lips. ''Shh.''

Tony gave a good-natured shrug and turned away, not watching as Joe pioneered a pepperoni pizza out of a huge wall oven. He boxed the pizza and stole toward the door. As he left, he grabbed an open bottle of Chianti his father kept back here for medicinal purposes.

He was pulling the back door shut behind him when he heard his father yell, ''Ant'ny! Where's my pie?'' The old man began cursing and yelling in Italian, wondering what had happened to the pizza he'd been about to take out of the oven. His brother winked at Joe and shrugged in complete innocence.

Joe whistled as he walked toward the truck. His first real date with his fantasy woman was gonna involve drinking house red right out of the bottle, and eating his family made pizza in a pickup truck parked in an alley.

Sounded like the beginning of a beautiful relationship.

CHAPTER FOUR

MEG HAD NEVER ENJOYED a date more. Sitting inside Joe Santori's truck, eating gooey pizza and licking grease off her fingers, ranked right up there among her best evenings ever. They wiped their mouths with the backs of their hands. They sipped Chianti to keep warm. They speculated over whether it was worse to freeze, or to risk fumes by leaving the engine and heater running. Eventually, they compromised: heater on once in a while, windows partially open, just in case.

Above all, they laughed and talked. For hours, until the wine was gone and the pizza cold. He told her what it was like growing up in a brood. She told him about growing up with Georgie the Goat. They argued over the Bulls, agreed on movies, and left politics alone.

Though the truck was a small one, leaving them in close proximity as she'd been with Ted in his car, Meg never felt one instant of unease. In fact, if she were to be perfectly honest, she'd have to admit a slight disappointment that he never tried to touch her. But it didn't matter. Whether they touched with their bodies or not, tonight they were touching with their laughter, with their conversation, with every breath shared in the close confines of the truck. It was incredibly intimate. But it wasn't quite enough.

Finally, needing reassurance that she wasn't the only one feeling affected by their closeness, she leaned over and touched Joe's cheek. "Thank you," she whispered as she ran her index finger along his jawline. She tested the texture of his skin, roughened during the hours since his morning shave. Then she lifted her thumb to his mouth, wondering if the wine had given her courage or just made her foolish. "Tonight has been wonderful, Joe."

He closed his eyes and took a deep breath, as if inhaling the scent of the perfume she wore. Then he caught her hand in his, pressing hers tighter against his cheek. He turned slightly, kissing the fleshy part of her palm. When his tongue tasted the pulse point in her wrist, she sighed. *He feels it, too.*

"I somehow suspect I might end up being thankful to Georgie for being such a creep," she whispered.

"Me, too," he whispered. "I can't believe I didn't know you really existed twelve hours ago." He didn't let go of her hand, still gently kissing her, driving her mad with the tiny flicks of his tongue against her skin.

Finally he entwined his fingers with hers and lowered their clenched hands to the seat between them. "I think I should probably get you home. It's pretty late."

Home. Yes. Glancing at her watch, she saw it was after midnight. Hopefully, the fates would be kind and her neighbors asleep. If they weren't...well, after hours sitting here in the dark, admiring his profile, dying to taste his lips, aching to be held by him, to feel that hard, masculine body beneath his clothes, she wasn't much sure she'd care.

Tonight she didn't much feel like the good little second-grade teacher. She felt very much like a grown woman with needs she'd buried for far too long.

When she told him her address, he glanced at her in surprise. "You said you live near your parents, right? Then we grew up a few miles apart. Ten blocks closer and we might have gone to the same school, though we wouldn't have been in the same class."

"So I might have gone to school with one of your brothers?"

He nodded.

She raised a brow. "Are they as cute as you?"

He shot her a look out of the corner of his eye. "Maybe it's a good thing you didn't. I'd hate to have had to steal you away from one of my little brothers."

"Confident, huh?"

"Only when it's important."

Like this? Like her? She didn't ask.

When they arrived at her building, she asked him to park a few spaces down from the entrance. Some of her neighbors were light sleepers. He did so, giving her a quizzical look, probably seeing the nervous way she chewed on her lip.

Meg sat in the passenger seat while he got out and came around to open her door. He walked quickly, his breath creating little clouds of condensation in the cold night air. Watching his every move, she saw him tuck one hand into the pocket of his soft leather jacket. *I'll warm you up.*

Meg couldn't believe she was about to do what she thought she was about to do. Invite a man into her apartment. Kiss him because if she didn't she'd never be able to sleep tonight, wondering what his mouth tasted like. And if it tasted as good as she suspected it would, she had a feeling she'd want more than one kiss. One of the books she sometimes read to her students flashed into her mind. *If you give a mouse a cookie...*

"She's going to want a glass of milk," she whispered.

Joe, who had just opened the door, smiled as he helped her out. "Pizza, wine and milk. Interesting flavor combination. Maybe I should ask right now if you can cook."

She shook her head. "Not very well. Does it matter?"

"Not a bit."

When they reached her front door, Meg fumbled with the keys. Dropping them, she winced at the klinking sound of them hitting the hardwood floor in the hall. She hoped Mrs. Mahoney wasn't awake, soaking her bunions or reading another of her never-ending tabloid newspapers.

Bending, she reached for the key ring, realizing when she had it between her fingers that the position was a very incriminating one. If Mrs. Mahoney opened her door right now, she'd see Meg, eye level with the impressively filled crotch of a pair of faded men's Levi's. She gulped, unable to look away from the lean hips, the long legs, the boot-covered feet.

Good Lord, was she really about to make a serious pass at this amazing man? Was she really going to find herself in his arms soon? Five minutes. Maybe less. *Just get the stupid keys in the door, Meg.*

"Let me," Joe said, reaching for the keys from her cold, shaking hand as she rose.

She did, passing the key chain to him, nearly unable to breathe from his closeness. His breaths touched her hair, his fingers sent friction shooting up her arm. His low, sultry whisper was only a tiny bit louder than the roar of her wildly beating heart.

Finally, when the door was open, she could resist no longer. She swung around, backing into the darkened room, throwing her purse to the floor. Grabbing the front of his jacket in both fists, she tugged him in with her. She noted the surprise in his widened eyes, but paid no attention to it as she leaned up on tiptoes and crushed her lips against his.

"Sweet Meg," he whispered against her mouth. He resisted for no more than a second, then wrapped his arms around her as if he were a man holding on to a life ring. Their lips parted. Breaths were shared. Tongues met and danced in a hot, wet frenzy that tasted like wine, pizza and frantic need.

And suddenly Meg knew she didn't want a glass of milk. She wanted the whole damn cow.

When he moved his hands lower, cupping her hips, pulling her tighter against him, she whimpered.

Feeling how affected he was by their embrace—hard and stiff against his jeans—her whimper turned to a moan. Instinct, not experience, made her grind her hips against him there. She needed so much more.

When she felt his hand slide up, under her sweater, to delicately stroke the sensitive skin along her spine, her legs went weak. He held her tighter, caressing the arch of her back, his fingers moving in tiny circular patterns near the edge of her skirt. She hissed when they dipped below the waistband.

Reaching for the door, intending to slam it shut, she suddenly realized Joe's other hand was already there. He was holding it open. He moved his mouth to her jaw, kissing her, pressing his lips to the nape of her neck, just under her ear.

"The door," she whispered. "Shut...the door."

"No, Meg."

She froze. "What?"

She saw the effort it took him to pull his hand from her body. "I should go."

Go? *Now?* "Why?"

"It's late. You've had a long day." He took a step back, separating them by much more than a few inches. The way he held his body told her they were miles apart. "Plus, we just met."

Oh, God, he thought she was a floozy. She, Meg O'Rourke, whose simple white underwear had served as an effective chastity belt for the past five years. Meg, who'd never initiated a kiss with a man in her life, had gone from nun to tramp in thirty seconds. *Must be a record.*

"I'm sorry," she whispered. "I didn't mean to, uh...you must think I..."

He shook his head hard, then cupped her chin to force her to meet his stare. "No, I don't. What I think is you've had a long, emotional day. As much as I want what you're offering, I'm not the kind of guy to take advantage of a very vulnerable woman."

Just her luck. She'd decided to go for it with a man who had a conscience.

"I'll call you tomorrow, Meg. And I'll *see* you tomorrow night. You can count on it. Okay?"

He was gone before she could agree, hurrying down the hall as if afraid that if he didn't leave right then and there, he might not leave until morning. That was some small consolation, she supposed. There was no way he could have faked his response. The evidence had been, uh, impressive. Meg stood in the doorway, listening to his steps on the stairs and the closing of the building's front door. Then she leaned forward, thunking her forehead on the door frame.

"Well, you certainly blew that one, didn't you, missy?"

Oh, please. Not this. Not now. She looked up and saw her neighbor scowling at her from the doorway across the hall. "Mrs. Mahoney. You're up late."

"Indigestion." The woman dropped a hand to her pendulous stomach and rubbed at it absentmindedly. "Rico at the deli put hot peppers on my hoagie. He knows my stomach can't take them. I think he did it on purpose because I didn't give him a big enough tip last time."

"Why didn't you pick them off?"

"Because I love the blasted things," the woman confessed. "Don't change the subject. How'd that hottie slip off the hook?"

Meg shook her head. "It's late. I really need to turn in."

The elderly woman, who was actually rather nice when she wasn't doing her imitation of Mrs. Kravitz from "Bewitched," smirked. "Tell me what happened and I won't tell your mother you went out with a blond-haired man in a sports car, and came home with a dark-haired man in a truck."

And to think she'd just believed the woman could be nice. Knowing the old battle-ax with the steely blue eyes would make good on her threat, Meg briefly explained how she'd switched dates. She never mentioned where she'd met Joe, though.

"He was being noble. So when you kissed him, he ran off." She crossed her arms. "Darlin', you really need to learn, men have to build up to these things. He looked upon you as someone he'd saved from a wicked man. The last thing he needed was to feel like he was a wicked man himself."

She almost laughed. Joe was one of the most decent guys she'd ever met. That, she realized, was probably Mrs. Mahoney's point. "Maybe you're right."

"You should have seduced him slowly, not jumped on him like a needy virgin."

It was on the tip of her tongue to tell the nosy old lady she wasn't a virgin. Not wanting such a juicy bit of news floating over the phone lines to her mother, however, she swallowed the comment. Mrs. Mahoney looked disappointed because her fishing lure had gone unnibbled.

"So," the woman said. "Do you know about seduction?"

"Seduction?"

The woman stepped into the hall, leaving her door open. "Look at you. You've got a beautiful shape under all that wool. Loosen up your hair." Mrs. Mahoney pulled her own blue robe tightly around her ample waist. "Wear some tighter clothes, and lower necklines." She tugged the edges of the robe apart until Meg could see a large expanse of flowered nightdress beneath. "Get a little sleazy and he won't be able to resist you."

Sleazy? Like the Meg she'd seen on the screen at The Red Doors? "I don't think so."

"Honey, men don't make moves on women who look like their maiden aunt Bertha. Believe me, I know something about sex. Haven't I buried three husbands?"

It made Meg wonder just how they'd died.

"I really need to go to bed now," she said softly.

"All right," the woman replied. "And, don't worry, I won't pass this on to your mother. If she thinks you can't even get the sex part right, she'll convince herself you'll never catch a man. I don't want to be responsible for her heart palpitations."

It took some serious self-control not to slam the door.

JOE SAT IN HIS TRUCK for a few minutes after leaving Meg's place. He watched her window, waiting for her light to flip on inside. When it finally did, he leaned forward in his seat, resting his crossed arms on the padded steering wheel. Then he saw her silhouette in front of the window, and sucked in a breath.

As the curtains separated, her face appeared. She spotted him instantly. Her eyes widened and her lips parted as they stared at each other.

He remained in the truck through sheer force of will.

After she mouthed, "Good night," and dropped the curtains, he started the ignition and slowly drove out of the parking lot.

Walking away from her, leaving her standing in the doorway after that kiss, had been one of the toughest things he'd ever done. It had been a pure case of mind over body, intellect over instinct. He'd been dying to stay, but he knew he had to leave.

Joe had only been partially honest with her. No, he truly couldn't take advantage of a woman he'd just met, who'd had such a bad day. There was more to it, though.

First, Meg was nothing like the more experienced women he usually dated. She wasn't an easygoing, free-spirited, single twenty-something who liked to play around as much as any guy. As a matter of fact, she was an awful lot like the kind of woman his mother had been trying to foist on him for the past year or two. A warmhearted, natural, delightful female. A woman with a genuine smile, a ready laugh, an open, honest personality.

Hell, that realization should have sent him running in the opposite direction.

It hadn't, of course. Because he'd been half gone on Meg O'Rourke before he'd ever met her, when she was an image on a computer screen. Now he knew she was so much more. As hokey as it seemed, he had a feeling she might be "the one."

Joe had never been a believer in love at first sight, nor did he fool himself into thinking that was what had happened here. Sure, he'd fallen madly in *lust* with her on Christmas Eve. Today, though, during the hours they'd spent together, the lust had smoothly transformed into desire, by way of genuine liking.

The minute she'd raised her head and walked through The Red Doors on his arm, he'd started to fall. He'd slid farther down the slippery slope of emotion with every shared laugh, every flash of her dimple or glimpse of her temper.

It was for that reason he couldn't allow himself any more than one heated kiss in her doorway. He still hadn't figured out a way to admit he'd been one of the lousy creeps ogling her on-screen for weeks. If he got sexually involved with her, and then she somehow found out, she'd never forgive him. He'd lose his shot at anything more permanent.

Yeah, he wanted to go to bed with her…now. But he had the strangest feeling he was going to want to wake up with her…forever.

"You're losing it," he told himself in the dark confines of the truck as he drove home.

Actually, he thought, he might already have lost

it—his head, and a little chunk of his heart. How crazy was that?

Maybe crazy, but true. So he had to come clean before things went much further. Judging by how quickly things were progressing between them, it would have to be soon.

She'll slam the door in your face.

She just might, which was why he had to make sure she knew he had a lot more at stake than his libido. He had to take time to reinforce the emotions already building between them.

Most of all, he had to figure out a way to make her believe what had started out as an infatuation with a computer image had evolved into much more than a case of lust at first byte.

SEDUCTION was still very much on Meg's mind the next afternoon. Not that she'd actually decided to try it…but she couldn't deny she was thinking about it. Mainly because of her dreams. Her entire night had been fitful and restless, with erotic dreams about Joe, interspersed with nightmares of her cousin Georgie hanging her underwear from the balcony of the mezzanine inside The Red Doors.

"Georgie," she whispered as she sat in her apartment Tuesday after school, "you'd better watch your back."

She hadn't confronted Georgie yet, not wanting to tip him off before she was ready with some payback. She hadn't figured out a way to even the score with her cousin, but she would.

Maybe she'd out him to his mother about why

Georgie had really missed Christmas with the family. He'd lied and said he had a big out-of-town job to do. Her aunt Lulu had been heartbroken because her baby boy had missed the holiday. Meg had found out later it was because he'd wanted to go to a Star Trek convention in Miami. "Knowing you, I bet there's a photo of you in a Ferengi costume on some Trekker's Web site," she muttered out loud, determined to do a Web search the next time she was online.

Not adequate revenge, but it was a start, anyway.

Though she still hadn't completely decided how to handle the Georgie situation, she had, at least, made a first step toward resolving the problem with The Red Doors. A phone call to one of the owners, Jamie Ruskin, had proven very productive. The woman had sounded truly horrified when Meg told her the situation, and had asked her to come in and meet with her and the other owner, a woman she called Faith, the following day.

Getting back to work on her lesson plans, Meg kept shifting her gaze between the clock and the phone. Despite his promise, Joe hadn't yet called. She told herself he'd just been busy today. But, deep down, she feared he'd merely been playing Mr. Nice Guy the night before, and she'd never see him again.

When the phone rang, she snatched it up so quickly she knocked the base off the coffee table. "Hello?"

"Hey, how about a picnic?" Warm relief flowed through her at the sound of his voice.

She chuckled. ''It's thirty-five degrees outside. I think you're about four months early for a picnic.''

''I might surprise you,'' he said. ''I'll pick you up at six.''

CHAPTER FIVE

MEG DEBATED over what to wear for their second date for more than an hour. "Sleazy?" No. Meg didn't own anything remotely sleazy. From her long sweaters and loose skirts to her pretty but plain underwear, her closet contained absolutely nothing that screamed seduction. Nothing that even *whispered* it.

Finally, figuring if Joe really did mean they were going on a picnic she ought to dress warmly, she settled on a pair of black cords and a sweater. The slacks were tighter than she usually wore—she'd bought them back in college—and she almost changed. "This is not a seduction, Meg," she told herself as she studied her reflection in her bedroom mirror. "These pants have nothing to do with what Mrs. Mahoney said. They're just warm."

Yeah. Sure. Right. It didn't matter a bit that they did really nice things for her legs, making them look longer and shapelier than anything she usually wore. Not to mention the way they accentuated her waist and the curve of her hips. And it certainly wasn't by design that she chose a cropped sweater to go with them, rather than one of her hip-length ones.

When Joe arrived to pick her up, his eyes widened in appreciation. She lowered her lashes to disguise the sudden rush of feminine pleasure. Maybe he was a nice guy, and he wasn't going to try anything. That didn't mean she didn't want him to *want* to try something!

He looked even better tonight than he had the night before. He'd obviously shaved before picking her up, and when he leaned close to help her don her jacket, she couldn't stop a tiny sigh of appreciation at the clean, masculine scent of his skin. His hair was still damp from a shower, and nearly touched the collar of his leather jacket. She wanted to run her fingers through it, wanted to open his jacket and to slide her arms around his lean body, to feel him against her the way she had the night before.

But Meg had made enough first moves for one week. Kissing the lips off him last night hadn't exactly inspired a madly passionate reaction. Drooling over him now probably wouldn't either. "So, where exactly is this picnic?" she asked as they exited her building toward his truck.

"It's a surprise."

He wasn't kidding. When they pulled up in front of a high-rise apartment building under construction a few blocks from Michigan Avenue a short time later, Meg definitely felt surprised. "Is there a park or something near here?"

"Or something," he said, a secretive twinkle in his eyes.

Waiting while Joe walked around to open the door for her, Meg watched in the side mirror as he stopped to remove some items from the back of the truck. A folded blanket. A picnic basket. And…''Hard hats?'' she asked as he opened the door.

He handed her one. ''Come on, I know you're not afraid it'll mess up your hair.''

Grinning because he was right, she plopped the bright yellow hat onto her head. ''Lead on.''

Meg had never been in a high-rise before it was open to the public, but she immediately saw that this one soon would be. The outside of the building looked ready for occupancy, but when they entered the lobby, she noted the absence of carpeting and fixtures. ''This is one of your projects?''

Joe nodded as he led her to a service elevator. ''My company is one of a group of contractors who went in together on this building. All of the units are already sold out.''

She whistled, knowing the price of real estate in Chicago. ''Nice. So your mother is entitled to do a little bragging.''

''Just a little. I'm only a minor part of the whole thing. But it'll definitely keep us in the black for a while.''

They rode up the elevator to the very top of the building. ''Good thing the power's on. Otherwise, we would have had a long walk up,'' Meg said with a laugh as they stepped out in front of a door marked Penthouse.

''Ready?''

She nodded while he unlocked the door. Flipping on a light, he led her inside. ''Watch your step. This is almost done, but it's possible somebody left something lying on the floor.''

''Wow,'' was all she could say, looking around at the huge luxury apartment. Though it wasn't finished, with bare floors and a few spackle marks on some drywall, it was easy to envision the final product. ''This is amazing.''

''Wait'll you see the view.''

He walked across the penthouse to a sliding-glass door that took up most of one wall. When she followed, she saw what he meant. The penthouse overlooked some of the downtown area. Twinkling lights of buildings, some higher, some shorter, mingled with the stars emerging in the night sky. ''Unbelievable.''

He looked as pleased as a kid who'd done well on a test. ''You like it? It's okay for a picnic?'' he asked as he spread a large blanket out on the floor in front of the door.

''Absolutely.'' She sat, still staring outside.

''Nothing fancy, just good Italian bread and cheese, and some fruit.'' He began to unload the basketful of food. ''Oh, and this.'' He removed a bottle of wine, uncorked it and poured them each a glass. Taking off his hard hat, he scooped some ice into it, and put the bottle inside.

''Can I take mine off, too?'' she asked with a laugh.

He reached for her hat and gently pulled it off. ''I think I can promise nothing's going to fall on you up here.''

Not even you? She couldn't blame the wicked

thought on the wine, which she hadn't even sipped yet. She looked away, not wanting him to see the needy look in her eyes.

Aside from the food, he'd thought of lighting and music. Candles and a battery-operated CD player set the right tone for their penthouse date. "This is a very romantic thing to do."

He shrugged. "Probably sappy. But, hey, Friday's Valentine's Day. Every guy ought to dig down and discover a little bit of romance in his soul for Valentine's Day. Even if it's just delivering something sweet wrapped up in a red satin bow."

"You obviously didn't have to dig too far. Thank you, Joe. No man ever went to this much trouble for me before. My typical Valentine's Day involves sticky little fingers stuck to red construction paper hearts, not red satin."

He chuckled, then met her eye steadily. "And I bet you keep every one of them, don't you?"

She answered with a slow nod. "In a box in my closet."

He seemed to like her answer. She held her breath as he reached out to touch her cheek, scraping the back of his finger from her hairline to her jaw in a caress so tender it made her sigh. She somehow resisted the urge to turn her face, to taste the tip of his finger, to press a hot kiss in his palm.

"You're so special, Meg."

She shrugged, reaching for her glass and sipping from it, trying to busy herself so she wouldn't throw her arms around his neck. "No, just sentimental."

"I like that about you."

"I warn you," she returned, "I cry buckets at movies."

He nodded and earnestly replied, "I cried when Dumbo's mother got locked up."

She rolled her eyes. "Everybody cried when Dumbo's mother got locked up. Besides, when did you see it? Twenty years ago?"

"Last Christmas," he replied, deadpan.

She lightly smacked his shoulder. "Smarty-pants."

"I'm serious. I bought it for my new baby god-son. I'm starting him a Disney collection."

"You really cried?"

"Well, okay, maybe not real tears. But, man, it came close when my sister-in-law came in to tell us dinner was ready, and that she'd made the turkey."

She snorted.

"She is the world's worst cook. I think even my brother Nick, the cop, cried then. And that started a fight because Mark, the marine, noticed and gave him crap about it. My mother came after them with a wooden spoon when they started yelling and woke up the baby."

"Aha!" She shook her index finger at him accusingly. "So the baby was asleep while *you* were watching *Dumbo?*"

He stared, obviously realizing he'd just been nailed. "Damn, you're quick. I'll have to remember that."

They both laughed as he poured them each more wine. He served Meg some bread, torn fresh off the loaf. Falling into the same easy sense of companionship they'd felt the night before in his truck, they spent another hour laughing, whispering, sharing cheese and grapes, and watching the stars come out above. At one point, when he tried to show her one of the constellations, Joe moved closer, sitting behind her on the blanket. It was the most natural thing in the world to scoot back between his parted legs, leaning back against his hard chest as he whispered in her ear and pointed up to Orion's belt.

Frankly, Meg couldn't care less about any belts except the one pressing against the small of her back. Somehow, the wine had made her lethargic and restless at the same time. She stretched against him, tilting her head to the side to put it on his shoulder. "This has been a wonderful evening," she said, whispering the words close to the bare, warm skin of his neck.

She saw him swallow, hard. Then he said, "Maybe I should get you home. We were out pretty late last night."

She closed her eyes. "I'm fine." Wriggling closer, she hid a languorous smile at the feel of his jeans against her backside. He was *very* fine, too. And obviously very aware of their closeness, if that hard ridge in the crotch of his pants was any indication.

"Meg..."

His voice was gravelly and thick with something she didn't quite recognize. She turned to face him and when she saw the way his eyes darkened as he stared down at her—their faces inches apart, their mouths so close they shared the same breaths—she suspected it might be exactly what she was feeling. Heat. Desire. Pure need combined with budding emotion. "Yes, Joe?"

"Did I tell you you look beautiful tonight?" he whispered as he cupped her waist.

She shook her head, licking her lips. "Did I tell you if you don't kiss me soon I might just open the door and throw myself off that balcony?"

He didn't even try to resist. With a helpless groan, he lowered his mouth to hers, catching her lips in a wet, deep kiss. She met his tongue with her own, wanting to taste every bit of him, to drink him in as she'd drunk the wine.

He moved his hand from her waist, sliding it up her body in a slow, smooth caress. She arched toward him, her breasts aching and heavy. He cupped her through her clothes, making her shudder in his arms.

As if unable to resist, he tugged her sweater up, revealing her stomach, inch by inch. The cold air in the room made her flesh pucker, but he warmed it with his touch. She whimpered against his mouth and shifted closer, until she nearly sat on his lap while they exchanged deep, slow kisses. When his hand paused below her breast, she wanted to cry, and sent him a mental demand to continue.

"Oh, yes," she said with a throaty sigh when he finally did. He touched the lace of her bra, then higher, slipping his fingers inside the fabric to brush his fingertips across her puckered nipple.

She felt an ache, low in her belly. No, *lower*...in the hollow place between her legs. She'd never felt this intense a need before. Even during her few sexual encounters, Meg had never been as aroused, as fully in tune with her body, as she was now in Joe's arms.

"Please, Joe," she whispered when he continued those maddeningly delicate touches.

"Please what? Please stop?"

"Stop and I just might have to shove *you* off the balcony!"

He grinned, then slid her bra strap off her shoulder, pushing it down until her breast fell free. "You are spectacular," he whispered as he looked at her, catching her fullness in his hand.

Frankly, Meg had never been too sure why men were so fixated on women's breasts. But the look on Joe's face now—adoration, appreciation, pure desire—made her very confident.

"I have to taste you, Meg."

He lowered his mouth to kiss her there, working his way in tiny tastes to her nipple. She took in shuddery, panting breaths, anticipation making her shake.

"Yes, please," she whispered, arching her back, wanting him to stop torturing her with the warmth of every exhaled breath and those gentle nips and kisses. Wrapping her fingers in his hair, she threw back her head and moaned when he finally moved his lips over the taut tip of her breast and sucked deeply.

Hot, liquid desire spread down through her body, settling with throbbing intensity between her thighs. "Oh, touch me, please," she said, needing more, needing him to do something about the awful, delicious, maddening, incredible fire.

He complied, stroking her stomach, then her hip. "Touch you where, honey?" His voice held a teasing note as he moved to pay careful attention to her other breast, increasing the pleasure even more. He lowered his hand and cupped her thigh. "Here?"

She shook her head, almost unable to speak.

When his palm pressed against the hot center of her, she jerked in response and moaned. "Yes, *there.*"

"You're burning up, aren't you?" he said, his voice little more than a growl.

"Joe, tell me you brought something else in that picnic basket of yours." She reached for his belt buckle. "I haven't had to worry about birth control for a long time."

Joe didn't make sense of her words at first. He was too busy enjoying the way she tasted, the heaviness of her exquisite breast in his hand. He inhaled her, noting the way her skin smelled of vanilla and the intoxicating scent of aroused woman. The damp heat between her legs had made him shake with the need to tug off her slacks and to explore her. Fully. Deeply. Thoroughly. But what she'd said finally sank in.

His hand stilled. He lifted his mouth from her and sucked in a deep, shaky breath. "I'm sorry, Meg."

He saw a veil of disappointment drop over her face. "You don't have..."

He stared at her for a long moment, then shook his head. "I meant what I said last night. I know it's too soon, and I didn't bring anything.'' He ran a frustrated hand through his hair, trying to find the noble instincts that had prompted him to remove the condom from his wallet before he'd picked her up tonight.

Maybe tomorrow he'd be glad he hadn't given in before he'd had the chance to come clean with her. But right now he was too aroused to muster up much appreciation. ''It's probably for the best,'' he said, trying more to convince himself than her.

She uttered the kind of four-letter word that he heard every day on this construction site, though usually it was spoken by sweaty men in hard hats. He almost laughed, in spite of the incredible sense of frustration rushing through him.

''I hope you have wings, Joe,'' she said. ''Because I *am* going to push you off the balcony.''

''SEDUCTION,'' Meg whispered out loud the next afternoon as she parked near The Red Doors. She didn't know which terrified her more: the idea of walking back into the place and speaking to the owner, or going ahead with her scheme to seduce a man she'd known for less than forty-eight hours.

Because of what had happened last night, she had no doubt about wanting to go further with Joe. She was ready to embark upon a wildly sensual affair with an incredible man. But first things first. She had to get him to want it, too.

After that embarrassing moment when they'd both realized they couldn't safely have sex, they'd tried to cool things down. Meg had straightened her clothes, then helped pack up the picnic basket. She could feel Joe's disappointment, but also sensed some relief. He'd gotten a little carried away, but still hadn't changed his mind about it being too soon for them to move into a sensual, erotic relationship.

As far as Meg was concerned, she was several years too late in starting her first sensual, erotic relationship. College groping just didn't count.

A nice girl would probably back off, let him set the tone and the timing. But, as Meg had learned the other night when she'd dutifully kept her date with Ted the Weasel, sometimes it didn't pay to be a nice girl. Not when being a bit of a bad girl could give her what she sensed would be the kind of pleasure she'd only ever read about in romance novels.

When she entered the complex, Meg beelined for the pickup counter inside the foyer. An attractive, middle-aged blonde, wearing a tight, pink sweater stood there. She was speaking with a balding, distinguished-looking older gentleman in a crisp, navy suit. Meg had seen them both working in The Red Doors the first time she'd come. The man's posture was so perfect, and his language so precise, she pictured him as an English butler. Quite a contrast to the blonde, whose honey-smooth words rolled off her tongue in a cadence that could only come from south of the Mason-Dixon line.

"If you're sure that's all, then, Mrs. Merriweather?" the man asked as Meg approached.

"Yes, it is," she replied. "But, Alfred, if you don't start calling me Dixie, I'm afraid I might just have to put some pepper in your tea to spice you up a bit."

The man pulled himself up even straighter and Meg thought she detected a hint of warmth in his eyes. "As you wish," he murmured, his voice low and sedate. But Meg heard a note of something—intensity?—which surprised her, coming from such a reserved-looking gentleman. As he turned to leave, he nodded to Meg, then left the vestibule.

As soon as he'd gone, the blonde turned to Meg. "Well, hello, sugar, aren't you a sight for sore eyes."

"You, uh, recognize me?"

"Of course I do." The woman—Dixie—came out from behind the counter. She walked slowly, with a confident swing to her hips and an assessing glint in her eye. "Though I couldn't have predicted the wardrobe. Child, where have you been shopping?"

Meg bit her lip. "I have an appointment with the owner."

Dixie tapped the tip of her index finger on her cheek, still staring Meg up and down, then said, "Yes, I heard about that."

"Could you ask Miss Ruskin to come out here?" She looked at her clenched fingers. "I really don't want to go inside."

Sliding a protective arm around Meg's waist, Dixie said, "Come on, we'll go up in the private elevator. You can get to the office without anybody seeing you. By the way, I'm Dixie."

"Nice to meet you." Meg let the woman lead her around the counter, watching as a nearly hidden elevator door slid open in the discreetly paneled wall. "Pretty ingenious."

"We strive for discretion. A gentleman places an order on the computer, it's brought down from one of the boutiques and waiting for him to check out ten minutes later."

"It's a great idea, and I'd probably love it if half the men of Chicago weren't viewing me wearing the kind of underwear I've never even tried on in my life," Meg said.

"Never tried on? Well, darlin', we simply must do something about that." Dixie's warm laughter allowed Meg to relax for the first time since entering the complex.

She felt even more relaxed when she met Jamie Ruskin, one of the owners of The Red Doors. The woman, an attractive redhead, didn't look the type to own a risqué lingerie shop. She was petite, with a short mop of red hair and an open grin.

"My business partner, Faith, asked me to apologize for not being able to meet with you. She feels as badly about this as I do." As soon as Meg sat, Jamie put a file into her hands. "I found the paperwork your cousin turned in with the program, including the release you signed. I never noticed it, but the name of the store is spelled shear, like scissors."

"He covered his bases." Meg shook her head in disgust. "If you had noticed it, you would have thought it a typo."

"Exactly. Listen, please don't sweat this," Jamie continued. "I've been working on the code all day myself, and I've called in another programmer.

We'll get you out of that program by tonight, I promise.''

''Thank you.'' Meg was so relieved she even managed a smile.

''In the meantime, aren't you a little curious?''

Meg had nearly forgotten Dixie was still in the room. The blonde gave Meg a Cheshire-cat grin as she sat on the corner of Jamie's desk. She crossed her legs, looking as sexy and confident as only a woman who's old enough to know what she wants, and young enough to enjoy the hell out of it, could. ''I mean, wouldn't you like to take a peek at some of the more popular items men have purchased after seeing your picture?''

Two days ago Meg would have laughed in the woman's face. But two days ago she hadn't been contemplating seducing a sinfully sexy man. ''Items?''

''Don't mind her. Dixie *loves* to dish out advice about sex and love.'' Jamie chuckled. ''But she sure can't take it herself.''

''Don't start,'' Dixie said, rolling her eyes.

''Did I miss something?''

''Oh, just Dixie's secret admirer,'' Jamie explained. ''She's going out of her mind because someone's been leaving her mysterious notes. Speaking of which, any new developments?''

''No. And I don't care since I'd never be interested in a man who can't damn well be honest about his feelings.''

Jamie shrugged. ''I'd be flattered.''

''Me, too,'' Meg said, unable to resist Jamie's playful grin.

Dixie sighed heavily. ''Back to your lingerie situation, missy.'' She glanced at Jamie. ''Our Meg here tells me she's never even tried out anything the least bit sexy. And judging by her outfit, I think we can take her word for it.''

''I teach,'' Meg explained defensively. ''I need to be comfortable chasing after seven-year-olds all day.''

''Well, sugar,'' Dixie said, her voice nearly a purr. ''If you want any twenty- or thirty-seven-year-olds chasing after *you* all *night,* you need a change of wardrobe.''

Meg thought about it. Then she nodded. ''Think you can dish out some advice along with that lingerie?''

Dixie clapped her hands together. ''Oh, my, did you come to the right place! Pull up a chair and let's get busy.''

CHAPTER SIX

NO MATTER WHAT HAPPENED, Joe was absolutely determined to keep his hands off Meg on Wednesday night. They were going out again, and this date, dammit, would be about fun, laughter and companionship. Definitely not about sex. Not about slow, wet kisses. Not about the way her nipples had tasted on his tongue, or the warmth between her thighs.

"Cool it, idiot," he told himself as he parked his truck outside his parents' restaurant.

Santori's was the perfect place for their date. It'd be loud, bright, filled with nosy family members and friendly diners. There was simply no way he'd be able to give in to attraction—okay, *lust*—in the middle of the mayhem. They'd simply spend another evening together, building the sense of liking they'd established from the first, and, he hoped, also building on the trust she'd begun to feel for him. Trust he was going to have to rely on when the time came to come clean.

Thankfully, Meg's own plans had coincided perfectly with his. She'd called him from her cell phone, saying she had to do some shopping and would meet him at the restaurant. So, they wouldn't have those long, private moments inside his cozy truck to deal with, either before or after dinner.

"You can handle this," he told himself. But when he walked into the restaurant and saw her standing there, chatting with two of his brothers, Joe's good intentions flew right out the window.

"Holy crap," he whispered.

His Meg, the second-grade teacher, was nowhere to be found. In her place stood a fantasy—the seductive, sultry Meg previously hidden within the computers at The Red Doors.

She wore a silky red blouse, the kind made with fabric so thin it probably whispered with her every move. The top draped each curve, not clinging, but sliding over those lush breasts Joe had kissed just twenty-four hours before. The deep vee of her neckline gave an enticing glimpse of her pale throat. Joe had to suck in a calming breath when he saw one of the waiters cast an appreciative look at her cleavage.

With the blouse, she wore a black skirt. But it was nothing like the one she'd worn Monday. This was skintight, clinging to her tiny waist, and to hips designed precisely to fit a man's hands. It ended a few inches above the knee, revealing perfect, long legs clad in shimmery black stockings.

If they had a seam, he was going to croak.

She turned slightly. "Sonofabitch," he muttered. *Seamed.*

"Joseph!" his mother cried, catching sight of him. She walked over, arms extended.

Bending for her kiss, he winced when she instead

rapped him on the head with a knuckle. "You're late. I taught you better. You kept your lady friend waiting."

Over his mother's head, he saw Meg grin. Even her face looked different. She wore more dramatic makeup that emphasized the delicacy of her skin and the depth of blue in her eyes. She'd done something new to her hair, pulling it into a loose braid, while leaving little curls around her temples. She looked like pure class and pure sin wrapped up in one mouthwatering package.

"Wow," he mouthed. Joe knew the heat in his stare told her he liked the way she looked. Her cheeks went a little red, but she managed to give him a sultry smile in return.

"It's all right, Mrs. Santori. I was early." Meg walked over to Joe, moving slowly, with an exaggerated swing to her hips.

He was drooling by the time she got within three feet. Then she stumbled slightly on her slim, high heels and fell into his arms—right where she belonged.

"Hi, Meg," he said, a laugh on his lips as he caught her.

She groaned. "Just call me Grace."

"I'll call you anything, sweetie, if you give me your number," Joe's younger brother said as he joined them. Lucas dropped his arm across Meg's shoulders with friendly familiarity.

"Lucas," Joe snarled, "unless you want to answer questions about your black eye tomorrow in court, you'll remove your arm."

Lucas, younger than Joe by only eleven months, merely grinned. "Nice to see you, too. And don't bother introducing me. Meg and I had a nice chat before you arrived."

He saw the merriment in Lucas's face and mentally sent up an apology for all the times he'd ragged on Tony for going out of his mind over Gloria. He now understood how his brother had felt.

"Now," his mother said, "go take the big table in the corner. Lots of room for everybody. Your sister has to work, but Gloria is on the way with baby Anthony."

Oh, ya-ay. A date with Meg...and several members of his family. His mother had obviously been busy ever since Joe had called earlier and asked her to hold him a table. The phone lines were probably still smoking.

But hell, he'd asked for it, hadn't he? His plan to make sure he didn't get the chance to lose his head the way he had the night before was obviously going to be completely effective.

Dammit all to hell.

MEG *LOVED* JOE'S FAMILY. His father, in particular, captured her heart because he and Joe shared the same smile. The older man had come out of the kitchen every ten minutes throughout the evening to make sure Meg's plate and glass were never empty.

His two brothers were incredibly handsome, and were outrageous flirts. Tony, the married one, stopped the flirting when his wife showed up. Judging by the way Tony and Gloria looked at one another, Meg had no question they were crazy in love. They could barely keep their hands off one another.

Meg kept her eye on Joe, and reminded herself about what Dixie had tried to hammer into her brain that afternoon. *You are a seductress.*

She didn't feel much like a seductress, unfortunately, because the man she wanted to seduce hadn't touched her all night. It wasn't Joe's fault, really. At least one member of his boisterous family had been between them at all times.

Right now it was his godson, little Tony.

"What did I tell you?" Mrs. Santori said when she spied Meg holding the baby. She clasped her hands in front of her and smiled widely. "That is what God intended for you."

Feeling sure her face was rapidly turning the same color as her blouse, Meg looked away. Her stare collided with Joe's.

"Don't be embarrassed, Meg," Joe's sister-in-law said. "This family has absolutely no understanding of the word 'tact'. Did I tell you what one of them gave me for Christmas during our Secret Santa exchange?"

She shook her head, finally pulling her gaze away from Joe.

"A gift certificate to a lingerie shop called Sheer Delights. I opened it up right in front of everyone."

Startled, Meg blurted, "Joe and I met there."

Gloria shifted her stare to Joe, who literally squirmed in his seat. "Joseph? So, it was you?" Standing, she leaned over the table, grabbed both of

Joe's cheeks, and pulled him closer. She pressed a loud, smacking kiss on his lips. "Bless you!"

Tony raised his glass to his brother. "Thanks for a great Christmas." Then he gave his wife a secretive smile. "And a very happy new year." The couple positively beamed at each other as everyone else at the table laughed.

Though she was thoroughly enjoying the company, Meg finally glanced at her watch and gave Joe a pointed look.

"I guess it's time to break up this party," he said.

Lots of loud exclamations and hugs accompanied their goodbyes, and it took at least another twenty minutes before Meg and Joe made it out to the parking lot. Holding her coat tightly around her body, Meg took a deep, fortifying breath as they reached her car. A light snow had begun to fall, the first in several days, and Meg watched as flakes landed on Joe's dark hair and long lashes.

She'd thought her attraction to the man was the most powerful sensation she'd ever felt. Now she wondered if her emotional feelings toward him were even more powerful. She was falling in love with Joe Santori. More in love with him every time they spoke, every time they touched, every time he looked at her and smiled that smile.

"Thank you for dinner," she murmured. Trying to remember to look hot and desirable instead of goofy and needy, she said, "Would you like to come back to my place? For a...cup of coffee?"

She saw his throat move as he swallowed hard. "Uh, I don't think so, Meg. I have an early walk-through tomorrow, and I probably should get home to go over some figures.''

The only figure she wanted him going over was her own! But Dixie had told her the keys were subtlety and patience. A man needed to be reeled in slowly, aroused by steps, she'd said.

Meg lowered her lashes. ''All right, Joe.'' Then, rising up on tiptoes, she slipped her hands behind his neck. ''Good night,'' she whispered before touching her mouth to his.

Gently parting her lips, she cajoled him to kiss her back. He did, sweeping his tongue against hers in a slow, languorous mating. It wasn't as frantic or frenzied as some of the kisses they'd shared. He took his time, tasting her with deliberation. For some reason, that made her want him all the more.

''Good night, Meg,'' he said when their kiss ended.

Though it nearly killed her, she got into her car and drove away, watching him standing there in the parking lot in the snow. He watched her, too, not moving a muscle as she drove down the street and turned the corner.

Knowing she was in for another long, restless, night filled with erotic dreams, Meg sighed. If Dixie had been in the car with her, she might have had to deck the woman. Because patience and subtlety might just be the death of her.

MEG HAD RUN OUT of patience and given up on being subtle. She and Joe had gone out again last night, for the fourth night in a row. She'd worn some of her new clothes, including a sexy black bra and thong she'd purchased at Sheer Delights. Not that he'd seen them, of course. Because after spending the Thursday evening watching a bunch of grown men on skates brawl like kindergarteners during a Black Hawks game, Joe had taken her home, kissed her lightly at her door, and left. She'd hurried inside her apartment the moment he'd walked away, not wanting to see Mrs. Mahoney's disappointed expression.

"A hockey game," she muttered as she got out of the shower. "Gimme a break."

It wasn't that Meg didn't like hockey—in fact, because she'd loved ice skating as a kid, she actually found the sport more interesting than others. But it wasn't exactly a thrilling date for the night before the most romantic day of the year.

"Enough is enough," she told herself. After drying her hair, she yanked on some clothes, and left her apartment. In spite of the rather thick snow that had begun to fall, she got into her car and headed toward Michigan Avenue.

Today was Valentine's Day. For the first time in years Meg had romance in her life. And tonight, without a doubt, she was going to get what every woman should get on Valentine's Day.

Some great sex with a man she'd gone absolutely crazy over.

NOTING THE ENDLESS STREAM of harried holiday shoppers had thinned, Dixie Merriweather glanced at her watch. It was five-thirty, and for the first time all day she had no customers waiting at the pickup counter at The Red Doors. She supposed it wasn't surprising since it was nearly the dating hour on Valentine's Day. With the holiday on a Friday this year, everyone had places to go... "And people to do," she whispered saucily.

Everyone except Dixie. Which made it perfectly reasonable for her to be the downstairs manager on duty tonight. Faith was around somewhere, probably up in The Diamond Mine, but Dixie felt sure she'd have plans in spite of the snowstorm brewing. And Jamie had a date. She couldn't have been happier about her young boss getting a little romance in her life than if she had some herself.

For a while there she'd thought she might. Her fingers moved to her throat, where the gold locket that she'd finally decided to put on rested. "Not that it did any good," she muttered. She'd been shocked to receive it this morning from her admirer and had expected him to reveal himself sometime throughout the day. She'd told Faith that if it turned out to be the studly young UPS guy, she wouldn't be back until next week. But if it was the cross-dressing former football player, who bought out their stock of extra-large women's underwear whenever they got a shipment, she was locking herself in the ladies' room.

She hoped nobody had seen through her attempt to make light of this secret admirer business. Because deep down, she'd been a lot more intrigued—and flattered—than she'd let on.

It hadn't mattered, because he'd never shown up.

Whoever the admirer was, he hadn't come forward to take credit for the necklace. He'd had cold feet, a better offer, or just a change of heart. Dixie didn't mind much. Whoever he was, he'd made her feel really good in the past few days. She hadn't felt as expectant and excited about anything in ages...not since her Lou had died.

Now, however, it was over. Because if the man didn't make his move today, on Valentine's Day, he never would. So, as it had been for the past eight years—since she'd become a widow at the much-too-young age of forty-six—her Valentine date would be a pint of Ben & Jerry's and a rented Cary Grant movie.

Absently sliding the locket back and forth on the gold chain, Dixie looked up as the doors opened. Meg O'Rourke, the pretty woman she'd met Wednesday, strode in, bringing a blast of thick snowflakes with her. Meg's expression was a combination of frustration, determination and a hint of terror.

Dixie smiled sympathetically. "No luck, sweetie?"

"Patient and subtle are out. I'm ready to try cheap and obvious."

Dixie tsked. Sheer Delights was never cheap. Not in price, nor in quality. "I can't believe the thong didn't do the trick."

Meg rolled her eyes. "It might have if he'd seen it. And let me give you some advice. Don't ever wear a thong under a skirt to a professional hockey game. My cheeks are still numb."

Dixie couldn't prevent a laugh at the younger woman's disgruntled tone. "All right, what's your plan?"

Glancing around to be sure no one could possibly overhear, Meg filled her in. When she'd finished, Dixie grinned and took the younger woman by the hand. "Perfect. Now, let's go upstairs to sample some Sheer Delights."

They spent the next hour shopping, and after Meg had finally picked out the perfect item, Dixie rang it up, wrapped it, wished her luck, and watched her leave. She smiled, having a pretty good idea of how Meg's Valentine's Day was going to end.

For the next two hours Dixie took care of the remaining customers trickling in, until it was nine o'clock. "Closing time. Cary, warm up the sofa for me, darlin'," she mused out loud.

Alone in the vestibule, she locked up, then glanced through the inner doors. The lounge was empty. The staff had apparently left promptly through the back, probably having plans themselves or wanting to beat the snow home.

Her gaze instinctively moved toward the counter, where Alfred Willis usually stood. He was always easy to spot, being so tall. But tonight he wasn't there. As a matter of fact, she hadn't seen him in a few hours.

He couldn't have a date. Alfred was a widower, and as far as she knew, didn't have a lady friend. Considering how perfectly reserved and formal he usually was, she couldn't imagine him asking out a stranger.

"Maybe he met someone," she whispered. Dixie could not begin to explain why that thought bothered her. She wasn't interested in the man. Heavens, they had nothing in common. Yes, she could admit, if only to herself, she occasionally enjoyed jabbing at that formal exterior of his. She liked seeing his fine, hazel eyes widen when she said or did something outrageous. She especially liked the way that incredibly attractive mouth of his, which had definitely made her stop and stare a few times, curved slightly into a mysterious little smile.

He never responded in kind to her teasing. No, most often he simply stared at her and murmured the same phrase—*As you wish*—while sounding as though he meant something else entirely.

"He probably means, 'Get lost, lady,'" she muttered.

He undoubtedly viewed her as a brassy, bossy, infuriating female. Not many people knew the sometimes outrageous, sexy exterior hid a rather lonely and vulnerable woman—which was just the way Dixie wanted it. She'd thought it best to be alone, rather than endure more than one crippling loss in her lifetime. Now, though, she wasn't so sure....

Needing to go back upstairs to check the locks, Dixie pushed the button for the elevator and watched the paneled door slide open. She blinked, twice, trying to make sense of what she saw on the floor inside. "Roses?" Stepping closer, she caught the sweet fragrance of the dozen bloodred blooms that stood in a vase overflowing with babies breath and greenery. She couldn't fathom how anyone could accidentally leave the lovely flowers behind.

"Happy Valentine's Day, Dixie."

The softly spoken words came as more of a shock than the flowers. Her jaw fell open as Alfred stepped out of the corner of the elevator. He held a single long-stemmed rose, which he extended to her with an expression so filled with tenderness, her heart clenched. "Alfred?" She touched the locket. "You?"

He answered with one of those small smiles.

"Why? You can't... I mean, do you...?" She finally shut up and stared at him in astonishment.

"Mrs. Merriweather, I think this is the first time I've ever seen you rendered speechless."

"Was that why you did it?" she asked warily. "Was this a joke, a prank to pay me back for teasing you?"

His eyes widened in dismay. "Oh, no. All of this, the notes, the locket...were only ever to make you smile. And to make you see yourself the way I see you." He stepped closer. She suddenly wondered why she'd ever thought of him as a cool, reserved man. Because his eyes literally glowed with suppressed emotion.

"How you see me?" She heard the breathless sound in her voice and felt the pounding of her heart within her chest.

He placed the rose in her hand and tipped her chin up with the tip of his finger. "As a very lovely, very desirable woman."

His unwavering gaze attested that he spoke the truth.

She tightened her fingers around the stem of the rose. There were no thorns, she realized. They'd been cut off. Feeling moisture in her eyes, Dixie blinked rapidly. In a moment no longer than a heartbeat, she felt her world go topsy-turvy as she acknowledged what a special man stood in front of her. He'd taken the time to painstakingly remove the thorns, not wanting her hurt.

She'd never expected to find such a man again.

"You're sure?" she finally asked when she trusted herself not to cry like a girl going to her prom.

"Quite sure, Dixie. I've been waiting until you were ready to let yourself care again."

Somehow, she knew what he meant. No, she hadn't been looking for romance for a long time. In fact, her soul-shattering grief for Lou had convinced her she never wanted to love again. But lately, working here, seeing so many relationships in all their different phases, she'd changed. She'd seen and recognized the signs of heady and sensual first love. She'd understood the looks of both naughtiness and tenderness in the eyes of older married couples. And recently she'd realized she wanted that for herself again. How perceptive of him to have known.

"Dixie Merriweather," he said, "will you do me the honor of joining me for a late Valentine's Day dinner?"

She nodded and slowly smiled. "Yes, Alfred, I will."

This time, his answering smile was broad and joyous.

"Can I ask you to do something for me first?" Swallowing to gather courage, she continued. "I would very much like a Valentine's kiss, Alfred."

He lowered his face to hers. Just before their mouths met for the first time, she heard him whisper, "As you wish."

CHAPTER SEVEN

JOE HAD DECIDED before he picked Meg up tonight that it was time to be completely honest. Somehow, though they'd known each other less than a week, he knew tonight, on Valentine's Day, was the perfect time for new beginnings and clean slates.

Besides...no way in hell could he gently kiss her and walk away again—not when those blue eyes begged him to stay. So he'd tell her the truth about where he'd first seen her, apologize, then, with any luck, they'd do what they'd both been dying to do since the night they'd met. Go absolutely wild together in bed.

When they arrived at the romantic restaurant, he helped her remove her snow-flecked coat. Seeing her fully for the first time this evening, he knew he'd made the right decision. The *only* decision. His jaw dropped. "Meg, you look incredible."

"Thank you. It seemed appropriate for the holiday."

He'd decided the other night that red was his new favorite color. Meg was wrapped in it, from shoulder to mid-thigh, clad in a glittery, tight little dress that clung to every seductive curve on her body. Even the coat-check guy stared.

He swallowed and said, "But, uh, it's kinda chilly. Would you rather keep your coat on for a while?"

She chuckled. "I'm sure I'll be fine."

As they walked through the crowded restaurant behind the hostess, Joe noticed a lot of eyes following Meg's every move. Waiters, the bartender, even men sitting with other women. Joe had never in his life been bitten by the green-eyed monster. But he was simply unable to stop himself from slipping a possessive arm around her waist as they approached their table.

After they sat and ordered drinks, Joe gestured toward her hair. "I thought you said it wouldn't hold a curl."

"A ton of gel," she confided with a grin, touching a thick lock of hair hanging over her shoulder. "It'll be flat as a pancake again by midnight."

He hoped it would be earlier than that, because he intended to tell her the truth over dinner, and be back at his place making it up to her by ten.

"I'd hoped this place would be a little quieter," he said, glancing around. "I should have known better because of the holiday. I really wanted to talk to you." As he glanced at nearby tables, he again noticed the stares Meg was getting. "I don't think I'm the only one who likes your new look," he muttered, unable to hide a frown.

She followed his stare. A faint blush stained her cheeks. "I'm not used to much male attention."

"You've always been a beautiful woman, Meg. That some men couldn't see it in spite of your clothes makes them pure idiots. I see you for who you are no matter what you wear."

Obviously noticing his discomfort with the attention she was getting, she asked, "Do you want me to go home and change into a skirt and sweater?" The humor in her eyes said she was teasing.

Only an ass would admit the truth…a tiny part of him *would* rather be the only man to see the incredible beauty of the woman he was falling in love with. Joe wasn't that stupid. Besides, it was easy to see her excitement and happiness tonight.

Before he could reply, an efficient waitress brought a bottle of red wine to the table. As the woman uncorked it, Meg said, "Thank you again, Joe, for the flowers. They were lovely."

"I hope they'll look nice with the twenty construction paper hearts on your coffee table."

Meg smiled and leaned across the table, reaching for his hand. But before she could slip her fingers into his, she accidentally jerked her arm and knocked the bottle of wine the waitress was pouring. As if in slow motion, the open bottle slipped to the table, landing on its side. Red wine literally gushed out, all over the pristine white tablecloth.

And all over Joe's lap.

"Oh, my goodness, I'm so sorry." Meg looked horrified.

The waitress reached for the bottle, but it was too late. The damage had been done. Joe was positively drenched.

AN HOUR LATER Meg found herself exactly where she wanted to be: inside Joe's apartment. She stood in the living room, waiting while he changed clothes…just as she'd planned. If he found out she'd intentionally spilled wine all over him, he'd probably think her insane. She hoped when she gave him his red-silk-wrapped Valentine's present, he'd be in a forgiving mood.

"Okay, Meg," she murmured. It was time to give him his gift. Now, before she lost her nerve, before he could emerge from the bedroom and insist they go back out to finish dinner someplace.

"No dinner tonight, sweetheart. We're heading straight for dessert," she murmured.

She turned off the lights in the room, leaving only the kitchen one on for some gentle illumination. Then she unzipped her dress, slipped it off, and tossed it to the sofa.

"Strike a pose," she mumbled, remembering what Dixie had suggested as she'd purchased tonight's provocative outfit.

A pose. She could do that. She jutted one hip out like a contortionist, and put her fist on it. Tossing her head back, she thrust out her chest, trying to look seductive and sultry. Probably, though, she just looked ridiculous and constipated, because a sudden ache in her lower back made her grimace. The horribly uncomfortable high heels had tortured her all evening. Now with all the hip-and boob-thrusting, her back screamed in protest. She'd be more likely to wind up in the chiropractor's office than in Joe's bed.

She bit her lip, dropped her fist and straightened. *Think sexy…not painful.*

But before she could come up with anything better, Joe returned. She heard his harshly indrawn breath and turned her eyes to see him standing frozen just inside the arch between the living room and the hall. "Oh. My. God."

Obviously a pose hadn't been necessary, after all.

"Happy Valentine's Day, Joe," she whispered.

He opened his mouth but didn't say a word. Somehow she didn't feel jittery or nervous under his hot, appreciative stare. Knowing Joe cared about her made her confident enough to want him to look. Judging by the way he had to grab the back of a chair, as if to steady himself, he liked what he saw.

JOE DEFINITELY LIKED what he saw. She wore a miniscule bit of red silk that masqueraded as a bra. It pushed up, rather than held in, and her amazing breasts literally overflowed the material. Only some peekaboo lace covered her nipples. Even from here, in the shadows, he could see them grow tight and pucker under his piercing gaze.

His mouth went dry and he swallowed, hard, remembering what she tasted like.

He watched as she ran her hand across her bare hip, sliding her pinky over the edge of a lacy garter belt. Unable to do anything else, Joe followed every movement with his eyes. Below the garter belt, which cinched her small waist and emphasized the curve of her hips, she wore the skimpiest pair of panties he'd ever seen. Sheer stockings covered those long legs. Her sexy-as-hell, red, spiked heels completed the outfit.

"Women are capable of romance, too. Something sweet wrapped up in a red satin bow?" she said as she took one step closer.

He instantly remembered their conversation during their picnic in the penthouse.

"You've said I'm sweet, Joe." She took another step. "And though this isn't satin, I think the silk works. Don't you?"

"It works," he whispered, hearing the thin, reedy tone in his voice. He cleared his throat. "Absolutely."

Meg closed the gap between them, step by step, until she stood just inches away. Her eyes were filled with promise and invitation. Joe couldn't even begin to try to resist her. Hell, he probably wouldn't have been coherent enough to notice if the building caught fire. Judging by the sparks in her eyes...and those shooting through his body...combustion was definitely a possibility.

"Are you going to open your present?"

He didn't answer with words. Instead he leaned down, swept her into his arms, turned and carried her back down the hall to his bedroom. Their mouths met in a hot, frenzied kiss, and he heard her throaty purr of feminine triumph. Not that he gave a damn. Things might have gone a little differently than he'd planned, but they were going to end up right where he'd hoped they would tonight. In his bed.

MEG DIDN'T CARE that she lost one of her shoes on the way down the hall. She just kicked off the other one, as well. When they reached his room, she noted the big bed with the bedding turned down, and shivered in anticipation. *This is really going to happen.*

Remembering the condoms in her purse, she whispered against his lips, "I brought some, uh..."

"It's covered," he muttered as he lowered her to the bed. Then he stepped back, never taking his eyes off her as he reached for the buttons at his wrists. She arched on the covers, feeling hot, achy and needy. Then she stilled, watching him undress.

Meg had seen men's bodies before. But seeing his emerge from his clothing, she knew she'd never seen anyone who could compare. Her pulse sped up like an out-of-control train as all that perfect male skin was revealed. If there was a sight more sexy than seeing a gorgeous man shrug off his crisp, white dress shirt to reveal an incredible body, she didn't know what it was.

She whimpered when she saw the thick, rippling muscles of his broad shoulders and hard chest. A light dusting of dark hair swirled between his nipples, trailing down to the waistband of his pants. She held her breath as he unfastened them.

"You take my breath away," he whispered, watching her as intently as she did him.

Then the trousers and briefs fell to the floor. "Oh, my," she whispered, astounded at how perfect he was. How big, hard and perfect. She marveled that this part of him would soon be a part of her, and knew he was going to fill her in ways she'd never even imagined.

Reaching up, she pulled Joe onto the bed. Their mouths met again and Meg arched into his hands, silently urging him to take her. Just rip off what was left of her clothes and *take* her.

He seemed to know she had no patience. He chuckled. ''Honey, I've been waiting for this too long to let it be quick.''

She groaned. ''I need you now.''

He wouldn't relent, torturing her by slowly touching her from neck to knee with deliberately light caresses. His mouth followed his hands, kissing her on almost every inch of her body. Almost. Because he avoided those inches she most wanted kissed. ''You're driving me crazy!''

''Good,'' he whispered as he deftly unfastened the garters holding up her stockings. ''That'll make it better. Trust me.''

She groaned as he moved his hand higher, passing right over the front of her panties, stroking her belly, then the vulnerable skin beneath her breasts. Her groan turned to a whimper as he slowly pulled down her bra strap, nibbling a path on each inch of her skin as it was revealed. She arched toward him, feeling something building deep inside her. More than need, more than want.

This was almost frenzy.

Finally, when she thought she was going to climb right out of her skin from wanting him so much, he sucked her nipple into his mouth. At exactly the same instant he slipped his fingers beneath her silk panties and caressed her throbbing center.

"Oh, yes," she cried as utterly unfamiliar, hot bolts of pleasure surged throughout her body, inundating her with indescribable sensation.

Before she could even fully acknowledge that she'd just had her first man-induced orgasm, Joe was reaching for the bedside table. She watched, wide-eyed and breathless, as he pulled on a condom. He pushed her silk panties down, not even bothering with the stockings, then moved between her legs. "I wanted to do so much more," he said, his voice thick with need and barely restrained passion. "But seeing you like that...I have to have you now, Meg."

She leaned up to kiss him, tangling her hands in his dark hair. "Then have me, Joe."

Their eyes never parted as he slid into her slowly, with agonizing restraint, until, finally, he was deep inside her body, touching her where no one had ever touched her before.

It was better than anything Meg had ever imagined.

And she knew it was only the beginning.

JOE WOKE UP FIRST the next morning and spent several minutes watching Meg sleep. He would have loved to make love to her again, to ease into her slowly, to wake her up with kisses and slow strokes inside her. But they'd made love several times throughout the night. While Joe knew she hadn't been a virgin, he suspected it had been a very long time for her. He didn't want to hurt her.

Easing out of bed, he headed for the kitchen to make some breakfast. They needed to talk—out of the bedroom. While they ate, he'd get things out in the open. Then they could move on—into what he sensed was going to be the most important relationship of his life. After last night, there was no doubt in his mind that he loved Meg. And no woman could possibly have been as passionately responsive if she didn't feel the same way.

He put some coffee on, then noticed how chilly it was. Quietly going back to the bedroom to grab some sweats, he peeked at the bed to see if she was awake.

Not only was she awake, she wasn't even in the bed. Startled, Joe looked around the room, and saw her standing in front of his open closet door, wrapped in a sheet. "Meg?"

"I didn't mean to pry." Her voice was soft. "I woke up and you were gone. I was looking for a robe or something to put on."

He finally realized exactly what she held in her hands. A sapphire-blue teddy. *Dammit.* "Meg, it's not what you think."

"Really? So you know what I think?"

"I have a suspicion."

She reached for the shelf, grabbing several pieces of tissue-wrapped, folded lingerie. "So you are not some kind of lothario who keeps up a nice supply of nightwear for all his overnight guests?" She tossed the clothes to the floor. "At least you have good taste. These are all from Sheer Delights, according to the receipts."

Cursing his own idiocy for leaving the lingerie in his closet, he approached her. She held up her hand, palm out. ‘‘Stop. Don’t touch me. Obviously we had different ideas about what last night meant. You’re a lot more used to this than I am.’’

‘‘Meg,’’ he said softly when he reached her side, ‘‘it was all for you. Every item you threw on the floor was bought for you.’’

Her eyes widened and her lips parted. Then she frowned. ‘‘No, that’s impossible. I saw the date on the receipt for the teddy, Joe. You bought it on Christmas Eve, long before you and I ever met.’’

He swallowed hard. ‘‘Maybe you should sit down. This is going to sound kinda strange.’’ She looked as though she wanted to argue. ‘‘Please, Meg, give me a chance to explain.’’

She reluctantly sat on the edge of the bed, still clutching the sheet around her body. Joe grabbed a pair of sweatpants off his dresser and pulled them on as he told her about going to shop for Gloria on Christmas Eve.

‘‘So, you bought the teddy for your sister-in-law?’’ she said, raising a skeptical brow.

He answered with a vehement shake of his head. ‘‘I got her a gift certificate and that’s all.’’

‘‘Then who was the teddy for?’’

Taking a deep breath, Joe told her the truth. ‘‘It was for you. I saw your picture in the computer system, wearing that teddy, and I just couldn’t leave the store without it.’’

Her eyes widened and the color drained from her face. There was nothing left to do but to tell her everything. He spoke quickly, wanting to get the story out in the open, begging her with his eyes to forgive him.

When he finished, she slowly rose to her feet. "So, last Monday, when I thought you were some wonderfully nice, thoughtful guy, you saw your chance and never let on you'd seen me before."

"Meg, it wasn't like that. I was really worried about you."

She continued as if he hadn't spoken. "I thought you saw and liked the real me, not the siren on the screen."

"I did see the real you," he insisted. "I've fallen in love with the real you every minute we've been together this week."

She didn't even comment on his declaration, instead laughing bitterly. "I spent a fortune on new clothes, trying to make you see me as sexy and desirable. I couldn't understand why you didn't want me."

"I *did* want you." He thrust a frustrated hand through his hair. "I was out of my mind wanting you, but I didn't want to take advantage of you. I needed to figure out a way to explain everything. God, it drove me crazy, trying to resist you while watching you come out of your shell. Seeing the way other men looked at you when we went out nearly put me over the edge."

Judging by the sudden fire in her eyes, *that* had been the wrong thing to say.

"Oh, so you want a frump who won't get any attention in public, and a sexpot in private?" She stalked toward him, poking him in the chest with her index finger. "Did you think you could separate me into two neat little parcels? The good girl Meg in the ponytail and bulky sweater for the world to see, and the bad girl in the G-string at night in your bed?"

She swept the sheet off her body, kicking it out of the way, not even allowing him to answer. Stalking down the hall, completely—gloriously—naked, she beelined for her discarded clothes. "Well, too bad, mister," she said as she yanked her red dress on over her body. "'Cause you just blew your chance with either one of us."

CHAPTER EIGHT

ORDINARILY, Meg would never have walked outside into a virtual blizzard wearing a dress without a stitch on underneath. Desperate times, however, called for desperate measures. And at least she had the long, wool coat to wear over it. She even managed to avoid tripping in the stupid spike-heeled shoes, which she almost couldn't get on over her bare, cold feet.

Joe had tried to talk to her, but she'd cut him off. He'd then insisted on taking her home. She'd refused, hurrying out while he grabbed his keys and shoes and came after her. Luckily, she was able to flag down a lone cab maneuvering through the snow as soon as she walked out the door of his building.

Though she'd expected him to try calling her after she left, the phone remained ominously silent throughout the morning. Meg kept picking it up, checking for a dial tone, even as she told herself she didn't want to hear from him.

''Bull,'' she muttered out loud as she sat in her bed, eating her breakfast: a package of Oreos. She couldn't even be bothered to separate them and lick off the cream. Emergencies like heartbreak required speed rather than precision.

She flipped the TV around the dial with the remote. Not that she was watching. No, her mind never strayed from what had happened last night. And this morning.

Last night had been pure heaven. This morning had...not.

Part of her was glad to know the truth. A bigger part wished she'd never found out Joe wasn't simply a nice guy who'd helped her in her moment of need. Okay, yes, he'd helped her, but only because he'd been lusting after her for weeks.

Lusting. She had to admit—especially after last night—lusting wasn't always such a bad thing. She'd never felt about Joe what she'd felt about Ted, or any of the nameless, faceless men who must have seen her at Sheer Delights. She'd never felt that Joe thought of her as an object. He'd wanted her, yes. But she'd wanted him, too, hadn't she? Nearly from the moment they'd met. So how could she hold it against him just because he'd seen and wanted her weeks before they'd met?

No, it was the dishonesty that really bugged her. That and her complete annoyance about the double standard he seemed to expect from her. "You jerk."

The dishonesty she could almost forgive. Because, no matter what, she knew the struggle he'd put up against going to bed with her too soon. She'd forced the issue last night. If she hadn't seduced him, she truly believed he would have told her the truth before taking her to bed.

She checked the phone again. It was still snowing,

and a line might have gone down. She heard the dial tone. "Damn."

It doesn't matter. This wouldn't work anyway.

So what if she could forgive the dishonesty? That didn't change the other problem. Any fool would have recognized the way he'd reacted to seeing her change in wardrobe over the past few days. He'd been delighted...and dejected. It was as if he'd felt happy to have discovered a pretty doll, and wanted to play with it—*really* play with it—but didn't want anyone else seeing how pretty it was.

A frump on his arm. A vamp in his bed. "Jerk," she repeated.

When she heard a knock on her front door, her heart leaped and her pulse raced. She tiptoed through her apartment, peeking through the peephole, expecting to see Joe's thick, dark hair and handsome face. Instead, she saw iron-gray hair and wrinkles.

Mrs. Mahoney knocked again. "I know you're in there, missy."

Opening the door, she forced a smile. "Good morning, Mrs. Mahoney. How nice to see you."

"Delivery came for you. I signed for it," the woman said. She bent and picked up something standing beside her. When Meg saw the bouquet of roses, her heart softened a bit. Then she crossed her arms and frowned. "I don't want them."

Mrs. Mahoney shrugged. "Great. I'll keep them for myself." The older woman turned around, crossed the hall, and walked into her apartment with Meg's flowers. She never even looked back.

Closing her door, Meg shook her head in disbelief. Mrs. Mahoney had just stolen her Valentine's flowers! "It's your own fault," she muttered, telling herself she didn't care.

They had to have been from Joe. Who else would have sent her flowers? Beautiful, fragrant, romantic roses that were now going to compete for table space with Mrs. Mahoney's medicine bottles and collection of ceramic pigs.

A half hour later she heard another knock. Again she peeked, hoping for dark hair. Again she sighed at the sight of her neighbor. "Hello again. Enjoying your flowers?"

The woman shrugged. "Not as much as I'll enjoy these if you don't want them." She held out a big, red-satin-wrapped box, obviously full of expensive chocolates. Then she gave her a look of exaggerated concern. "You probably shouldn't. A few too many of these and those hips of yours could go from curvy to tubby."

"Keep them," Meg snarled as she shut the door.

She watched out the peephole as Mrs. Mahoney strolled back to her own apartment, opening the box and popping a chocolate into her mouth even before she went inside.

"Flowers and chocolate," she muttered. "How original, Joe. Maybe Mrs. Mahoney will go out with you. You'd probably at least approve of her wardrobe." She stalked into her kitchen to make lunch. The Oreos were gone; it was time to move to ice cream.

My hips are not tubby. But she grabbed some yogurt instead.

The next time she heard a knock, Meg was determined not to lose her temper. Didn't she deserve to keep at least one gift she was given for Valentine's Day? Even if it was a day late, and from a man who was currently number one on her hit list.

Mrs. Mahoney held two wrapped shirt boxes. "Shook 'em," she said. "Can't tell much, though. Want me to open them?"

Meg stepped out. Instead of answering, she countered, "Have you called my mother yet?"

Mrs. Mahoney sniffed. "Before the big finale? Puh-lease!"

Finale? Meg frowned. "Why are these deliveries coming to your place, anyway?"

The woman merely smiled, shoved the boxes at Meg, and walked away. "I wondered when you were gonna think of that," she said over her shoulder. "Maybe it's 'cause the delivery man thinks you won't open the door to him."

Joe. She stepped out, shutting her door behind her. Glancing down the hall, she failed to see his lean form and dark hair.

He could have already left the building. Or he could be in the stairwell. Either way, curiosity made her open the first box right there outside her door. Tearing off the pretty paper, she saw something wrapped in tissue inside. There was a note taped to the tissue. Opening it, she read, "'For you to wear whenever you go out, anywhere you damn well please.'"

More curious than ever, she opened the tissue and saw a mound of shiny tan spandex. Leaning down, she placed both boxes on the floor. Then she pulled out the fabric and held it up.

"Good Lord," she muttered when she saw the slinkiest, tiniest, skimpiest dress she'd ever seen in her life. It was the color of skin, and would fit like it. The plunging V-neckline was lower than any dress she'd ever dreamed of wearing, and the slit would risk showing off anything its wearer had on underneath.

To wear in public? Sure. Right. As if that'd happen.

But, she acknowledged, at least he'd admitted she had the right to do so if she wished. A smile curled her lips and, in spite of herself, she felt her reservations slipping away.

Her heart pounding in earnest now, she reached for the other box and tore away the wrapping. Inside, another note was attached to the tissue paper covering some soft material. This one read, "For you to wear in our bed. I'll want you no matter what, Meg."

When she pulled out the two white cotton items, she nearly choked. Joe had sent her the most unattractive, plain undergarments she'd ever seen. The cotton underwear was huge and hideous, looking more suitable for a grandmother—or Mrs. Mahoney. And the bulky bra, complete with five rows of hooks, had probably been in style in the fifties.

A bubble of laughter burst from her lips as she

dropped the box to the floor. She had to lean against the wall and bend over to chuckle in pure delight.

He understands. Had he sent her red silk, or that blue teddy, she would have tossed them in the trash. But Joe knew her well enough to figure out exactly how to make her understand his feelings. His gifts proved it.

Still grinning, she suddenly noticed someone standing a few feet away. She slowly lifted her gaze and saw Joe. His tender expression reinforced everything she already knew. "Thank you," she whispered with a smile. "I think."

"I know your neighbor—Mrs. Mahoney?—kept the flowers and the candy, so you didn't get to read those notes," he said quickly, as if afraid she wouldn't listen. "The first one said 'I'm sorry for being a letch who ogled you at Sheer Delights.' The second said 'I'm *more* sorry for not being honest from the start.'"

The third set of notes was just as important, but she didn't tell him that. "You went to a lot of trouble. What if I hadn't opened these, either?"

"I would have kept right on going until Mrs. Mahoney had a stack of notes and gifts piled up in her apartment."

Curious, she asked, "What would have come next?"

"Handcuffs."

Her jaw dropped.

"Plus a complete description of the plan my cop brother and I came up with to get even with Georgie the Goat."

Flowers, chocolate, clothing and revenge? *What a man.* "It involves handcuffs?"

"And a real goat," he said with an evil chuckle. "I'll tell you all about it if you'll let me."

She tapped her index finger on her cheek. "Do I get to keep the cuffs afterward?"

He nodded again, a twinkle in his brown eyes. "You can keep anything you want, Meg."

Lifting her chin in challenge, she said, "And you really don't mind me wearing that dress?"

His eyes darkened with appreciation as he looked at her. "I'd love to see you wearing that dress. Anytime, anywhere."

She raised a skeptical brow.

"I'm not a caveman, honey—I promise." He touched her shoulder, gently tracing a path along her collarbone with the tip of his finger. "But I knew I was walking a tightrope until I told you everything. I didn't want any other man to sweep you away before I had a chance to prove how I felt about you."

She closed her eyes and took a deep breath, focusing on the way his light touch infused her with energy and warmth.

"I believe you," she admitted softly.

"Thank you." He lowered his head and pressed a gentle kiss to her lips, not taking any more than she offered.

When he let her go, she gestured toward the undies. "I still can't quite picture you shopping for these."

He winced. "I think the salesclerk thought I was

a cross-dresser. Or a gigolo shopping for my elderly sugar mama.'' He took her hand and earnestly said, ''Wear whatever you want, but *please* don't ever make me shop for anything like that again.''

She giggled. ''Deal.''

Leaning close, he tucked a strand of hair behind her ear, touching her so tenderly she sighed. ''I needed to make you understand, Meg. I *wanted* the woman I saw. I fell in *love* with the woman I got to know.''

She leaned closer, until their bodies were a whisper apart. Looking into his eyes, she murmured, ''That's the second time you've mentioned the L-word.''

''I do love you, Meg.''

She absorbed the moment, letting the words soak into her brain, making a memory of it to last forever.

''I know it's too soon,'' he continued, ''but I also know I'm going to love you just as much in fifty years as I do today.''

''It's funny, but I have no problem believing you,'' she replied, knowing he saw the emotion in her eyes. ''Because I feel the same way, Joe. I started to fall the minute you stepped into the computer kiosk at The Red Doors.'' Sliding her hands up to his neck, she curled her fingers into his hair. ''And I know I'm going to love you forever, too.''

He answered with a slow kiss that overflowed with gentle passion. He held her close, as if afraid she might disappear. She tightened her arms around his neck as their kiss deepened, assuring him she wasn't going anywhere.

"I want you again," she whispered against his mouth as they exchanged kiss after kiss. She needed him to take her on the same wild roller-coaster ride of pleasure he'd shown her the night before. She slid her hands down, beneath his jacket, to stroke his strong body and feel his heat.

"The door, open the door," he muttered as he kissed her neck then her throat.

Feeling his desperation and excitement, she reached blindly for the knob, needing to get him into her apartment—and into her body—before she went out of her mind.

"Can't you two take that inside?"

Meg winced as Mrs. Mahoney's voice intruded. Joe groaned and dropped his head in frustration. Keeping his arms around her waist, he looked over his shoulder at the woman. "We're going."

"Good. *Now* I can call your mother!"

Meg just sighed.

"And thank you for your help," Joe added with a chuckle.

"You're welcome," the woman said. Then her sharp gaze shifted downward to the open boxes on the floor. "For me, too?"

Eyeing the bra and underwear, Meg nodded mindlessly. She edged closer to the door, still frantic to make love with Joe. "Definitely for you," she said. "Happy Valentine's Day."

When the woman bent over, snatched the spandex dress out of the box, then disappeared back into her apartment, Meg couldn't even murmur a protest.

Because Joe finally got the door open.

EPILOGUE

March 15, 2003

JAMIE COULDN'T DECIDE which to focus on, last month's profits displayed on her computer screen, the diamond winking on her left hand or the full-page, going-out-of-business-sale ad for The Gift Program. The diamond won out, although those big, fat numbers had tremendous appeal and she loved knowing that The Red Doors had beaten their copycat competition into a bloody pulp. February had been a dynamite month all the way around.

"C'mon, Jamie." Faith poked her head around the divider that separated their office cubicles. "It's time for the big powwow."

Jamie shut down her computer and rolled back her chair. "You still have no idea what this is all about?"

"No, and I can't believe Dev didn't tell you, either."

"He didn't." Jamie stood and grabbed her purse.

"Not even a hint last night?"

Jamie had trouble sifting through all the wonderful lovemaking they'd shared to search for possible hints. "I don't think so. When he called the office this morning, I got the impression it was something that had just come up, but he said we needed to talk about it in person.''

Faith walked beside her down the hall toward the mezzanine. ''And whatever it is, he thinks Carter should be in on the discussion. I can't imagine what this could be.''

''A hot stock tip he thinks we should take advantage of when the market opens Monday morning? If he gets us all together, he'd only have to go through it once.''

''That's as good a guess as anything, I suppose. But I have to say he's being overly dramatic. Why not just tell us that's what he wants to talk about, instead of all this mystery?''

''I haven't a clue, Faith. He's your brother.''

''And he's your fiancé. I thought you told each other everything.''

''Well, we do.'' Jamie remembered the disguises she and Dev had hidden behind in the beginning of their relationship. ''Eventually.'' As she and Faith headed for the red-carpeted stairway leading down to The Red Bean, they had to maneuver past several groups of shoppers, and the only holiday on the horizon was St. Patrick's Day. ''Totally off the subject—but don't you love how busy we are?''

''Absolutely. It's as if Chicago has fallen in love with The Red Doors. I hate to say it, but the publicity surrounding the robbery probably helped.''

Jamie gave her a playful nudge. ''Didn't hurt yours and Carter's cause any, either.''

Faith smiled as they descended the stairs. "No, it sure didn't."

"Say, there are a couple of hotties sitting at a table in the far corner. Think we should try to pick them up?"

"I'm game if you are."

"Let's go for it. I'll take the guy in the Armani. You can have the one in the jeans and leather jacket."

"Thanks. He looks like exactly my type."

Jamie walked toward the table where Dev and Carter sat watching them approach. Dev's eyes glowed with such appreciation and love that Jamie wondered if he was thinking about the peppermint oil massage she'd given him last night. And what had happened afterward. She certainly was thinking about it.

Both men rose and pulled out chairs. Jamie scooted into the one Dev held for her.

"I ordered you an espresso and Faith her vanilla-flavored coffee." Dev gave Jamie a quick kiss as he scooted her chair in. "With Mr. Willis on his honeymoon with Dixie, we can't count on this substitute guy to bring it over automatically."

"I sure miss Mr. Willis," Jamie said. "Both of them, in fact. But I'm thrilled with the way everything turned out."

"I'm dying to find out how they liked the Caribbean cruise on that new cruise line," Faith said. "Carter and I might book one if Dixie gives it a thumbs-up."

Carter laughed. "Are you kidding? You know

Dixie—she wouldn't let the cruise line get away with making it anything but the best."

Dev leaned his elbows on the table. "That fits in perfectly with what I wanted to talk to everybody about. I—"

"Cruises?" Faith asked. "If I'd known that I'd have brought my brochures. I have—"

"Hold on a minute." Jamie touched her arm. "That's Meg O'Rourke coming out of the kiosk over there." She blinked as a man followed Meg out of the kiosk. They both looked a little rumpled, but happy. "Ohmigod. I'll bet that's Joe Santori with her. He dealt mostly with Dixie, so I never got a good look at the guy, but he fits Dixie's description."

Faith turned to look. "Isn't Meg the woman whose image was accidentally programmed into our software?"

"Yeah." Jamie grinned. "And she freaked, but I guess she feels comfortable coming into the store now."

Carter glanced at the couple. "I'd say they look *real* comfortable. I'd go so far as to say they did a little canoodling in the kiosk, wouldn't you, Dev?"

"Looks like it."

"I'm sure it was a sentimental journey for them," Jamie said. "They met in one of those kiosks, and then Meg came in a couple of times to buy some lingerie to catch his eye, but I never heard the end of the story."

Dev laughed. "You don't need to. Just look at them."

"I want to hear it from the source," Jamie said. Standing, she waved her hand over her head. "Meg?"

Meg glanced her way and her eyes widened. "Jamie! I didn't see you over there."

Carter lowered his voice. "She wouldn't have seen a charging rhino. That woman has it bad."

Faith tweaked his ear. "People in glass houses shouldn't throw stones."

Carter turned in surprise. "Me? I never—"

"That's not what your friends down at the station say about you." Faith smiled at him.

Meg and the guy who'd shared the kiosk with her walked over. Sure enough, Meg introduced her fiancé, Joe Santori, and displayed a stunning engagement ring.

After Jamie introduced everyone at the table to Joe and Meg, Faith took Meg's hand to study the ring more closely. "That's one of ours!"

"Yep," Joe said. "But you weren't there when we bought it the Saturday after Valentine's Day. Someone said you'd taken the day off for personal business."

"Um, yes, I did." Faith blushed and glanced at Carter, who gave her a wink.

"We came in today to look at trousseau stuff," Meg explained. "I know it's a little unconventional for the groom to help pick out the bride's lingerie, but—"

"It was more to revisit that particular kiosk," Joe said. "We met there, and as of today we've been engaged exactly one month."

Jamie realized today was the fifteenth. ''You know, all of us got engaged February fourteenth. And Dixie and Mr. Willis got engaged that night, too.''

''You're kidding!'' Meg grabbed a chair from another table. ''Pull up a chair, Joe. I have to hear all about this.''

Another cup of coffee later, Meg and Joe left, but not before addresses were exchanged and promises made to send out wedding invitations all around, once the dates had been set.

''I suppose we do need to think about that,'' Faith said. ''Carter and I have been so busy that we haven't looked at a calendar.''

''I know.'' Jamie glanced at Dev. ''All we decided was to wait until it was a little warmer, so we could have it outside.''

''Thanks for the perfect lead-in.'' Dev took her hand before glancing over at Faith and Carter. ''Mom called this morning. She asked me, as the oldest son—''

''I'm the oldest daughter!'' Faith lifted her chin.

''See, that's exactly why she called me, the accommodating one.''

''I'm very accommodating!''

Dev grinned. ''Then you should be more than happy to go along with Mom's plan of a double wedding.''

Everyone stared at him. Then Jamie glanced over at Faith and discovered Faith was studying her, her eyebrows lifted in question.

Jamie held up both hands. ''Don't ask me to decide. Dev knows I want something simple, but that's all I care about.''

''And Faith knows I want something simple,'' Carter said. ''A double wedding sounds like it would be anything but.''

Dev sighed. ''If you want the truth, I don't think a Sherman wedding could ever be simple.''

''He's right.'' Faith gazed at her fiancé. ''Every time you've said that you only want a small ceremony with a few family and friends, I've agreed, but in my heart I knew that plan was doomed. I just hated to tell you.''

Dev squeezed Jamie's hand. ''Same here. Unless you want to start married life by totally alienating your in-laws, we have to have some commotion attached to the wedding.''

Jamie had no intention of alienating anyone. She looked over at Carter, who had suddenly become her ally. ''If an extravaganza is inevitable, maybe better one ceremony than two. And, Carter, you and I can ride shotgun on all the plans, and slash and burn whenever possible. One of us alone against the tide would certainly drown, but together we might be able to nix the strolling minstrels and the champagne waterfall.''

''Maybe the minstrels,'' Faith said, laughing, ''but no Sherman ever got hitched without a champagne waterfall.''

''Oh, I think the strolling minstrels are a given, too,'' Dev said.

Jamie threw up her hands. ''Oh, who cares?

We're marrying Shermans, Carter, so I guess we have to accept the bad with the good."

"Hey, it's mostly good!" Dev said.

"You bet it is!" Faith added.

"I agree." Carter smiled at his fiancée.

Jamie gazed into Dev's eyes and realized that nothing mattered but spending a lifetime with this amazing man. "You know what? It's *all* good."